Evelyn James

Evelyn James has always been fascinated by history and the work of writers such as Agatha Christie. She began writing the Clara Fitzgerald series one hot summer, when a friend challenged her to write her own historical murder mystery. Clara Fitzgerald has gone on to feature in over thirteen novels, with many more in the pipeline. Evelyn enjoys conjuring up new plots, dastardly villains and horrible crimes to keep her readers entertained and plans on doing so for as long as possible.

Other Books in
The Clara Fitzgerald Series

The Traitor's Bones

by

Evelyn James

A Clara Fitzgerald Mystery
Book 14

Red Raven Publications
2019

Chapter One

Drizzle quietly dripped down the windows. It was a rainy early summer's day, the sort farmers crave and everyone else grumbles about. People were coming into the Brighton Pavilion shaking rain off their hats and coats, muttering that they had not brought umbrellas to protect themselves against the unexpected downpour.

Clara Fitzgerald, Brighton's first female private detective, was already inside and had avoided the showers. As a member of the Brighton Pavilion Committee, (the volunteer organisation that had valiantly fought to save the eccentric building from destruction) she had been there since the break of dawn making sure everything was in order for their latest open day fundraiser.

Clara discreetly yawned. She had spent too many sleepless nights over this whole affair. Certain sections of the pavilion were regularly opened to the public, these included the exhibition gallery and some of the more interesting rooms. But the majority of the apartments were reserved for private use only. The large banqueting room, for instance, with its many nice paintings, was only for private hire and they charged a sum in keeping with its grandeur. Other areas of the Pavilion were considered too fragile or valuable to be constantly open to the general public. Some had exquisite, but easily damaged, furniture or wallpaper that was rapidly fading and needed to be kept in near permanent darkness. Some people complained over this, which Clara thought was childish. They were preserving something for the future, for a time, hopefully, when it would be easier to keep such delicate things in pristine condition.

Not everyone saw things this way and ultimately a compromise was needed – one that would also supply the committee with much needed funds to maintain the pavilion. For, as Clara well knew, the building's structure was in serious need of attention. For every leak they found and fixed, another would spring up. For every rotten window frame they repaired, a floorboard would spring or a lump of plaster would fall from the walls. Some of the jobs required experts in preservation who knew how to charge for their skills. Clara had to wonder how many of the people who filed into the building were aware of the ongoing battle the committee was facing, or the fact that some of them (Clara included) distinctly felt they were losing.

The people who were now arriving through the main doors had paid for tickets to go on a guided tour around the usually inaccessible rooms. The tickets were not cheap, but did include refreshments and dinner in the banqueting room. Clara had chipped in with the rest of the committee to make sure all the rooms were fit for visitors. There had been mild panic when it was discovered that the Chinese room had developed a severe case of damp seemingly overnight, which had required a rearrangement of some furniture to mask it. And only that morning Clara had stepped into the crimson room to discover another plaster fall had occurred, this time from the ceiling right onto the bed. She had personally fetched a brush and pan to deal with the miniature disaster.

She was still anxious that something unexpected might happen and interfere with the day ahead. The last thing the committee wanted was anyone to see how poorly preserved the fabric of certain parts of the pavilion was. The committee had promised to keep the pavilion in perfect condition, preserving and saving it for future generations. A noble promise, if you had the cash. They didn't, and everyone was worried that their guests would notice and criticise their efforts. The last thing the committee needed was someone thinking they were not doing their job. They tried their hardest, they really did. They just did not have the money to keep up with all the repairs the pavilion required.

Sometimes Clara wondered if their desperate efforts were worth it all. Today was one of those days. She was feeling tired and despondent, and not at all inclined to marvel at the pavilion's fabulous gilt-work, ornate decoration, randomly sensual architecture and all the other things that made the crumbling building too unique and too special to lose.

"Are you Miss Fitzgerald?"

Clara glanced to her right and saw a woman stood there. She was a decade or so older than Clara and wore nothing but black. Clara guessed she had recently been widowed. She was short, a little stout, but not in an unattractive way, and had dense curly brown hair. Clara smiled at her.

"I am."

"I hoped you were," the woman fiddled with her handbag. "I hoped to find you here. Not that I bought my ticket for that reason."

The woman looked suddenly appalled that it might be imagined she had bought her ticket for reasons other than to support the pavilion. Clara was really not fussed why she bought the ticket, as long as it was another one sold.

"You don't need to explain yourself to me," she said.

The woman relaxed a little, but her hands still gripped tightly to the handles of her handbag, as if she was clinging on for dear life.

"I almost did not approach you," the woman continued. "I bought the ticket to see the private rooms, I really did. It was only afterwards that I remembered you were a member of the committee here and I hoped I might bump into you."

"You could have come to my office," Clara said lightly. "I am always open to enquiries."

"I couldn't do that," the woman shook her head. "Someone would see and then they would talk about it."

She bit at her lip anxiously.

"No, I had already discounted that possibility and then this opportunity arose and I thought I might just happen to bump into you and it would seem all so natural," the woman glanced about her. "No one must know what I am up to. They will say such horrid things."

Clara was not sure what the woman was talking about, no one else seemed bothered, or even aware that they were talking. But the woman's agitation was catching and she was starting to feel that this was important.

"Why don't we get a cup of tea?" Clara suggested.

A long table had been laid out with teapots and cake. Clara poured two cups and then offered the woman a piece of shortbread. The woman took it without really appearing to notice what it was. She was still surveying the room as if at any moment a person would spring out and accost her.

"Would you like to go somewhere quiet we can talk?" Clara asked.

"Yes…" the woman blinked. "No, it would seem more obvious that way. Why don't we go over to that wall of pictures and pretend we are talking about them?"

The woman pointed to a selection of nautical themed paintings, including a portrait of Nelson, which hung on the long wall of the reception room. Clara was amenable to the idea. They stood before the paintings and the woman gave a long sigh.

"You may think I am crazy," she said softly.

"I would never presume," Clara reassured her. "I get the impression that whatever the problem you are enduring is, others have been less than sympathetic?"

"You could say that," the woman nodded. "My name is Emily Priggins, by the way."

Emily spoke with her eyes fixed on the paintings.

4

"And what has happened that brings you to me?" Clara asked.

Emily seemed to freeze a little bit, as if whatever she wanted to say was almost impossible to spit out. She blinked back tears and then took a trembling breath.

"I want to know what happened to my brother," she said at last, still keeping her attention fixed on Lord Nelson's portrait. "He disappeared in the war."

Clara felt her heart sink a little. She had pursued a number of such cases and, as the years rolled on, so the likelihood of her searches being successful became less and less. To find someone alive after they had been absent all this time was unlikely. If they were still alive, then they had to have strong reasons for not wanting to be found. Her lack of a response prompted Emily to speak up.

"I know he is probably dead," she said hastily. "But I need to know for certain. Also, I need you to find out the truth about his actions in Belgium."

Clara was curious.

"What do you mean?"

Emily was really struggling with her tears now.

"It is hard to speak aloud, though so many have said it to me in the past. I don't like the words coming from my own lips. My brother has been accused of being a traitor to his king and his country. He has been accused of working with the Germans against his own people. I cannot believe such lies, but many feel his disappearance during the war confirms his guilt," Emily paused, too choked for a moment to carry on. "He was a good man, Miss Fitzgerald. He would not have betrayed us. Yet, nearly all my friends and family are convinced that is exactly what he did. Even our parents…"

Emily hastily found a tissue in her bag and dabbed at her eyes.

"The army would have conducted an official investigation into these accusations," Clara said carefully.

"He was not in the army," Emily shook her head. "My brother was a Catholic priest. He went to Belgium to bring some sort of hope to the unfortunates there and to strengthen the brave souls fighting for freedom. This is why I know he did not betray us. It was not who he was."

Clara frowned, finding it hard to know how to reply. She had seen many things and knew that no one was perfect or free from vice. The devotion of a loved one was no real confirmation that that person was innocent of their crimes. Love was blind, as they said, especially the love of a loyal family. Though clearly Emily's parents thought differently. The fact that they had accepted that their son was a traitor was just as damning as the accusations in the first place. Their reasons for such acceptance had to be based on a greater knowledge of their son's character, or so you would imagine.

"When was the last time you heard from your brother?" Clara asked Emily gently.

"The first of October 1917," Emily answered promptly. "That was the date of his last letter to me. We learned two days later that he was missing by telegram. The accusations began a week after that."

Emily rummaged in her handbag and produced a grey envelope. It had a Belgium postmark. She handed it to Clara.

"His last letter. I have found nothing insightful in it, but maybe you will see something I do not."

Clara gingerly removed the extremely thin paper from the envelope. By 1917 shortages meant that paper pulp had to be stretched to the limit to make the most product from each batch. The result was tissue-like sheets, thin enough that the writing on the back could easily be read from the front. Clara could see the pink of her finger as she held the fragile paper in her fingers. The missive had been read over and over, removed and replaced in its envelope so many times that the edges were torn and damaged. It would not be long before the letter was completely unreadable.

Clara turned her attention to the script. It was written in blue ink, the hand bold and free, the letters looping and clear to read. She scanned the message which was rather typical of the sort of letters sent home from the Front during the war.

It started with the usual formalities – hoping everyone was well and noting that the writer, himself, was fit and hail. It then went on to discuss a few mundane things, such as the difficulty in getting any sort of bread or fruit. Next the writer mentioned an outside religious service he was hoping to hold for the local families. Without the date for context, the letter would seem quite innocuous, but Clara knew what was happening in Belgium at that period of time, how many parts had been overrun by the Germans. She could only guess what was really going on in the background.

Clara glanced at the end of the letter.

"Your brother's name was Christian Lound?"

"Yes," Emily nodded.

Clara folded the letter and returned it to her in its envelope.

"I see what you mean, the letter gives no real insight and no indication that he was fearful for his life or was about to commit an act of treason."

"Thank you," Emily sighed with relief. "I have felt the need so desperately for someone else to say that. I am sure my father thinks there is some code in this letter, some detail we are missing. My brother wrote nearly daily from Belgium. I have all the letters he sent to me, but I cannot say about the ones he sent my parents."

Emily gulped back tears.

"It would not surprise me if my father burned them all. He was so quick to believe the worst about Christian."

Behind them, a voice called out that the tour was about to begin and everyone should gather. Clara felt now was the time that they should retreat to somewhere private to discuss matters further. She just had to persuade Emily.

"I have an office here in the pavilion," Clara said. "We could go there to talk further, I want to know all the details about your brother's disappearance. If we remain here, it will seem more obvious that you are talking to me."

Emily was reluctant, that was apparent. She glanced at the other guests rapidly vanishing to gather in the main hall.

"I can only be sure I can help you if we speak in detail," Clara persisted. "This is not the place for that."

Emily dabbed at her eyes again. Clara sensed that her reluctance was waning. She had come this far and could not turn back now. If she left, Clara felt she would not return. She waited for Emily's decision, ultimately it was up to her.

"I am assured you are discreet, Miss Fitzgerald."

"Absolutely, and call me Clara," Clara smiled.

"Clara," Emily seemed to test out the name. "I have wanted to speak with someone for so long, yet I have held myself back for what seems like forever. I feel so torn."

"I am your opportunity to speak," Clara said. "The real question is whether you want me to listen or not."

Emily turned her attention back to Lord Nelson. Slowly her face hardened into a look of determination. She squeezed the handkerchief into a ball in her hand.

"I must speak with you," she said at last. "I cannot abide the silence any longer."

Clara smiled, then she quietly guided her through a side door and to the staff rooms at the back of the pavilion.

Chapter Two

When Clara had said she had an office in the pavilion, what she actually meant was that the committee reserved a room near the kitchens for their administrative work, and it was used by all the members. Clara was relieved to find it empty. She had hoped it would be considering most of the committee would be concentrating on the tour, but someone might have slipped away to do some work.

She pulled out a wooden chair for Emily and then secured one for herself. She dug among some paper on a desk and produced a clean sheet and a pen.

"Now," she said, "let's go through this from the start."

Emily gave that familiar shaky sigh.

"I don't know where to begin."

"Tell me about Christian," Clara nudged.

"Christian is my junior by four years," Emily explained. "He was a brilliant scholar as a boy. So very bright. My father is a politician, you may be familiar with Amadeus Lound?"

Clara paused. She knew the name. Amadeus Lound had served as the MP for Brighton close to two decades, before losing his seat at the last election. He was known for being outspoken, somewhat brusque and a complete philistine. He had been firmly set on seeing the pavilion sold off, wanting the land to be reused for luxury houses. There had been talk at the time that he was good friends with the developer interested in purchasing the site. Clara had not personally crossed swords with the man, but some of her colleagues had and considered him a wolf masquerading as a lamb. All he was interested in was feathering his own nest, pleasing his influential friends and keeping his seat in parliament. There had been genuine delight when he had lost his place to another, more community-minded politician.

"I had not connected your name with Mr Lound," Clara said diplomatically.

"You need not mask your feelings. I know my father," Emily shrugged. "I suspect his instant acceptance that Christian was a traitor was sparked by his instinctive and completely selfish sense of self-preservation. It would never do for his political career, you see, if it became public knowledge his son had betrayed his country, so he never pushed to learn the truth. He let it all disappear."

Emily looked angry, Clara could hardly blame her. If someone accused her brother, Tommy, of being a traitor, she would fight tooth and claw to have him absolved.

"Anyway, father was already angry with Christian," Emily continued. "He wanted Christian to go into politics too. My father is not a religious man, but if you asked him he would most certainly say he was Church of England. For his son to not only defy his wishes, but to defy them by becoming a Roman Catholic priest was beyond the pale. They never really spoke after Christian joined the priesthood, though he always wrote to mother and father. I suppose it all made things too simple for father when the rumours surfaced. He could write him off as a bad egg, and pretend he never existed. It almost made him feel as if he had been right all along."

A tear trickled down Emily's cheek.

"I am sorry," Clara said softly.

"Honestly, I am used to it all by now," Emily gave a weak smile. "I just want to do right by Christian. He always watched over me."

"When did he go to Belgium?" Clara asked.

"Early 1915. I think it was the March. He had talked about it for a while, but my father was very against the idea. He was still certain he could get Christian to change his mind about politics and he didn't want him going out there and getting shot. My father is very self-absorbed," Emily said this as a statement of fact, rather than a criticism. "Christian eventually left in secret, my father was appalled. That was when he started to disown him. For months he would not even have Christian's name mentioned in the house."

Emily groaned at the memory.

"Christian seemed to flourish in Belgium. He found his calling there. He helped to start a retreat for soldiers, where they could go and take a pause from the fighting. It was a joint effort of Catholic and Anglican priests and it welcomed everyone, from privates to colonels. He wrote all about it in his letters and I know he felt a sense of worth in his work. He hoped he was bringing peace to men whose souls were in turmoil," Emily explained. "They also ran services for the Belgians, trying to keep their spirits up too. He felt especially sad for the children caught up in the conflict. They held special Christmas parties for them and tried to bring them some joy amid the madness. It was such a noble thing to do, and my father just laughed bitterly when he read about it. He thought Christian was wasting his time."

"Some people do not understand why it is so important to look after people spiritually as well as practically," Clara replied, hoping it was a tactful comment.

"I don't think my father cares much about people at all," Emily said with no humour. "He thought the Belgians had got themselves into a mess and should get themselves out of it."

"Tell me about Christian's disappearance," Clara nudged. "I take it you had no warning?"

"No. Well, you saw his last letter and there was nothing in that," Emily frowned. "Two days after that letter the telegram came. It was all very formal, just said that

Christian had been reported missing to the British authorities. That was it. Didn't even mention if they thought he was alive or dead. I didn't know what to do. In the end, all that seemed possible was to wait.

"At first there was nothing but silence, then my father received a letter from a colonel he knew. I was never supposed to see the letter, but I stole a look at it while it was on my father's desk. It stated that there were suspicions that Christian had been working with the Germans."

"Did the letter explain why they suspected this?" Clara asked.

Emily shook her head.

"It was very vague."

Clara was not entirely surprised. With a war raging, censorship was considerable and the colonel would have been extremely cautious about what he wrote, even in a private letter.

"After the war, did you learn anything else?"

"No," Emily sighed. "Nothing. Christian was just gone. No one could explain what had happened to him. Nor did anyone elaborate on the claims he was a traitor. That is why I do not believe it. There is no proof. But, my father refuses to listen, and my friends are sick of hearing me talk about it. They seem to think it's a case of 'no smoke without fire.' They are convinced I am wasting my time. The only one who supported my opinion was my late husband."

"I noticed you were in mourning," Clara said sympathetically.

Emily gave a bitter smile.

"Gerald was always sickly, I was under no illusion we had a long future together ahead of us," she said, toying with the wedding ring on her finger. "He was a brilliant lawyer, if his family had had money he could have been a barrister. Even my father was impressed by him, and that is something. Gerald was asthmatic and then he developed TB. We knew his time was limited, though we tried everything we could."

Emily's hands were trembling and her voice had cracked a little.

"He died last month," she managed to say. "With him died the last ray of hope I had in this life. I was so happy with Gerald, he made me feel like I was worth something. Now I am back living with my parents, and I…"

Tears made Emily's eyes look watery, but she refused to let them fall. There had been a lot of tears shed over the last few years. Too many. They had become a burden rather than a release.

"I have nothing now, Miss Fitzgerald. The two people I loved most in this world are now things of my past. There is just one thing that is keeping me going, the hunt for the truth about my brother. I don't know if learning what became of him will make me happy or sad. Whether it will give me the strength to carry on or leave me wishing I never knew. But… what else is there?"

"I understand your mixed feelings," Clara promised her. "I am willing to take on this case, as long as you are aware that I can only reveal the truth, whatever that may be. If your brother did somehow betray his country, I shall have to reveal that to you, as much as if I discover he was innocent."

"I am fully aware of the risk I am taking," Emily replied, her voice now stronger. "I know there is a chance you will discover my brother did something he should not have done. Yet, I also know in my heart that he was a patriot and loved his country. I could just ask you to find out what became of him. But I would still have questions. Knowing why he disappeared is just as important as learning where he ended up."

Emily paused, biting her lower lip.

"I know the chances are he is dead. If he was not, he would have contacted me somehow, I am sure of that."

"There is another possibility I must raise with you," Clara said gingerly, feeling awkward to mention the concern on her mind. "Considering your brother disappeared in Belgium, it would seem likely that I would need to travel abroad to pick up his trail. That raises the question of costs. My usual fees would apply, but also the price of travelling abroad."

"Please, say no more," Emily held up her hand to politely bring Clara to a halt. "I have taken that into account too. I inherited my husband's estate and that has provided me with a suitable sum to employ your talents. You need not worry if you have to travel abroad."

"I would only go for the minimum of time."

"Miss Fitzgerald, I trust you, I would not have come to you otherwise. This matter needs to be resolved and I am prepared to spend the money such a task requires."

Clara relaxed, with that difficult matter out of the way she could get on with business.

"I shall need to begin by examining the letters your brother sent you during the war. The ones he sent your parents would be helpful too, but I appreciate they will be difficult to come by."

"I can look for them," Emily nodded. "I shall try to get them."

"I will also need to interview the colonel who first told your father about your brother's supposed treachery. Do you know his name?"

Emily rummaged in her handbag and hastily produced a slip of paper.

"Gerald planned on contacting him, but he ran out of time. He found his address, however."

Clara took the paper and was mildly disheartened to see that the colonel's home address was in Durham County, a considerable distance from Brighton. If he was not available on the telephone, it would mean a lengthy train journey.

"You say your husband supported your views on your brother, was he researching his case too?"

"He was. Any spare moment he had Gerald was trying to piece information together. I have a folder of papers that he compiled. I didn't bring them because I was not sure what would happen when I saw you, but I shall make sure you get them."

"I would also like to know the Seminary your brother attended and the names and addresses of any of his friends and fellow priests who were acquainted with him at the time of his disappearance. That is quite a number of people."

"I shall do all that," Emily said without flinching at the daunting task. "I very much appreciate this Miss Fitzgerald."

"It is my job," Clara smiled. "I shall do my best for you. Though, I warn you, five years is a long time. Information gets lost, memories fade, people forget."

"Then best the effort is made now rather than later," Emily said firmly.

Clara could not agree more, though she had her doubts about the whole matter. She was going to find out some dark secrets, she was certain of that. People, especially priests, do not just disappear without a good reason. And people aren't accused of being traitors lightly, not when the punishment for such a thing was death.

Clara expected to make Emily unhappy with whatever she discovered, but it was not her place to determine whether that was right or not. She only served her client and she let them decide whether they were prepared to risk unhappiness or not.

"I'll start looking into this right away," she promised.

"Thank you," Emily looked very relieved. "I really can't express how good it feels to have someone else on board. It is a lonely business believing in someone that everyone else has condemned."

Clara only hoped she was not about to discover that condemnation was justified. She shook hands with Emily and escorted her back to the main hall to await the return of the tour party. In the meantime, she was heading for home. She needed to host a council of war, so to speak, and figure out just where to begin in this complicated case.

Chapter Three

Tommy sat opposite his sister at the dining room table in their home. Next to him was Captain O'Harris. Both men were veterans of the last war and knew about the atrocities that had occurred in Belgium. They also knew how men could simply disappear into thin air and about treachery in the trenches. Clara outlined Emily's story to them, hoping for their insight into the matter. Both men were sombre when she had finished.

"I met a few priests during my time at the Front," Tommy said after a moment. "Brave souls, usually. They put themselves in harm's way to help men who very often wanted to deny God rather than be saved by him."

"What was the establishment he was part of again?" O'Harris asked.

Emily had written down the name of the sanctuary Christian had helped to found.

"Albion Hope," Clara read off the paper Emily had handed her. "Ever heard of it?"

"I have this vague feeling I went there once," O'Harris mused. "I'm not certain. I did spend a lot of time around Belgium in 1916. I was flying reconnaissance across the border into France. I recall visiting a house that my friends had mentioned. It was a place of peace in the midst of war. I am sure there were religious services going on there too, but God and all that was not rammed down your throat.

There was a good library, I remember that. I only got the chance to visit it once though."

"Had I known such a place existed I would have paid a visit," Tommy interjected. Out of the three of them, he was the one who still retained his religious spirit. The years of war and bloodshed and made him hold firmer to God, rather than the other way around. He was very spiritual, in his own way. "I was deeper in France than you, old boy."

"We could have done with a few more places like that dotted around," O'Harris nodded. "I remember thinking that at the time. But, you know how it is, the next moment you are on a mission or struggling to survive the latest German push forward and you forget all about that other stuff."

"You don't think you ever met Father Lound?" Clara asked O'Harris.

"Name doesn't ring a bell," O'Harris shrugged. "Sorry. I confess I was not really paying attention to who was running the place. Names were blurring into one at that point."

"What about this Colonel Matthews who wrote to Mr Lound to tell him his son was a traitor?"

Both men looked blank.

"There were plenty of colonels going about," Tommy explained. "Sometimes seemed like there were more officers than regulars. Of course, every time an officer got shot someone had to replace him. A few colonels got their rank by filling dead men's shoes."

"I know Amadeus Lound, however," O'Harris spoke. "On a professional basis, that is. He knew my uncle, they moved in the same circles. Though my uncle disliked him a good deal. I met him at a few formal events over the years. He is a man acutely aware of his position and petrified of losing it, which of course he now has. I'm not going to say he was a bad fellow, just weak. He buttered up people he thought he needed to, to keep himself in his position. They say all his political decisions were prompted by the friends he desired to keep on side. I say, name me a politician who doesn't, on occasion, think like that?"

"Emily seems to think her father was so quick to believe the worst of his son because he was fearful of losing his seat. If he had made a fuss, or tried to find out more, then others would have learned of the situation and that might have dented his reputation," Clara said. "It was easier, and safer, to accept this colonel's word and pretend he never had a son."

"That sounds like Lound," O'Harris agreed. "Not in essence a bad fellow, not even that bright. Just cowardly and inadequate."

"Aside from Colonel Matthews' letter, what other evidence is there that Father Lound was a traitor?" Tommy asked.

"As far as Emily is aware, none. But I can't rule out that her father knows more and has kept it from her. Equally, there may be more in official documents that Emily cannot access. I'll know more if I can speak to Colonel Matthews," Clara explained. "Though Father Lound was not a military man, there would have been some sort of official investigation into the matter, I presume?"

"You are right," O'Harris answered her. "The army had an intelligence division working throughout Belgium and France, and later, Germany. They were badly stretched, of course, but they would be the ones to take up this case. The rumours could not be ignored. They would have tried to track down Lound and pursue the accusations. They probably have a file on him somewhere, but you will never get access to it."

Clara was disappointed to hear that.

"There has to be a source for these rumours," she said. "Something the Father did or said that made people think he was helping the Germans. That is what I need to find out. The start of the puzzle will help me figure out how this all ended. I hope…"

"I assume you have prepared Emily for the possibility her brother is dead?" Tommy asked Clara.

"I think we all know that is the most likely scenario,

otherwise why has he made no contact with her? For that matter, if a traitor to King and country was on the loose, would not the government still be trying to track him down?"

"Depends," O'Harris shrugged. "If they felt he was no further risk, or perhaps they considered he was long gone and too much effort to chase, they would probably forget about him. From the way things are stated, it doesn't appear as if his treachery came to much."

Clara agreed with him.

"Really, until we know more we can make no assumptions about this man. Emily is bringing me all the papers and letters she can and that may help us. I need to contact this colonel and see why he accused the man in the first place. Then I shall know where to go next," Clara placed her hands on the table. "Which reminds me, I must see if my passport is in order."

"Passport?" Tommy frowned.

"The chances are I shall need to pursue this trail back to Belgium. I doubt I will find my solution in England."

"You won't go alone?" O'Harris said tentatively.

"Why ever not?" Clara asked him back. "Emily has agreed to pay my travel expenses, I can hardly ask her to pay for a companion too."

"You don't know the language," Tommy pointed out.

"Did you when you first went over? Quite frankly Tommy, you might have a bit of French but you are not fluent. I studied the language at school."

"Don't get prickly," Tommy rebuked her. "This is not about us questioning your independence or abilities."

"Isn't it?" Clara replied, but she moderated her tone to sound less defensive. "If one of you was going abroad alone, would you make such a fuss?"

O'Harris and Tommy glanced at each other.

"You think some harm will come to me," Clara prodded them. "You think I shall not be able to cope."

"I think you poke your nose into places it is not wanted and end up in trouble," Tommy answered.

"That is the nature of my work," Clara agreed. "But I always get myself out of trouble too."

"True," O'Harris admitted. "You never seem to need me to play the knight in white armour coming to your aid. A less secure man might feel threatened by that."

Clara tried to look annoyed, but his jest had lightened the atmosphere. She smiled.

"I agree there are hazards going abroad, though this is Belgium we are talking about, not some remote jungle full of tigers and cannibals," Clara smirked. "I hear it is really quite civilised."

"And, on the other hand," Tommy interrupted, "it would surely be beneficial for you to have a guide, someone who knows what Belgium was like in the war and can guide you to the right places. You need someone with inside knowledge."

"I cannot ask Emily to pay for a second fare, if the need arises," Clara pointed out. "That is simply that."

They were silent a moment, then O'Harris shrugged his shoulders.

"Look here, I am not exactly strapped for cash. I'll pay an extra fare," he said.

"You would accompany me?" Clara asked, feeling slightly eager at the idea. Clara and O'Harris had an understanding, they were not quite prepared to move that understanding on to an actual romance, but they were certainly heading that way.

"Ah," O'Harris looked embarrassed. "I could not. The convalescence home is just up and running, I can't leave things. I'm sorry. But I could pay for Tommy to go."

"Me?" Tommy suddenly looked appalled. "Go back to France?"

"Belgium," Clara corrected.

"Near enough!" Tommy stretched back from the table in horror. "I swore I would never set foot on foreign soil again after the war. Especially soil where I helped kill men."

"One of us has to go, old man," O'Harris coaxed. "I

really can't abandon my duties here. If I could I would have been delighted…"

"You don't understand, I swore never to go back, never!" Tommy looked at them both with an accusing expression, as if they had just asked him to cut off an arm. "I promised myself, promised!"

Clara said nothing. She knew the demons Tommy had fought and did not want to push him to do something he was so clearly afraid of. She was not really worried about going to Belgium alone, it seemed like a good excuse for an adventure. She had never been to the country, but had heard it was beautiful, even in its war-torn state.

"I can't go," O'Harris repeated. "Maybe this is a prime opportunity for you to challenge your demons?"

"Whatever for?" Tommy glared at him. "Who says I have demons that need to be challenged?"

"It might not seem important," O'Harris said steadily. "But the moment we say we can never do such and such a thing, we are instilling in ourselves a sense of defeat. It can spill out into our lives in other ways which we never expected."

"Stop the mumbo-jumbo," Tommy said crossly. "I am not defeated, I just have no intention of going back to a place where I nearly died, thank you very much!"

"What are you all arguing about?" Annie, the Fitzgeralds' friend and housekeeper entered the dining room with a plate of freshly baked sausage rolls. "You are making such a racket. Where will you not go to Tommy?"

She punctuated her question by drawing a smaller plate out from under her arm and placing a sausage roll on it. She put this before Tommy.

"The meat is from a different butcher, I want to know your thoughts on the taste," she continued, supplying each of them with a plate and sausage roll.

There was nothing like Annie's cooking to defuse an argument. No one was going to remain so cross they could not enjoy sampling her food.

"I might be off to Belgium for a case," Clara explained

to Annie, since neither of the men were speaking. "The boys are arguing about who should accompany me."

She almost rolled her eyes, but remembered Tommy and O'Harris were facing her just in time.

"Belgium," Annie mused over the word. "I read about that a lot in the war. Seemed a nice place until the Germans marched in. Why don't they just both go with you?"

"I can't leave my convalescence home just at the moment," O'Harris pointed out. "It would seem very wrong of me to up and leave my patients so soon after opening."

"I am not going to Belgium," Tommy was pouting again. "I swore I would never go back."

"Oh well, Clara will just have to go alone," Annie said, giving Clara a wink.

"No!" Both men said in unison.

Clara groaned.

"Really? I am sure there is no more harm going to come to me in Belgium than if I were in London."

"I went with you to London, remember?" Tommy reminded her. "I know the trouble you get in to."

"And out of," Clara said proudly.

"You really are such big gooses," Annie tutted at O'Harris and Tommy. "If you won't let Clara go alone, which is daft, by the way, then you must decide on one of you going. And, as I see Captain O'Harris is in a bind, that leaves you, Tommy."

"Annie, I can't!"

"There is no such word as 'can't' Mr Fitzgerald," Annie told him sternly. "I said once, 'I can't cook pastry' and my old mother said 'can't' is an excuse for not putting in the effort. It took a long time, but now you are eating the result. Can't is a very bad word."

"That is different," Tommy said sulkily. "And you know it is different."

"Well, if needs be I will be going to Belgium," Clara said calmly. "I really can see no way around it. Whether I am accompanied or not, I do not mind."

Clara bit into her sausage roll.

"Nice pastry Annie."

Annie smiled proudly.

Chapter Four

Emily kept her word and delivered all the papers and letters she could find concerning her brother. It came in a large box and Clara felt slightly daunted by the task of sorting through it all. To put off the moment, she sat down and composed a letter to Colonel Matthews and sent it off with the afternoon post. With any luck it would be with him in the morning.

Tommy came into the parlour and saw the large box on the table. His eyes widened.

"That is a lot of correspondence."

"Father Lound was a prolific writer, by the looks. Those are only the letters he sent to his sister during the war."

Tommy took a handful of letters out of the box and glanced at them, then he turned his attention to the other papers.

"What else is in here?"

"I don't know entirely. I suppose there is the file Emily's late husband compiled on her brother's disappearance, and there are possibly papers concerning Lound's seminary training and work in Belgium. Basically, anything Emily thought might be relevant. She is still trying to get hold of the letters he wrote to her parents, if they still exist."

"Do you think it is odd Mr Lound was so quick to believe his son a traitor?" Tommy asked.

Clara frowned.

"How do you mean?"

"It is a shocking thing to be told about your only son. Yet, he seems to have just accepted the news, almost as if he had known something before?"

"A bit soon to be making inferences like that," Clara replied. "Emily says he just accepted the news, but it may be her memory of events. It might actually have taken days, or weeks, for him to really accept the news. In the meantime, he did nothing as it seemed the safest option for his political career. I don't think at this point we have to see it as anything but the selfish nature of the man."

Tommy dug in the box deeper.

"Look at this," he produced a large leaflet. It was high quality, the front and back pages printed on thick card and the contents professionally laid out. It was bigger than a standard pamphlet, about eight by ten inches. "St John's Seminary, Worthing. Religious Education at the Highest Standards. I guess this is where Christian went to become a priest."

Tommy flicked open the pamphlet.

"Very nice, they have their own tennis courts."

"Might be worth contacting the seminary and seeing what their views on Christian were. I doubt they can tell me if he was a traitor to his country, but they might give me an insight into his temperament," Clara took the pamphlet off Tommy and glanced through the pages. It was a brochure for a school like any other. There were stories of students who had achieved great things, lists of accolades the seminary had won, images and descriptions of the classrooms, sleeping quarters and curriculum. There were a lot of pictures of smiling priests.

"Do you want a hand going through all this?" Tommy pointed to the box.

"I wouldn't mind," Clara agreed. "I was thinking of starting by going through the contents and arranging items into three piles. One for documents I think can be useful for the case, one for documents completely irrelevant and one for documents I am not sure about."

Tommy pulled up a chair to the table in the parlour and took a large handful of letters from the box which he gave to Clara. He took a second bundle for himself and they began to work. The task was time-consuming and many of the documents were irrelevant. Clara read letter after letter that kept to the same mundane topics of the weather, the services Christian had performed for the British troops and the latest book he was reading. Christian wrote so often, that the majority of his letters had to be filled with these somewhat boring subjects. Occasionally there was something more dramatic; one letter described how an artillery shell had landed not far from where Christian was holding mass and had showered him and his congregation with mud.

Clara could not help but wonder how much Christian had not mentioned in his letters to his sister. How much had he self-censored his own writing to avoid worrying Emily? There had to have been many more disturbing and upsetting situations occurring than he wrote about. If you took Christian's letters at face value, it would almost appear as if nothing much was happening at all on the Front and everyone was really quite jolly, and people were not being blown-up, shot or buried alive on a regular basis.

"The letters feel like a dead-end to me," Clara said to Tommy.

"Typical of the sort of stuff you write home," Tommy nodded. "All the ordinary things you can think of, so as not to worsen the concerns of those left behind. I imagine most of my letters were the same."

"They were," Clara nodded. "You know, you could have been more open with me back then, if you had wanted to. I was not oblivious to what was occurring."

"No," Tommy shook his head. "In a way, writing the dull as dishwater letters was cathartic. It made you focus on the ordinary, sane stuff, rather than the madness that was happening all around. I didn't want to put down in ink or graphite what I was enduring. Somehow that would have made it all the more real."

Clara placed another letter into the 'not relevant' pile and gave a sigh.

"I wonder if Christian's letters to his father were more insightful?"

"I have a hunch they have been all destroyed," Tommy said grimly. "I just get the impression that was the sort of man he was. He made the effort to pretend his son never existed after he learned of the rumours. He would not have wanted to keep something so incriminating as letters."

"Then we will never know if there might have been something in them that made Mr Lound have his own doubts about his son," Clara added.

"Ah, so you are reconsidering my suggestion that he already had suspicions of something untoward, which made him quicker to accept the news that Christian was a traitor?" Tommy grinned.

"All right, I may be considering that possibility. But what I meant was that maybe Mr Lound sensed an undercurrent in his son's writing that made his disappearance seem understandable. Maybe Christian sounded depressed in his letters to his father? Or wrote of the horrors he was witness to?"

"We'll never know. I imagine you are not going to attempt to talk to Mr Lound?"

"I thought about it," Clara admitted. "But the man is an accomplished politician and capable of avoiding answering any question put to him. I very much doubt I can persuade him to talk about his son. Though I never rule out anything."

Clara had been glancing at a letter as she spoke, and suddenly she paused and drew the paper closer to her eyes.

"Tommy, does it look like something was removed from this letter?"

Clara handed over the paper. It was a thicker type of stationary than that which Christian had used later in the war. He had been writing in blue ink, but at one point it appeared that a word had been carefully scraped out with a knife, and another written on top. The paper showed the marks of the alteration, and there were faint traces of the previous word.

"I think you are right," Tommy agreed. "Seems to me he has changed the name here."

The sentence in the letter read; 'there is an abandoned orchard nearby and I went with Ramon to collect apples for the children.' Someone had scrubbed out a word in the space where 'Ramon' was written.

"Ramon has been mentioned in several letters," Tommy noted.

"I found one where he is identified as an older Belgium boy who did odd jobs about Albion Hope and was given food and clothes in return for his family," Clara quickly returned to the 'irrelevant' pile and went through the letters until she came to the one she meant. "Here it is. Ramon is described by Christian as being aged about sixteen and a keen sportsman. He says the boy has a mother and three sisters. His father is dead, and he would take on any work to help support his family."

"But Ramon was not the original name written here," Tommy said. He was tipping the paper from one side to the other, to try to get the light to catch on the altered section. "You don't waste paper in a war. The wrong name was put here and rather than throw the sheet away and begin again, Christian did what he could to correct the mistake."

"Are we making more of this than needs be?" Clara picked up another letter. "He accidentally wrote the wrong name in this letter too. He put 'John' from what I can make out, then crossed it through and wrote 'Ramon' next to it."

"That's the thing, I have seen him make errors in his other letters and he has just crossed them through and carried on," Tommy said. "This is different. In this one he went to a great deal of effort to erase whatever was originally there. Maybe that is meaningless, or maybe it is significant. It is extremely hard to scrape ink off paper without simply ripping it. He must have spent ages picking out the original word."

"What he would not be able to scrape out is the

indentations his pen had made," Clara added. "Try rubbing over the spot with a pencil and see if anything is revealed."

She handed a pencil to her brother and he lightly rubbed the tip over the correction. The paper had become fluffy in this spot, as the pulp fibres had been pulled up by the work of the knife. The impressions made by the pen nib were therefore fuzzy and unclear. However, a letter B appeared where the R of Ramon now existed. The base of the B could be seen beneath the feet of the R. The next letters were difficult to make out, but the original name (for it seemed certainly to have been a name starting with a capital) appeared to have been longer than Ramon. Past the N of the replacement name there was a faint trace of 'ice'. There was also a hint of a taller letter overwritten by the M. It might have been an L or a T, but it was certainly something that reached up higher than the loops of the M.

"I can't work out the name, but there was something else here," Tommy said. "Something he wanted to hide."

Clara frowned as she studied the marks on the paper.

"I can think of a name," she said. "But, I don't want to get obsessed by one name in case I am wrong. I think we can agree the name begins with B, so let's go through the letters and keep our eyes open for anyone Christian refers to with a name beginning with B."

They went back to work and for a while were silent. The letters were frustratingly sparse in details on the people Christian socialised with. Ramon was one of the few mentioned often and it felt as if Christian was fond of the boy, but his other colleagues and the people of the town were rarely listed. Clara was starting to feel this was deliberate, as if Christian was keeping his two worlds carefully divided. Yet, if that was the case, why was Ramon allowed to cross that divide? The boy was the only one to slip between both aspects of the priest's life.

As the correspondence started to run out, Clara felt disheartened. There had been no mention of a person with a name beginning with B, and no further carefully erased errors.

Tommy had finished with his pile of letters and was dipping back into the box. He drew out a folded piece of paper, it was a newspaper clipping.

"I saw this mentioned in one of the letters," he said to Clara. "The local mayor died in 1917. Natural causes, not because of the war. Christian conducted the funeral service. It was the first time he had officiated at a funeral, as usually the older priests took the task. He found it a very moving experience and wrote about it to Emily. He said he was sending her the newspaper clipping. I suppose he was a little proud of his first funeral."

"Seems slightly odd," Clara was surprised.

"Well, I think he was nervous about it. He had hinted about that in his letters. Guess he wanted to show his sister how well he did."

Tommy flattened the clipping on the table and started to tentatively read it.

"It's in French, of course," he said. "Oh, here is the part where he is mentioned. 'Father Christian Lound, a British Catholic priest, performed the service. His readings were considered appropriate and respectful by those gathered in attendance.' Rather dull praise."

"You can't say much about a funeral service," Clara shrugged. "Does it mention any other names? Such as one beginning with B?"

"Let's see. There is a list of the pall-bearers, ah, here is Ramon. 'Of the four pallbearers, the youngest was Monsieur Ramon Devereux, who, despite his youth, performed his task both nobly and with great dignity," Tommy drew his finger down the paper. "It is very detailed, I suppose because it was the town mayor's funeral. Here is a list of those who sent flowers and messages of sympathy. A bit further there is a detailed account of the mourners in attendance. I don't know if in Belgium they rank the mourners in relation to the deceased – family first, then friends and business associates. There are a lot of names."

Tommy was silent as he read through the list. Then he

glanced at Clara.

"That's rather interesting."

"Do tell," Clara said, trying not to be impatient as he paused for effect.

"Among those listed at the funeral is Madame Devereux, I assume Ramon's mother, and her full name is Madame Beatrice Devereux."

Clara sat back in her chair and took this in. She had wondered if the obscured name was Beatrice, the B and the 'ice' would fit, also she was struggling to think of any other names that ended with those three letters. But the woman was mentioned nowhere else, and it would seem that Christian had gone to great efforts to keep her from his writing. Why?

"Of course, it is easy to think scandalous thoughts," Tommy vocalised Clara's own musings. "Madame Devereux was a widow. And Christian seemed to have sympathy for her situation, he certainly made sure Ramon had plenty of work, so his family could be supported."

"All of which may have been done out of philanthropic generosity," Clara pointed out. "Though it does seem slightly odd that Christian did not want his connection with the widow known. Why would he make such effort to scrub her name from a letter, for instance, if the situation was purely innocent? Or did he have a strong sense of reputation like his father and fear that mentioning the woman would harm it?"

"I have a feeling those are questions that will not be answered by the contents of this box," Tommy remarked.

"I think you are right," Clara nodded.

She looked at the three piles on the table. They had catalogued most of the letters, but there were still a lot of loose papers and the file compiled by Gerald Priggins to look through. Clara stretched her shoulders out.

"You know Tommy, I do understand your reluctance to go to Belgium," she said as casually as she could.

"I don't want to talk about it," Tommy said sharply.

Clara picked up one of the few remaining letters to sort.

"You don't have to talk about it. You just have to understand that there is a very good chance I shall have to go to Belgium," she said. "I would never push you to join me. I just need you to understand."

"Really, must we? I know my own damn limitations!" Tommy abruptly pushed back his chair and rose. He stalked to the door of the room.

Clara called out behind him.

"You know as well as I do that the only limitations we have are the ones we impose on ourselves. You are your own worst enemy, Tommy. I can't change that, only you can. What you really have to ask yourself is whether this is a battle you think necessary to fight, or whether you can live with the restrictions you are imposing on yourself."

Tommy had stopped in the doorway. He was listening, but Clara could not see his face to know if her words had caused hurt, anger or perhaps realisation. She was not trying to upset her brother, but sometimes he needed a firm nudge in the right direction. The only question that remained was whether he cared that his inner demons were confining him to England.

She thought he would say something. She thought he might snap back. Instead, Tommy walked out the door and disappeared. Clara rubbed at her eyes, feeling tired and foolish. Had her words been rash? Tommy had suffered deep mental trauma during the war and maybe she had no right to question his decision to never set foot out of England again.

Then again, maybe each little nudge to shrug off those demons was a step to helping him to have a sounder, more balanced existence? She just wasn't sure. Probably no one was.

She sighed and went back to the letters. What demons was Christian Lound hiding beneath the talk of rain and church services? Was it just such a demon that had caused him to disappear?

Or was it something happier? Had he fallen in love with a woman? It was too early to say for sure, but Clara was going to resolve the mystery. One way or the other.

Chapter Five

The following day Clara caught the train to Worthing to pay a call on St John's Seminary. She was not sure what sort of reception she would receive, being as she was a woman striding into a man's world. But she hoped they allowed visitors. After all, even priests had mothers and sisters.

The rain had let up and a fragile sun was hovering in the sky. Clara was travelling alone. Tommy had been sombre the previous evening and had barely talked at dinner. Clara had confessed to Annie what she had said and her guilt over her words. Annie was not concerned. She told Clara to go about her business and leave Tommy to her.

Worthing seemed a nice town; Clara glimpsed it as she headed out of the train station to one of the cabs standing nearby. She asked the driver to take her to the seminary and she felt slightly more confident when he did not seem surprised. Maybe the priests quite often received female visitors?

The hooves of the horse clicked a steady rhythm over the cobbles and she settled into her seat, contemplating what she would say when she arrived at the school. It was hard to know the best way to approach the subject. She wasn't going to mention the rumours about Christian being a traitor, she hoped she could get away with just saying he had disappeared during the war and his sister had asked her to find him, which was perfectly true. Hopefully the priests would be accommodating to her enquiries.

It took half-an-hour to reach the seminary which was on the outskirts of town; it was set in large gardens and as private as it was possible to be with a town nearby. The cabman took her right up to the door and then charged her a small fortune for the privilege. Clara decided she would be walking on the return trip. The cabman still made no comment about a woman coming to a seminary and abandoned her the second she had paid him. Clara was certain that Brighton cabmen were much better mannered.

She walked up to the front door, (or at least the door she assumed was considered the front door) and rang the bell. She quickly looked about for any notices that might indicate women were not welcome, but saw no such signs. She was still feeling rather agitated when an older man in a priest's cassock opened the door.

"Good morning," Clara said.

"Good morning, daughter. Have you come for Father McKelly's women's netball team tryouts? If so, you are an hour too early," the priest said mildly.

Clara was thrown by this statement. She opened her mouth to explain why she was really there and then hesitated.

"Women's netball team?"

"Ah, you are not here for that," the priest picked up on her tone. "May I ask, how I may help?"

"Oh, I am Clara Fitzgerald," Clara started to hold out her hand for him to shake and then stopped herself. Did priests shake hands? And if they did, did they shake hands with women? "I was hoping to speak to anyone who knew a former student of the seminary."

"Has there been an issue?" The priest looked concerned.

"He is missing," Clara elaborated. "Actually, he has been missing these past five years and his sister would like to know what became of him. I am trying to find people who knew him and, of course, this seemed a logical place to begin."

"Naturally," the priest looked a touch relieved, as if he had expected a worse problem than a missing man of the cloth. Perhaps he had feared a scandal was brewing. "Why don't you come in to Father Creek's office, he is in charge of the seminary and will be best placed to answer your questions."

"Thank you," Clara stepped through the door and followed the priest. "But, I am curious, why is there a women's netball team at a seminary? Surely this is a male only establishment?"

The priest gave her an amused smile.

"The seminary is not as busy as it used to be, not so many young men choosing to become priests. We have time on our hands and have chosen to branch out into community projects. To help those around us is part of our Christian duty. We heard that some of the girls in the villages around here were interested in playing sports, but had no equipment nor a suitable venue. For that matter, they didn't have any idea of which sport they wished to try or how to play it. Father McKelly used to be a sports coach and offered his time and experience," the priest laughed. "I suppose there were some raised eyebrows at first, but once the idea got going a number of girls came along. Now Father McKelly is organising a team to attend the South West Netball Championships."

They had come to a door and the priest opened it and motioned for Clara to enter.

"It is also good for our students to work with the community. A priest does much more than just give mass. He is a fundamental part of the parish, spiritually and socially. We must make sure our priests are prepared for such a role."

"That I understand," Clara nodded.

"I shall find Father Creek for you," the priest said. "Can I get you some tea?"

"Thank you."

The priest quietly closed the door and Clara was left alone in the office. She didn't quite know what to do with herself. She had never been in a priest's office before. She walked to the window and looked out into the grounds. She could see a couple of men in cassocks walking briskly along a path, deep in discussion. Somewhere deep in the building a bell rang, but Clara had no idea what it meant.

She wandered about the room. There was a large bookcase filling the entire back wall opposite the office desk and she glanced at the titles on display. As she had expected, they were all of a religious nature, from academic essays on the saints to books of hymns. Clara never knew so much had been written about religion. She found one book which was a directory of priests living in the British isles, both retired and active. She lifted it off the shelf and scanned the index for Christian Lound. She found him and then flipped to his entry. The book had been published in 1915 and all it stated under his name was that he had become an ordained priest in 1913 and was currently working in Belgium. She replaced the book.

The door opened again and the priest who had guided her into the house appeared with a tray of tea things.

"Father Creek will be here very shortly," he promised, placing two cups and saucers on the table along with the teapot and milk jug. "I'm sorry for the delay."

"That's all right," Clara moved back to the desk. "It is not as if you were expecting me."

"May I ask, who is the priest you are enquiring about?"

Clara saw no harm in answering.

"Father Christian Lound," she said. "He left the seminary in 1913 and not long after went to Belgium to bring comfort to the troops."

The priest frowned for a moment, then he went back to laying out the tea things, finishing his task by placing a bowl of sugar next to the teapot.

"I remember Father Lound," he said. "I was here from 1910. He was a good man, a very dedicated student. An idealist."

Clara thought that sounded worrying. Idealists did not always see the world the way others did. They might just happen to do something that they felt was right, but which could seem to the rest of the world to be treachery.

"I did not realise he was missing," the priest continued. "Of course, there were priests lost in the war."

"What is this? What are we talking about?"

A man had appeared at the door. He was also dressed in a cassock and Clara guessed this was Father Creek. He was short and very stout. He rather looked like someone had made him out of wax and then sat him on a sunny windowsill and left him to melt a little. His flesh seemed to sag, his whole body melting into rolling layers. He had such a belly on him, that it caused him to walk with his back heavily arched to counterbalance the weight. He reminded Clara of a heavily pregnant woman trying to negotiate about the room.

"Father Creek, this is Miss Clara Fitzgerald. She has come to make enquiries regarding one of our former students."

"He hasn't run off with a parishioner, has he?" Father Creek scowled.

"Nothing like that," Clara hastily said though, in truth, she had no idea what Lound had done and it was entirely possible that his reason for vanishing was of a much more serious nature than just breaking his priestly vows. "He went missing in the war. His sister fears he is dead, but would like to know what became of him."

"Well then, how can we help?" Father Creek blustered. "We had nothing to do with sending priests out to the Front. We are a place of learning."

Clara was starting to feel uneasy. She was not sure she wanted to reveal her true reasons for coming to this man. He gave the impression of being very narrow-minded and not the sort who would be discreet with the information that one of his former students might have been a traitor. Clara did not want to spread the rumours about Christian any further. That would be awful for Emily and was not the purpose of her enquiries. She had promised to be discreet, and she would abide by that.

Father Creek was not giving the impression of a man who would keep such a thing secret.

"I was hoping to get a better idea of Father Lound's character," Clara explained.

"I thought you were working for his sister? Surely she can tell you what he was like?" Father Creek muttered.

"Family always tends to be biased," Clara continued patiently. "Equally, they often will only see one side of a person. Friends and acquaintances will have different views which can be useful for creating a clearer picture of the individual."

"I think you are barking up the wrong tree with that," Father Creek flopped down in a chair behind the desk, it gave a considerable groan. "Family knows family best. In any case, I don't remember this Father Lound. I do have a directory…"

Father Creek waved a hand at the bookcase.

"I saw it while I was waiting," Clara interrupted him, feeling annoyed with the man. "I did glance at Father Lound's entry. It was not very enlightening."

"Well, I can't see how I can help you," Father Creek snorted. "I don't keep track of all the students who come through our doors. Did the family not receive a telegram telling them what happened?"

"No," Clara said, not feeling the energy to explain further. She had had enough. "I am sorry to have wasted your time. I shall continue my enquiries elsewhere."

Clara could see that she was going to achieve nothing with Father Creek. His attitude was one of disinterest and no amount of talking was going to change that. She rose and left the room, not really caring if Father Creek thought her rude. She had made it to the front door before the friendly priest caught up with her. He had been present for her brief interview with Father Creek and had followed her as she left.

"Please wait a moment," he now called to her.

Clara had stopped by the door, she didn't want to hang around. She was annoyed that her trip here had been a waste of time, not because of a lack of information, but because Father Creek was so unwilling to help her. She could tell that he was a man only interested in the reputation of his seminary. That was why she could not tell him about the rumours concerning Lound. She feared he would react in a similar way to Christian's father, accepting the gossip at face value and instantly going to work to cover-up the seminary's connection. He would be of no use to her. She only paused now because the friendly priest seemed to genuinely want to speak with her, and he had been pleasant.

"Father Creek can be brusque," the priest began.

"Please," Clara interrupted before he could carry on, "I really do not need an apology, or for you to defend him. I've met plenty of individuals like Father Creek, who are so obsessed by their own world and their role in it, that they cannot be bothered to consider the importance of other people's lives. For him Christian Lound is irrelevant and I don't need to waste my time attempting to change his mind. I know too well I won't succeed."

Clara opened the front door, ready to leave. The friendly priest placed his hand on the door, preventing her from pulling it open.

"Would you talk to me?" He said.

Clara glanced at him.

"Why?" She asked.

"Because I knew Christian Lound," the priest said. "And I would like to help you find out what became of him. I did not know he had vanished during the war. I have lived in happy ignorance that he was continuing on his life without a problem. To learn otherwise is a shock."

Clara removed her hand from the door and took a better look at the priest. He was much younger than Creek and in far better physical shape. He was unremarkable in appearance, though his face was open and gentle, which added a certain attraction. Clara decided she should give him a chance, after all, he probably knew more about Lound than Father Creek did.

"All right," she said, "let's talk. Father…?"

"Father Dobson," the priest introduced himself. "Might I suggest we go somewhere private?"

"Lead the way," Clara said.

Father Dobson gave his warm smile, then showed Clara out of the front door.

Chapter Six

There was a large summerhouse in the garden. Father Dobson led them there. He explained that it was a place often used for meditation, but was typically empty at this time of the day when the students were attending to their lessons.

Father Dobson gave Clara a brief guide to his life as he showed her where to go. He was just turned forty and had spent his whole adult life in the priesthood. Coming from an impoverished background, there had not been much time for religion in his early days, in fact, it was deemed an unnecessary luxury in the day-to-day existence of his parents. Survival was the name of the game. If they all got to eat a square meal once a day, then they were happy.

Dobson had been a sickly child, probably some sort of deficiency, he confided lightly. He struggled to learn to walk and he was never very strong. He was rather useless in his father's eyes, though the man was kind enough not to make a huge drama of his disappointment. It was just hinted at now and then. Dobson was never going to be able to bring money to the family through manual labour, he knew that early on. The best he could do was find a way not to be a burden upon their meagre resources.

He had considered joining the army when he was old enough, but his health and fitness excluded him. It was by chance he learned of the priesthood. He had been caught in the rain while walking home from school one day. His mother always insisted he avoid getting wet as she feared it would ruin his already poor health. Knowing this, when the heavens opened he had dived for cover in the nearest place he could find. It happened to be a Roman Catholic Church.

"That was the turning point, my eyes were opened," Dobson explained.

He was taken under the wing of a kindly old priest, who taught the boy what he could about God and religion. Dobson became fascinated, but was at first reluctant to pursue his new passion as it was not practical or capable of putting food on the family table. To encourage the boy, the old priest explained to Dobson that he could become a Father too one day. He would have a job and money to send to his family, without having to perform the manual labour he struggled with.

"And that was that," Dobson smiled. "My father was unhappy at first, my mother thought I was going to be snatched away. But my mentor came to see them and explained everything in detail. I never looked back. I live a frugal life and all my spare money I send back to my parents. It feels good knowing I can help them at last."

Dobson opened the door to the summerhouse and Clara stepped inside. It was several degrees warmer in the building, the large windows having channelled and contained the sunshine outside. It was very pleasant. There were several wicker chairs in the building and Dobson motioned for her to take one. He sat nearby.

"I sympathised with Christian when he arrived. His father had not understood his calling either, but whereas my father was prepared to accept my decision, Christian's nearly disowned him," Dobson leaned back in his chair. "Christian wanted to achieve so much. He was driven, determined, but I feared his passion would get the better of him."

"How so?" Clara asked.

"I feared he would exhaust his enthusiasm," Dobson

said, frowning as he endeavoured to compose his thoughts. "Sometimes people think they have a calling and go for that calling with such passion that they burn themselves out through their endeavours. I don't know, I felt that Christian could become disillusioned, perhaps even turn his back on religion. He was too over-zealous.

"The other tutors here did not seem to see it. They loved his enthusiasm. Any task, challenge or outside course they came up with Christian instantly volunteered for it. He would take on anything as if that was the only way he could prove himself good enough for the clergy. I soon saw a great cloak of weariness overcoming him. He was so tired, so worn out that he struggled to remember why he was studying in the first place. That is a dangerous thing. He was in peril of growing to resent the very calling that had brought him here in the first place."

"However, he did become an ordained priest," Clara said.

Dobson nodded.

"There were a couple of occasions when I thought he was going to give up. I had words with him, said he needed to be less intense about his training. He did not have to volunteer for everything to prove himself worthy."

"He felt unworthy of becoming a priest?" Clara asked.

"Yes. Another of Christian's failings was his own self-doubt. He questioned himself constantly, believed that he was somehow more flawed than anyone else. He thought that none of the others ever had doubts or sinful thoughts. He was trying to hold himself to an impossible standard and I had my concerns that one day this would overwhelm him."

Clara felt this was a good time to reveal her true reasons for being there.

"There were rumours, after Father Lound vanished in Belgium, that he had committed some form of treachery against his country," she said carefully. "His sister does not believe this and has asked me to get to the bottom of the accusations. Part of the reason I came here was to discover

44

if Christian Lound had the potential to be a traitor. You said he was an idealist, does that mean he might have done something which could have been perceived as betraying his own people, for an idealistic reason?"

Dobson had seemed surprised by her statement, but he shook this off rapidly and considered her question.

"Christian was a man of principle. I don't think he would have betrayed his country, at least, not for financial gain. And he never struck me as a man who was anything less than patriotic."

"But what if a situation occurred that placed him in a difficult position, torn between his principles and his patriotism?"

"What sort of situation?" Dobson asked.

Clara could only shake her head.

"That I don't know."

"Christian was different, but different does not mean wrong or bad. He just saw things in ways that others did not," Dobson mused. "He judged people by their actions, not their nationality or their gender, or even their job. If he thought a priest was a bad man he would not be afraid to say as much. Even to their face."

"Did people like him at the seminary?" Clara asked.

"He had many friends," Dobson agreed. "I could give you some names, if it would help? Unfortunately, he also had enemies. When he saw hypocrisy or simply behaviour that was inappropriate for a would-be priest, he called it out. People don't like that sort of thing."

"Would these enemies be prepared to slander his name and reputation?" Clara asked.

Dobson did not answer at once, his gaze drifted out the window to the sunny gardens. He pursed his lips.

"Maybe," he said at last. "He never cared about that, of course. He was a good man. But then, everyone always says that about the people they like. His sister would not have asked you to look for him if she thought any differently."

"Do you think he could have betrayed his country?" Clara decided to be more direct. Dobson, like everyone else, was hedging.

Dobson's frown deepened, he seemed to have trouble conjuring up the right words, when he spoke it was with hesitation.

"I want to say no, I want to say that Christian's patriotism was unquestionable. But the truth is, I am not sure. Patriotism is not a real thing, it's not a person. It is a concept and it is hard to be loyal to a concept. It is just as hard to be loyal to a country, which again is a concept. You could argue that your 'country' is its people, or it might be considered the king and what he stands for, or it could be some artificial notion of place and being. Whichever way you look at it, it is vague.

"Place next to that notion a person – a living, breathing person – and you have to ask yourself, would I do something for this person at the expense of my country? Of course, it depends on your relationship with that person, but there is a good chance that the answer, if you cared enough about that individual and believed in them, would be yes. Supposing you had a choice of helping someone in desperate danger at the expense of your country? Where does patriotism stand in such an equation? As a priest, I am afraid the needs of a person must come before any concept of loyalty to a place, a king or even the conventional politics of war."

Clara considered this.

"What you are saying is that Father Lound may have betrayed his country, but not for the reasons we might imagine traitors consider, rather, for Christian principles?"

Father Dobson shrugged his shoulders.

"If he betrayed his country. And I might be wrong. Christian, however, struck me as a man who was always trying to do what was right, and what is right is not always what you are supposed to do."

Clara sat back in her chair, taking in this information. It was not the sort of thing Emily would want to hear. She believed her brother incapable of betrayal, whatever she said to the contrary, Clara saw in her eyes and manner that she was convinced Christian was innocent. It was going to hurt her a lot to be wrong.

"Do you know anything about Albion Hope, the organisation Christian worked for in Belgium?"

"I do," Father Dobson nodded. "I visited it once. Father Creek was very angry about my insistence on going abroad during a time of war, but I needed to see for myself what war did to men. I had to see the blood, the bullet wounds, the dead, all for myself. I have always been something of a pacifist. My experiences in Belgium only confirmed my belief that war is evil."

"We had to stop the Germans," Clara pointed out. "Should we have just stood by and let them overrun Belgium?"

Father Dobson frowned.

"I like to think there was another way, a peaceful way."

"If a man is determined to attack you, kill you even, then peaceful words rarely change that. Sometimes you have to fight back in self-defence. I don't like it, but when a nation draws arms on innocents, we have to act," Clara sighed sadly. "I hope we never experience such a war again."

"Man is a destructive creature," Dobson mused. "I saw that in Belgium. But I was given hope by the sight of a house dedicated to restoring some peace to the men serving. If only such a thing could have been multiplied a hundred times over, all along the Front."

"Did you see Father Lound there?"

"He invited me," Father Dobson smiled. "We exchanged letters quite often."

"You have letters from Father Lound?" Clara said, feeling a sudden pang of excitement. "From his time at the Front?"

"Yes, a few," Dobson said. "Up until early 1917, I believe, then we stopped communicating."

"Why?"

Dobson blushed and dropped his head, looking embarrassed.

"I had a crisis of faith," he admitted unhappily. "At that

time I was helping a lot in the local villages, assisting them to fund raise for the troops and put together care packages. We raised enough to buy a tank, you know."

"Impressive, especially for a pacifist," Clara said, though her words were not sarcastic.

Father Dobson tilted his head.

"Fair point. I did not always abide by the principles I held, not in that instance, at least. I also had other things on my mind, which swayed my judgement," Dobson groaned to himself. "You must not repeat any of this, I am only telling you this in case it has any bearing on the situation with Father Lound. Perhaps the fact I cut off our friendship contributed to his later disappearance, I do not know. I have always felt bad that I behaved so churlishly, but by the time I was suitably contrite, the war had ended, and I did not know where Christian was to write to him and apologise. Besides, the longer things went on without me apologising, the harder it felt to compose a letter. Maybe Father Lound needed me later on and I was not there."

"You cannot really know that," Clara gently reassured him.

Father Dobson just sighed.

"You are kind, but the truth is I know that Christian felt alone and isolated. He had the other priests at Albion Hope, yes, but they were much older than him and he saw them as superiors rather than friends," Dobson's mouth drooped sadly. "It all came down to my own silliness. I became infatuated with the woman in charge of the fund raising. I began to think I was in love and, of course, that was completely against my oath to God. I was confused and worried. I wrote to Christian about it, he was the only one I dared reveal myself to. It helped that he was abroad and I did not have to look him in the face to confess. However, his reply shocked me."

"Why was that?" Clara asked.

"Christian told me that God would not deny me love, that he had placed this woman in my path for the very reason of giving me the chance to be happy. He said I should consider ignoring my spiritual promises and abandon the priesthood to go with this woman if I truly loved her!"

Father Dobson looked appalled and amazed by the suggestion, as if it had only just been made to him. Clearly it had shocked him senseless.

"Quite a remarkable thing to say," Clara noted.

"I was angered by his response. It was suggesting that there were things out there greater than the promise I had given to God, a promise that I had sworn to uphold all my days! I am not the sort of priest to ignore my vows, I know some would..." Father Dobson became solemn. "I did not think Christian was that sort of priest either, but his words shamed me and made me so upset that I became quite petty about it all and never wrote a reply. I suppose Christian guessed, as he only wrote a couple more letters and then desisted. I failed to be forgiving and all these years that fact has haunted me."

"Could I see the letters you did receive from Christian? They may be of use to me."

"You can have them," Father Dobson said. "Now Christian is missing, I cannot ask his forgiveness and they sit and taunt me instead."

"One last thing," Clara said. "Did you ever meet a boy named Ramon at Albion Hope?"

Father Dobson frowned.

"I may have done. There were several lads who helped out at the house from time to time. They were paid to do odd jobs and run errands. I never really paid attention to their names, however."

"No matter," Clara smiled. "You have been very helpful."

Father Dobson shrugged.

"Not to Christian," he said miserably.

Chapter Seven

Annie took a cup of tea to Tommy, who was sitting in the morning room at the back of the house. At one time this had been changed to a bedroom for Tommy. He had come home from the war in a wheelchair and had been unable to go upstairs to use his original bedroom. Four years later, he had regained the use of his legs and the morning room had been returned to its former function.

Tommy's legs might be fixed, but the demons that had chased him home from the Front still clung to him. Shaking them off might be the work of a lifetime. There was just no telling when they might spring up. Like this moment, right now; talk of Belgium had stirred the monsters within Tommy's psyche and left him restless and unhappy. Annie did not know how to fix that, so she did what she knew best, she made tea and cooked comforting food, in the hope that this would solve the problem.

Tommy was stood by the tall windows looking out into the garden, which was a fraction overgrown. He glanced up as Annie entered.

"More tea? That is my fifth cup today," he said, teasing.

"It will do you good," Annie set the cup on a small occasional table.

"If only tea was the solution to life's endless battles," Tommy said gently. "Thank you."

Annie frowned, annoyed she had been caught out in her efforts.

"I did not mean it harshly," Tommy apologised. "I

appreciate your concern."

"Tea made me feel a lot better when I was recovering from my operation," Annie said, still annoyed that her secret efforts had been noticed. "Tea is very good for you."

"It is Annie, and your tea is certainly the finest," Tommy came over and gave her a hug, holding her tight.

For a moment Annie was surprised, then she relaxed and put her arms around him. Tommy dipped his head down, resting it on the top of hers and gave a long sigh.

"When did life get so complicated Annie?"

"It isn't complicated," Annie answered. "You just take it moment by moment. And if things get upsetting, you have a cup of tea."

"Oh, if only I could be so sensible!" Tommy squeezed her lightly and then stepped back. "I am afraid my old head is a muddle of thoughts right now. Stuff full of jumbled nonsense, like a messy bundle of string that has been allowed to develop into lots of twists and knots."

"Then we have to unknot you," Annie reached up and stroked his cheek.

"If you have any ideas how, just say," Tommy chuckled, trying to seem easy-going about it all. The chuckle was forced, and it was apparent he was hurting quite deeply inside. "I would gladly get my head fixed."

"I know where you can start," Annie said softly.

Tommy hesitated.

"Really?" He said uneasily.

"You know how to start too," Annie added. "That is why you are in such a pickle. You know the answer, you are just afraid to admit it to yourself, because acting on the solution seems scary."

"You are speaking in riddles," Tommy pulled away and walked back to the window.

Annie stood with her hands on her hips for a moment, contemplating leaving the room or continuing the discussion. She tapped her foot twice, then decided she was not leaving.

"Thomas Fitzgerald, I can tell you how to unloosen one

of those knots in your head, but I would only be repeating to you what you already know."

"What do I already know?" Tommy grumbled, folding his arms.

"That you have to go to Belgium."

Tommy flashed a sharp look at her, his eyes blazing for a moment with a mixture of anger and hurt. Annie stood her ground.

"The reason you are in such a dither is because, deep down, you know that going back to Belgium would help you. It would scare off some of those demons that won't leave you be. It would also make you feel better about yourself."

"I feel perfectly all right about myself!" Tommy snapped.

"No, you don't," Annie softened her tone. "You are angry that you are afraid to go back. That makes you dislike yourself a little, and that is a very bad thing. If you didn't feel like that, you wouldn't be spending all this time moping."

"I'm upset because I don't want Clara to go to Belgium alone, and no one else seems to appreciate that."

"Yes, you are upset because you don't want Clara to go alone, but you also feel unable to go with her," Annie explained to him patiently. "You need to realise that."

Tommy turned his back on her and glared out the window. Annie had known this conversation was going to be hard and was not surprised that he was fighting her. She didn't need him to change his mind at that immediate moment, she just needed him to start thinking about changing his mind.

"We all have things we are scared of, that is nothing to be ashamed about. The only time it hurts is when it prevents us from doing something we really want to do, or feel we should do," Annie went back and fetched the cup of tea she had brought in. "That is when I make myself a fresh brew and let the tea leaves do their work."

She offered him the cup. Tommy did not look at her.

"My nan could read the leaves," she said, trying to move the conversation along and distract them both from the situation. "She reckoned that the leaves would tell you what to do when you had a dilemma. If you thought about your problem while drinking a cup, then the leaves at the bottom would reveal the solution. Then again, my nan had a very poor tea strainer, so she did end up with a lot of leaves at the base of her cups."

Tommy grudgingly looked over his shoulder.

"Do you believe in that?"

Annie shrugged.

"It made my nan feel better. She based many life decisions on the leaves," she said. "She bought a cow based on the leaves."

"A cow?" Tommy asked.

"She was trying to decide whether to buy a cow or a goat to provide her with milk and she could not decide, so she asked the leaves. The leaves formed a picture of a cow. So, she bought Daisy and never looked back."

"Your nan really believed in the power of leaves," Tommy was starting to mellow. "Maybe there is something in it? Who are we to judge?"

Annie offered him the teacup again.

"You think a cup of tea can provide me with the answer to whether I should go to Belgium or not?" Tommy asked her in disbelief.

"Nothing ventured..." Annie replied.

"Fine," Tommy groaned and then walked to the sofa in the room and sat down.

He sipped the tea, conscience of Annie watching him.

"Will you sit down beside me rather than hovering over me like a nurse or something?" He grumbled.

Annie tried to hide her smirk as she sat beside him. Tommy continued to drink and silence crept over them. Annie attempted to keep her eyes on the window and the garden outside rather than watching Tommy. She didn't really believe in tea leaf magic, or all those weird superstitions her nan clung to. On the other hand, she did think that sometimes silly games could open your eyes to a solution to a problem. It wouldn't hurt, anyway.

Tommy drained his cup.

"Now what?"

"There are a few ways to do the next bit, but my nan was not fancy. She just would look into the teacup and see what shape the leaves had formed."

Tommy glanced into his cup.

"I see a heap of tea leaves."

Annie took the cup off him. She did have to admit that the picture they painted was not very clear.

"Hang on," she said.

She put the saucer on top of the cup and gave the whole thing a swirl while it was held in her hands. Then she removed the saucer and took another look.

"That's better. The leaves have separated."

She gave the cup back to Tommy, who was still looking sceptical.

"Let your mind relax and think about nothing as you concentrate on the leaves," Annie said, remembering her nan's words. "Try to find pictures in the leaves."

"I don't think I see anything, maybe you should look," Tommy responded.

"It has to be done by you, it's your thoughts and questions," Annie shook her head.

Tommy gazed at the leaves for a long time. Then he gave a little sniff.

"I think I see the letter B," he said.

"Anything else?"

Tommy curled up his face in concentration then shook his head.

"Give it another swirl," Annie suggested.

Tommy obeyed and the leaves shifted position. He stared at them for even longer this time, a frown growing on his face.

"What is it?" Annie asked.

"Just a moment," Tommy rose and went to a bookcase in the room. He selected a large size folio volume from the shelves and brought it back to the sofa. Scanning the index first, he opened it to a specific page and then pressed his finger down onto the paper.

Annie was looking over his arm and saw that he had turned to a double page spread showing a map of Europe. Tommy's finger was sitting on Belgium.

"It's a load of rot, of course," Tommy grumbled to himself. "Just because the tea leaves look like the shape of Belgium, it means nothing."

Annie took the cup from his hands and then compared the pattern in the leaves with the picture of Belgium on the map. The outline of the borders of the country did seem to match the shape that had formed in the tea leaves. Annie was rather astounded.

"I've never seen anything like that before!"

"It's like the games psychologists play with funny blots of ink," Tommy was still protesting. "You can read anything into a shape."

"What about the letter B you saw?"

"Again, I was seeing what I wanted to see," Tommy argued. "The mind is clever like that. It's the unconscious part that does all this."

"Then, you saw the letter B and you saw the shape of Belgium because you unconsciously feel you should go there?" Annie asked tentatively.

"Or because it is on my mind," Tommy countered.

"But, why would it be on your mind if you did not think you should go there?"

"Look, it's just a bunch of tea leaves," Tommy slammed shut the atlas. "It doesn't mean anything."

Annie decided it was best to say no more. She had nudged Tommy in the right direction and she didn't think pressing the matter further would do any good.

"I imagine my fruit cake must be done by now," she stood up and started to leave the room. "Would you like a ham sandwich for lunch? I have leftover ham from Sunday's dinner and there is homemade pickle?"

Tommy was silent, sitting forward with his hands

clenched on his knees and looking miserable. Annie felt bad. She had meant to help him, but it looked more like she had added to his woes. She headed for the kitchen feeling awful.

Truth was, she could never understand what he was going through. It was outside of her own experience. Maybe pushing him was not the answer. Maybe he should just blank out that piece of his past. Trouble was, the more Annie thought about it, the more her instincts told her that Tommy had to face his demons and that meant going back to Belgium and walking in his past footsteps. Annie's instincts were rarely wrong, and she trusted them. But was she right to trust them now?

Annie had become so distracted that it took her a moment before she realised that there was a smell of burning in her kitchen. With a flutter of panic, she raced to her oven and pulled her fruit cake out. It was charred a little at the edges and there was a fair chance it would be rather dry.

"Oh, for crying out loud!" Annie declared forcefully, slamming the offending cake down on the kitchen table.

Bramble, the Fitzgeralds' black poodle, bounced into the kitchen and pranced on his back legs to see what the commotion was.

"You're not getting any of it," Annie told him firmly. "Do you know the last time I burned anything? Anything at all? It was 1918, and that only happened because someone shouted that a zeppelin was coming over and we all had to run for cover. And they were wrong, so it was not my fault I burned the pork joint that day."

"Annie, what's wrong?" Tommy entered the kitchen after hearing the noise.

"I burnt my fruit cake," Annie puttered.

"Oh," Tommy looked at the cake and then grinned. "Didn't see that in the tea leaves."

"You're horrible," Annie flapped a tea towel at him. "You know how I feel about burning food. It's an awful waste!"

"It will be perfectly edible," Tommy reassured her. "And you have to have these odd moments of imperfection so that us mere mortals know you are still human when it comes to cooking."

Annie raised an eyebrow at him. He was stepping into dangerous territory.

"If I get this out of the tin and get it cooling quickly, I might just salvage my pride," Annie said in a mock haughty voice.

She grabbed up a cooling rack and inverted the cake onto it, shaking and tapping the tin to loosen the contents and free it.

"I've made a decision," Tommy said while she was distracted. "But it has nothing to do with tea leaves."

"Oh?" Annie said, not really listening.

"I'm going to go to Belgium," Tommy said.

The cake loosened at the same moment and crashed out onto the wire cooling rack with a thud. Annie stared at it, then smiled.

"Good," she declared. "In that case I am coming too. I want some new cake recipes."

"You could have told me you were going to go sooner," Tommy complained.

"Would it have made a difference?"

He had no answer.

"Then that's settled," Annie deftly turned her cake over so it was sitting properly on the rack. "Clara will be delighted."

Chapter Eight

It was another two days before a reply came from Colonel Matthews. It was blunt and to the point.

"Thank you for your letter. I must decline your request to speak to me regarding Father Lound. I am not at liberty to speak on official matters concerning him."

Clara was annoyed. There were no 'official matters' as far as she could tell. The matter had gone no further than a few rumours. She had not even mentioned that she was investigating Father Lound's supposed treachery, only that she was trying to discover what had happened to him after he had vanished. She was not, however, defeated. She had been researching Colonel Matthews in Brighton's library and had discovered which regiment he had served with. As it happened, she knew someone locally who had served with him.

Colonel Brandt was a friend of the late uncle of Captain O'Harris. He was long retired from the army and rather unsettled in civilian life. He had never married and his loneliness was palpable, so much so, that when Clara became involved in unravelling the mystery of what happened to the late O'Harris, she had ended up befriending the good colonel and inviting him for Sunday tea. He now visited them at least once a month, usually when Annie was doing her beef roast, which was his favourite.

Clara was hopeful that Brandt might be able to offer her an introduction to Colonel Matthews, but first she had to track him down. When Brandt was not at home he tended to be at the Brighton Gentleman's Club which, as the name suggested, did not entertain women. Clara had never been one for listening to rules, however, and strode into the club without hesitation. The porter spotted her with a look of alarm and started in her direction. Clara held up a hand to halt him.

"I'm not here to cause trouble," she assured him.

"That would be a first," the porter grumbled.

Clara was amused, not offended.

"Is Colonel Brandt here?"

"He arrived an hour ago," the porter replied cautiously.

"Could you pass a message to him saying that I would like a word," Clara smiled politely.

The porter was suspicious, but he obeyed, deciding that was the safer option than resisting. Clara might do something awful like barge into the smoking room and disturb the gentlemen if he protested. It always puzzled Clara as to why the presence of a woman should be of such alarm to these men. Why were they so determined to flee from the feminine element of the population? Considering many were not married or were now widowed, it could hardly be blamed on a nagging wife at home they were aiming to escape.

The club butler bustled past as she was waiting and gave her a dark look. Clara responded with a wink and he hurried on even faster. Clara shook her head. It was really remarkable.

It was not long before the porter returned with Colonel Brandt. Brandt smiled at Clara and greeted her warmly.

"You look very well," he said.

"And you," Clara responded. "Annie says you must take some more of her homemade marmalade when you next visit."

"Splendid! She does make it nice and tart, as I prefer. Care to come into the visitor's lounge?"

Clara glanced at the porter who had a face like thunder. "I wouldn't mind," she grinned.

Colonel Brandt showed her into the cosy lounge which was set aside for club members to meet with non-members. A number of the club's patrons were businessmen who liked to arrange meetings within the private confines of the club. The lounge, however, was not supposed to ever have women inside it. Clara sat down in one of the huge leather sofas, almost disappearing. Colonel Brandt took a seat in the opposite sofa, settling down with a groan.

"Now, how can I help you?"

"I am hoping you know a gentleman called Colonel Matthews. He was in your regiment."

"Not just in it," Brandt chuckled. "He replaced me when I retired. They promoted him to fill my shoes, so to speak. What do you want with him?"

"I am working on a case that I think he has information about," Clara explained. "No, actually, I know he has information, but I have to find a way to get him to talk to me. I wrote him a letter, but he refuses to discuss the subject."

"And what is the subject?" Brandt asked.

"In essence, it is about a Catholic priest who vanished in 1917. Matthews wrote to the priest's father informing him that there were rumours his son was a traitor. I want to know what evidence there is for that statement and whether Colonel Matthews knows anything more."

Brandt whistled.

"That is a very serious allegation, especially against a priest. I assume the man was British?"

"Yes, and he has been missing since 1917. His sister wants to know what happened to him, she would also like it proved that he was not a traitor."

"Messy business," Colonel Brandt shook his head. "War makes men do funny things. Still, to write to someone to tell them that their son is a traitor is rather unpleasant."

"Matthews was a friend of the family and I believe his letter was to act as a forewarning of potential trouble. The man in question was the son of Amadeus Lound."

"That pompous politician!" Brandt gave a dismissive snort. "Yes, he would be having kittens if he thought his son was a traitor. Would tar his reputation. But nothing was ever said."

"No, it would seem the situation went no further," Clara agreed. "Possibly because Father Lound was simply impossible to trace."

"And you want to know what really was going on? If there was anything to back up the accusations?"

"Yes, I want to know why Colonel Matthews wrote that letter. He must, I would hope, have had good reason. He is my only link with that element of the case."

"I can see why Matthews would be cautious to speak with you," Brandt said. "Treachery is a very sensitive subject. It may even be that he feels he was wrong in mentioning it in the first place."

"If so, he does not appear to have made the effort to clear Father Lound's name," Clara replied. "You can't go around accusing men of treachery and then pretend it never happened. He either had evidence for it or he did not. And if he did not, then he was wrong to cause the family such pain by mentioning the possibility."

"I agree," Colonel Brandt said gently. "But Matthews is not an ogre. He genuinely cares about his men and I always considered him a good officer. Very loyal, very patriotic. Perhaps a little stubborn, but not in a bad way. He was always very concerned about doing things properly. It would surprise me if he acted without genuine reason. He would not just report rumours."

"Can you persuade him to speak to me?" Clara asked.

Colonel Brandt frowned.

"He was under my command for a time. I might be retired, but I still have a degree of authority, even if it is out of respect for the position I once held rather than anything official. Matthews went back to normal duties after the war, you only need so many colonels in peacetime, but Matthews is a career man. He has his regimental office in London."

"I wrote to his home address," Clara said.

"He will spend much of his time in the city," Colonel Brandt tapped his fingers on the arm of the sofa. "There is still a lot of post-war regimental work to do. Men are still being slowly discharged and then there is all the pension business and general paperwork. The further up the ranks you get the more time you spend behind a desk. I'll see about arranging a meeting with him."

"Thank you," Clara was very grateful, having feared she might be stuck in this case before she began. "That will be much appreciated."

"He is a good man," Brandt repeated himself. "If he has called a man a traitor then I would not doubt him."

Clara could offer no comment on that. She thanked Colonel Brandt again and then made her farewells. The club butler was very relieved to see her go.

Back on the street outside, Clara considered her options. So far everything was proving a dead end. Father Dobson had raised possibilities and given her an explanation for why Lound might betray his country, but no real answers. Clara wanted to speak to the other priests who had worked with Lound, but so far she had not been able to discover where they were. Albion Hope had ceased to exist in Belgium, from what she could tell, and those that had once worked there had moved on. Clara was reaching a point where the only reasonable next step was to go to Belgium and speak to the people who knew Lound when he was in the country. They were the ones who were with him before he vanished and might have some knowledge of what was going on at that time. The odds of solving this case from Britain were looking slimmer by the day.

The letters she had borrowed from Father Dobson had not revealed any great insight into Lound's time in Belgium. They were almost as bland as the letters he wrote to his sister, though he did occasionally discuss ecclesiastical issues that were worrying him. Lound clearly felt that he should not take sides in the war, that his work meant he ought to be neutral and serve all as equals. He had raised the subject at a time when several injured German soldiers were being held prisoner in the little town where Albion Hope stood. He had visited the men to offer them spiritual comfort and had been admonished by a British officer. He had felt stung by the rebuke and was trying to justify himself to Dobson. Clara had no idea what Dobson's reply was, but by the next letter Lound seemed to have regained his former confidence.

He appeared to be a man who cared deeply about others, whatever their nationality, but who resented having his patriotism and loyalty to his country questioned. At least, that was what he wrote in 1916; unfortunately, situations and people changed. Might Lound have altered his opinion? Maybe he felt that his religious calling overruled any loyalty he had to a country? After all, as a priest his fundamental function was to serve God and God was nationless.

Clara was starting to think it was possible Lound had betrayed his country, not out of sympathy for the German cause, but for some sense of humanity she had not yet grasped. The real question was, why had he disappeared? And was he dead or merely in hiding?

"You! Young lady!"

Clara did not at first realise she was being accosted. When she did she stopped in her tracks and glanced over as an older man ran across the street. He narrowly missed being run down by a grocer's cart, the horse veering around him just in time, causing the driver to swear.

"You!" The man barked again at Clara.

Clara realised the figure fast approaching her was Amadeus Lound and she braced herself.

"I need a word, at once!" Amadeus demanded.

Clara frowned at him.

"I do not believe we have anything to discuss."

"We do and you will talk to me," Amadeus was loud and people were taking note, though no was attempting to intervene.

"What do you want?" Clara asked him.

"We should…" Amadeus had started to notice how many people were nearby. His initial anger had forced him across the street, now he was feeling reluctant to speak out. "We should go somewhere private."

"I only intend going home," Clara told him.

She did not like the way he had yelled at her across the street and was not about to give him the opportunity to berate her in private. She knew very well why he was chasing her down. Somehow, he had learned she was investigating his son's disappearance, more than likely through Colonel Matthews who seemed very keen to protect Amadeus' reputation.

"No, you will come with me and we shall talk," Amadeus puffed up his chest, but Clara was not going to be bullied.

"I have no intention of going anywhere with you after the way you have just spoken to me," Clara told him coldly. "You can speak to me here, or not at all."

Amadeus looked like he might grab her arm and drag her away, Clara took a pace back from him and was ready to put up a fight if needs be.

"Look, you…" Amadeus ground his lips together as if not sure what name to call her. He spoke low. "I know what you are up to and I will have none of it."

"What am I up to?" Clara asked him, not intending to give him an easy time.

"You know," Amadeus snapped, his eyes slipping from side-to-side, looking at the people walking past them. "This whole matter should be forgotten about, do you hear me? No more poking your nose in it!"

"What matter?" Clara pressed him, feigning ignorance.

"Don't play dumb!" Amadeus growled and his voice had risen again, but he was not going to say the words Clara wanted him to.

In that case, Clara would say them for him.

"You mean I should stop looking into the disappearance of your son in 1917?" Clara said in a very clear and loud voice.

Amadeus shook his fist at her.

"Shut up!" He yelled at her.

"I would have thought that any father would want to know what happened to his son and why he never came home," Clara persisted. "Why have you abandoned your son, Mr Lound?"

People had stopped and were now paying full attention. Lound glanced around him and his nerve went. There were too many eyes on him and his fear for his reputation was his weakness.

"My son is dead," Amadeus hissed at Clara.

"You have proof of that?" Clara replied.

Amadeus turned on his heel and stormed off. Clara watched him go and felt herself relaxing again. Amadeus clearly believed his son was a traitor and did not want his disappearance investigated for fear of what might be found. Well, tough. Clara was poking her nose in, she was going to root around and find out the truth.

That is, as long as Emily had the courage to stand up to her father. If she asked Clara to stop, then Clara would. And that would really annoy Clara. She hated being pulled off a case, especially when she had just got her teeth into it.

Chapter Nine

Clara was not entirely surprised when Emily Priggins appeared on her doorstep that evening. She had been expecting her. Emily almost stumbled in through the door. She looked in a dreadful state and there was a nasty red mark on her cheek suggesting she had been struck. Clara took her through to the kitchen and sat her by the fire to warm her. She was shaking all over, but that might have been from shock.

The second Annie saw the woman she knew there was a great need for a fresh pot of tea. Clara pulled a chair up in front of Emily and clutched her hand.

"Your father?" She asked.

"He knows I have hired you to investigate Christian's disappearance."

Clara nodded. She had feared as much.

"I think Colonel Matthews may have revealed us. I am so sorry Emily. I was trying to contact him about your brother."

"I understand," Emily squeezed Clara's hand. She had been sobbing, but had stopped by the time she had reached the Fitzgerald house. Now she was breathless and hiccoughing from crying.

"Emily, if you wish me to stop…"

"No!" Emily's voice was so firm that it sounded just like Amadeus when he had accosted Clara. She suddenly saw that there was a lot of the father in the daughter. "You must carry on. I knew this could happen, I won't be defeated."

"Good," Clara smiled at her. "But what about you?"

Emily's head drooped. Despite her words, she looked at the end of her tether.

"We have a spare room," Clara said. "You can stay here."

Emily said nothing for a moment, then she drew herself up straighter.

"I don't intend to give my father the satisfaction of seeing me run away," Emily replied. "In any case, I need to get hold of anything that relates to my brother from the house. I can't do that here. I shall go home."

"That is very brave."

Emily snorted.

"I am too damn stubborn to do anything else. More than ever I want this matter resolved and my brother's innocence demonstrated. I want you to prove this stupid Colonel Matthews wrong, so I can throw that in my father's face!"

Clara hesitated. She was not certain Matthews was completely wrong, though the betrayal he and Amadeus Lound imagined might not be what really happened. It worried her that there could be a grain of truth in the accusation, just a grain.

"I can only find out the facts, Emily," Clara said carefully. "They may or may not prove your brother innocent."

"I appreciate that," Emily said, though Clara was not convinced.

She decided to change the subject.

"I was going through your late husband's file on Christian before you arrived."

Annie appeared with a hot cup of tea and a slice of fruit cake. She had discreetly cut off the edge where it had charred in the oven. Emily accepted both tea and cake.

"Gerald was very supportive. He would have solved the mystery of my brother's disappearance, if only he had had more time."

Emily fell silent, a new sadness creeping over her. She

was a woman who had lost an awful lot in her short life and for reasons out of her control. Clara felt she was clinging to her brother's memory as a means of surviving her grief for her husband.

"Your husband confirmed my suspicions that nothing much was ever officially done by the military over this matter. The intelligence service does not appear to have delved deeply into the situation. I think someone covered it up, probably to protect your father more than your brother."

"Colonel Matthews," Emily said.

"I would imagine so. What is his link with your family? Why is he so determined to shield your father?"

"I don't know much about him," Emily replied. "He and my father are old friends. From before I was born. I think they went to school together, but I have never personally met Colonel Matthews. I think if I did I would slap his stupid face, so it is probably just as well he has never come to the house."

"Your husband did as much as he could in England," Clara continued. "After the official military records proved unenlightening, he traced the priests who worked with your brother. I shall follow up on them. It doesn't appear that he had the chance to interview them."

"No," Emily looked bleak. "His illness overtook him. He never was strong. The work you speak of took him months, and there is so little of it. He could only bring himself to work on the problem when he was well enough and that was rarely. The long hours at his office took their toll. When he came home, he was simply exhausted and could do no more. I understood that, though I know he felt awful about it, as if he was somehow negligent.

"In the last weeks of his life, he became distressed that he could not complete the task he had set himself. I told him it did not matter, but he could not accept that."

Fresh tears trickled down Emily's face.

"At some point, this became about finishing my husband's work as much as being about finding Christian.

Can you understand that?"

"Yes, I can," Clara promised her. "I will do what I can to solve this mystery."

"And you will not let my father intimidate you?"

Clara laughed.

"Never! I think I gave him a fright anyway, he thought I was going to say aloud in the street that your brother had been accused of treason. Of course, I wouldn't do that, as I don't want to tarnish his memory. But if your father thinks I just might do something like that, all the better."

"Hopefully he will stay clear now," Emily nodded. "Life is so complicated!"

"Sometimes," Clara agreed.

They drank tea and ate cake until Emily had fully calmed down. Then she declared that she was heading home.

Annie shook her head sadly once Emily was gone.

"Some people are so afraid of the truth," she sighed.

"I haven't said anything to Emily, but there are elements in her husband's file on Father Lound's disappearance that suggest he had a feeling there was truth to the rumours."

Annie looked surprised.

"But surely Emily has read the file?"

"I can't say if she has, or whether she is so blinded to the truth that she overlooked the clues in her husband's notes. Whatever the case, I think there is more to this than just nasty gossip."

"Have you ever thought about it, Clara, how a man might betray his country?" Annie asked.

"I can't say I have," Clara shrugged. "I suppose I should now, but, well, it's hard when you are in a time of peace and war seems very far away. It's difficult to really imagine those desperate times. And I never was at the Front. I can only picture it in my mind."

"I think there are a lot of reasons someone might betray their nation," Annie said. "I have been musing on it a lot. I think there is the obvious one – greed. Financial gain might be all some people require, they perhaps have no real links to their nation and no attachment to it."

"I don't think that was Father Lound," Clara replied to her. "I could be wrong."

"Another reason could be that the person feels an affinity with the enemy, maybe they believe in their cause more than their own nation's."

"An ideological traitor," Clara nodded.

"Then, you might betray your country to save yourself," Annie added. "I can see that being a very powerful motive. If you are surrounded by the enemy and the only way to live or avoid being tortured is to reveal some secret about your country, then I think it takes a very brave man to remain mute."

"You have spent a lot of time thinking about this," Clara remarked, raising an eyebrow.

"Making bread dough is an excellent time to let the mind wander," Annie said with pride. "I have a final reason."

"Go on."

"Love, you might betray your country for the love of a person. Not necessarily a lover, but a parent, a sibling, a child, even a good friend. You might do that if your love for that person meant more to you than notions of honour," Annie paused. "I would betray this country for you or Tommy, you know."

Clara smiled, that was a very personal confession coming from Annie.

"Thank you, I hope to never put you in a position where you have to."

"Any of those reasons could explain what Father Lound did," Annie said. "That is, if he really did betray his country. Do you think these rumours of treachery stem from the fact he disappeared?"

"I guess so," Clara said uncertainly. "They seem to have been spread after he vanished. Which brings us back to that fundamental question: why did he disappear?"

"Was he murdered?" Annie clasped her hands together.

"By this Colonel Matthews, perhaps? Then he spreads rumours that Father Lound is a traitor to cover up what he did!"

"That might be pushing the evidence we currently have," Clara almost laughed at Annie's wild idea, but restrained herself. After all, she had uncovered far more bizarre motives for murder in the past. Nothing could be ruled out at this stage.

"When I have more evidence, then hopefully this will all make sense," Clara explained. "Hopefully."

"We are still going to Belgium?"

"Most likely, unless Colonel Matthews is willing and able to tell me exactly what became of Father Lound. Which I doubt. I think he is going to be a hard nut to crack," Clara winked at Annie before heading back into the parlour.

Lying on the parlour table was Gerald Priggins' file on Father Lound. As Emily had said, it was a thin file and it was obvious Gerald had not been able to devote much time to the effort. But what he had uncovered was troubling. Gerald had somehow managed to get cuttings from Belgium newspapers, remarkable for two reasons – that newspapers had been printed at that stage in the war when paper shortages were rife, and that they had survived. Gerald apparently had a contact in Belgium, someone who had access to wartime newspapers, specifically the ones produced for the town where Albion Hope had once stood. A handful of these cuttings had been about the founding of Albion Hope and events happening there. There had been a copy of the cutting about Father Lound conducting the town mayor's funeral and another about an Easter party held at the house, where Lound was briefly mentioned for organising an egg hunt for the children.

However, the cutting that had caught Clara's eye had come from a newspaper printed at the end of the war. The slip of yellowed paper had been dated at the top in pencil – 1 October 1918. Almost a year after Father Lound had disappeared.

There was not much to the article and it was all in French, perhaps the reason Emily had overlooked it – if she had read her husband's file. The font was rather archaic and challenging to read. The title said simply – Body Found in Woods. Clara had transcribed the rest of the article into English so she could take better account of what it said. It seemed important as well as alarming.

"Body Found in Woods. Yesterday a body was discovered in woodland by two local boys. The remains were badly decomposed and appear to have been there for some time. They had been partially buried, but recent rain had washed the upper soil away to reveal a skull.

"The police attended with a local surgeon and the remains were fully removed. Apart from a few missing finger and toe bones, the skeleton is complete and appears to have been untouched by wildlife. It is believed the skeleton is that of a man, however, it has so far been impossible to identify the victim as there were no personal belongings with the bones except for a gold crucifix found near the neck and a rosary which appeared to have been clutched in the deceased's hands.

"Death occurred due to a gunshot wound to the back of the skull and there is every reason to believe the individual was a victim of callous murder. Fragments of clothing revealed little and it is felt that unless further evidence can be found the identity of the man, and that of his killer, will never be determined."

Clara read through her transcript again. She could see why the cutting had been sent to Gerald. The body in the woods had the trappings of a priest and the only person known to have vanished without explanation from the town (as far as Clara knew) was Father Lound. The link was casual, admittedly, but it was worrying.

And if this was Father Lound, it raised a variety of new questions. The bullet wound suggested an execution killing, the rosary in the man's hands suggested he was praying or at least clutching them at the time of his death. The presence of the gold crucifix ruled out robbery as a motive. But no one appeared to link the discovery with the disappearance of Lound or, at least, so it appeared from the newspaper. Clara would need to find out more and she would need to do that in Belgium by questioning the relevant authorities.

Unless Colonel Matthews really did know more and was willing to help her.

Clara sighed. She had had enough for one evening. She tidied up the file and put it away in the box with the letters. Why would anyone want to murder Father Lound? A good question, but there were no answers to that in the box. She had a tiny window into Christian's life from these letters and papers and that was simply not enough. There was too much she didn't know about that period of his life in Belgium, when he decided he must vanish or, perhaps, someone decided for him.

Clara gave up on the unanswerable questions for the time being. When she had the right information she would know what really happened to Father Lound. It was finding that information that was the tricky part.

Chapter Ten

Colonel Brandt called on Clara a couple of days after their meeting to say he had managed to make contact with Colonel Matthews and had persuaded him to speak to Clara. The appointment was arranged for the following day in London, where Matthews had his regimental office. Brandt would accompany her to make the relevant introductions and keep Matthews in line.

They travelled on the early train the next morning, Brandt explaining that Matthews had been reluctant to agree and Brandt had to pull rank (or rather he played on the fact he had once ranked higher than Matthews) to secure the meeting. Clara was extremely grateful, but also concerned that Matthews would only tell her the bare minimum of what he knew.

They arrived in London in plenty of time for their meeting and walked to the building where Matthews had his office. Brandt took a deep breath as they stood before the tall structure with its fine Victorian architecture.

"Seems so long ago I was last here," he said. "That window, third floor, fourth from the right, was for my office. I spent so many hours looking out onto this road. But, my, that must be ten years ago now."

Brandt whistled through his teeth.

"I was damn old before the war, too old to be worth anything to the army. I'm even older now."

"You are worth an awful lot to me," Clara reminded him

gently. "And you are not that old."

Brandt's frown lifted and he smiled at Clara.

"Let's find out what my replacement has been up to, shall we?"

They walked in and introduced themselves to the concierge. After he had looked through a book to confirm they had an appointment, he took them upstairs to the third floor and knocked on Colonel Matthews' office door. Brandt was amused that Matthews now occupied his old office. Amused, but a little saddened by nostalgia too. Matthews asked for them to enter and they obeyed.

Sitting behind a very grand desk, Matthews looked imposing. He was tall, at least six foot in height, even sitting down he seemed to tower. He had lost nearly all of his hair and this was unfortunate as his ears jutted quite proudly from the side of his head and, without a mop of hair to mask them, this anatomical defect was extremely noticeable. He had a pudgy face, but was not fat, far from it. He clearly took great pride in his physique and Clara noted numerous athletics trophies dotted about the room, along with photographs of Matthews proudly winning races. He had extremely pale eyes that were slightly sinister, especially when they peered from behind his horn-rimmed glasses. He took these off as his guests entered and rubbed the bridge of his nose.

"Colonel Brandt," he rose and offered a hand to his former commander. "And you must be Clara Fitzgerald?"

Clara was surprised when he offered her his hand too. It was not every day that a man, especially an army officer, shook her hand. In her experience, the military were some of the worst for accepting that women were capable of independence and worthy of being treated as equals. She gladly shook Colonel Matthews' hand and her impression of him dramatically improved.

"Take a seat," Matthews pointed to the chairs before his desk.

The concierge had retired and the door was shut behind them. Colonel Matthews took his own place and folded his hands together on the table.

"I have a broad idea of why you are here," he said, largely to Clara. "Of course, I had your letter earlier too. This is not a meeting I ever wanted to have."

"May I just say that I will take everything you say to me in complete confidence," Clara swiftly promised. "I am seeking out answers, that is all, I am not here to question your actions or your reputation."

Colonel Matthews tilted his head, almost surprised by her words, then he smiled.

"And I shall just say that were it not for Colonel Brandt's persuasion, you would not be here at all," he said. "I had no intention of ever discussing that horrid affair, for my own reasons. Personal ones."

"Your silence has left people with a lot of questions," Clara pointed out.

"What people?" Matthews asked.

Clara knew that he was implying that he had done his duty by Christian's father and no one else's curiosity should matter.

"Father Lound's sister has spent the last five years confused and forever wondering what became of her brother. Five years in which she could not grieve properly or know what became of him. Your silence has done her a grave disservice."

Colonel Matthews dropped his head and it seemed to Clara that he regretted this. At least she hoped that was what he felt. When he looked up again he seemed resolved.

"I will answer your questions just this once, and then I shall never speak of Father Lound again," Matthews told her bluntly. "This is a very delicate matter, the consequences of the truth getting out could be more hurtful to Christian's family."

"You mean to his father's political career?" Clara was equally blunt. "Which is pretty much finished in any case. I am curious, why do you care about the family's reputation?"

Matthews' smile became wistful.

"A favour for a favour," he said softly. "It is really rather simple. Amadeus Lound was not always the selfish oaf you see today. He entered politics because he once cared about other people, and then he lost his way. But I am not here to redeem his character, only to pay him back for a great thing he did for me. He saved my life."

Colonel Brandt started to take interest.

"Really?" He said. "In the army?"

"Before then," Matthews explained. "When we were boys we were at the same public school. We were both keen swimmers and there was a lake in the grounds where the boys were allowed to swim. I went out one day as usual. It was cold, but not so cold I was concerned about swimming. I started out just fine, but halfway across the lake I suffered a terrible cramp in my side and stomach. I was incapable of swimming and I started to sink under. I would have drowned that day, only Amadeus Lound swam out and rescued me.

"I promised to one day repay the favour. To one day save his life. Well, that day never came, but an opportunity to save his reputation did and I took it. I warned him that his son's actions could harm him and then I took steps to see that the matter went away."

"You hushed it up?" Clara asked, her tone a fraction accusing.

"No, I did my job, I just didn't push too hard," Colonel Matthews did not take her words to heart. "No one was harmed. I would not have allowed Christian's treachery to disrupt the war effort."

Clara frowned.

"Why did you suspect Father Lound was a traitor?"

"There had been talk," Colonel Matthews said. "This is to go no further, you understand?"

His tone had suddenly become alarmed. Clara just nodded.

"I understand. I don't intend to tarnish Father Lound's reputation this late in the day."

Colonel Matthews gave the impression that he didn't

think Father Lound had a reputation to tarnish.

"For some time I had been aware of rumours that a person connected to Albion Hope was passing information to the Germans. It was not vital stuff, mostly, but information garnered from men visiting the house. To test my concerns, I sent one of my officers to the house with a document in his pocket that supposedly showed our local gun emplacements. Of course, it was all false, but I knew that this paper would tempt out our traitor.

"My officer pretended to be careless, letting the paper fall out of his pocket in public so its contents could be seen, then hastily retrieving it. The trick worked, when he left his tunic jacket hanging on a hook in the hall, the paper was taken from his pocket. He reported back at once and I arrived at Albion Hope and insisted everyone there was searched.

"There was naturally a lot of upset. I remember Father Lound stood very calmly and berated me for causing chaos in a house of peace. He did not resist me searching his own office however, and there I found the paper. He would not say how it came to be there. He did not even deny he had taken it. He just said nothing."

"Isn't that slightly odd?" Colonel Brandt interrupted. "If the man really was a traitor, why did he let you search his office when he knew you would find the paper?"

"He had no choice," Colonel Matthews shrugged, thinking that was obvious.

"He gave you no explanation for his actions?" Clara asked.

"None," Matthews shook his head, and now he paused, as if a thought had just come to him. "That did seem slightly odd. I thought he might have offered a religious or moral explanation. Something along the lines of pacifism. Priests are always pacifists and that makes them a nuisance among the men. They never understand the point of war."

Clara's mind went back to Father Dobson, she understood how there could be conflict between priests and military officers.

"But you did not arrest Father Lound?" She said.

"I was already aware of who Father Lound was, and I had not expected to find the papers in his office and that threw me at first. I had to go away and think about things. Had I not been so shocked I would have reacted better, I would have arrested him at once."

Colonel Matthews paused, realising the implications of all he had just said. He had not performed his duty as he should have done. He had neglected it. He shook off the thought and the regret.

"I had to go away and think about things. By the time I returned, intending to arrest Father Lound, he had vanished. I thought that for the best and did not make an effort to pursue the matter. He could do no more harm now he was exposed," Matthews paused. "Few people knew about the papers being found in Lound's office. I could keep the matter quiet. I don't believe I did anything wrong. I ensured a traitor could no longer operate and protected his family, who were innocent in all this, from being treated like criminals along with him. Can you imagine what would have happened to the Lounds had it become public knowledge their son had betrayed his country? I had to consider all that. His father would have been hounded from politics, his mother would have never been able to hold her head up again. His sister would have been an outcast. His treachery would have claimed far more victims after it was discovered than it ever had before."

Colonel Brandt was nodding his head along with this.

"Sometimes we have to look at the bigger picture," he mumbled.

Clara was not listening to them. She was thinking that a single stolen paper in an office did not add up to a criminal case. It was worrying, of course, but did it make sense? Father Lound had never denied or confessed to his crime. He had never explained himself. Also, she wondered if he was really stupid enough to leave the paper to be so easily found?

"Did you know that in 1918 a body was found in the

woods near the town, and it might have been the body of a priest?" Clara asked. "The victim had been shot in the back of the head."

"I didn't know that," Colonel Matthews replied. "By 1918 I was in another part of the country. I am sorry to hear that was the case. Presumably someone caught up with Lound. Maybe the Germans slew him for his failure."

"The man had lain in the woods a long time. Probably he died around the time Father Lound disappeared. Maybe, in fact, that is why Father Lound disappeared?"

"You are suggesting I had the man executed?" Matthews grasped her implication. "To protect the family name? No, I did not do that. Sorry to disappoint you."

"Matthews, was there any reason, other than the paper, to suspect Father Lound was unpatriotic?" Colonel Brandt asked, side-stepping Clara's unsettling implication that his comrade might have murdered a man.

Colonel Matthews paused, the question causing him some concern.

"To be perfectly honest, no, he is the last man I would have suspected," Colonel Matthews finally said. "But, then again, that is how these things go sometimes. A good traitor will not make himself obvious."

"A good traitor," Brandt chuckled at the choice of words. "An ironic thing to say."

"You get my point," Matthews looked mildly embarrassed. "I was greatly disheartened to find it was a man of the cloth behind such activities. Perhaps more so because I felt that Father Lound had a deep concern for the troops and was keen to support them. He cared, or so I had imagined, and it seemed odd that he would be doing something that put them in harm's way. If he had passed on that information about the guns, and had it been accurate, then he would have been setting up his own nation's men to be slaughtered by the Germans in a ranged attack. I still find it hard to imagine he would do such a thing."

"Might there have been a mistake?" Clara asked as

delicately as she could. "Might Father Lound have realised the paper had been left in a dangerous place and removed it for safekeeping?"

"Then why did he not say as much when we raised the alarm about it being missing?" Colonel Matthews said.

"The other possibility is that the good Father was protecting someone," Brandt mused.

That caused everyone to briefly fall silent. Clara shook her head.

"That means he willingly protected a traitor. It seems just as unpatriotic as stealing the paper on purpose."

"He would have been an accomplice to the crime," Colonel Matthews added. "I would find it hard to have sympathy for a man who acted in such a way. Protecting a traitor who has caused harm to the very men attempting to protect Belgium? It beggars belief."

"He might have had a reason," Colonel Brandt continued with his train of thought. "Not everything is black and white. Maybe the traitor was not a willing one. Perhaps they were being blackmailed by the Germans?"

"That is a supposition based on no evidence," Colonel Matthews dismissed the idea out of hand. "From my perspective, it seemed, and still seems, that the traitor was Father Lound. His reasons I do not know. I should have arrested him there and then, but I explained why I did not. I am even prepared to admit, all these years after the war, that there was a part of me that hoped he would run and spare me the complication of charging a priest with treachery. In that regard, he behaved as I expected."

"There has to be something more to this," Clara frowned. "Or am I just trying to hope too hard that Father Lound was not a black-hearted traitor prepared to sell out his own people?"

"Every traitor has his reasons," Colonel Matthews said quietly, his hands still folded on the table before him. "None of us is privileged to look into another man's heart and know what lurks there. Whatever the logic Father Lound used to convince himself to do what he did, I certainly do not know it and, as it seems he is dead, no one ever shall.

"You ought not to chase these shadows, Miss Fitzgerald. They will only cause you disappointment and misery."

Chapter Eleven

Clara had come to the end of what she could achieve in England. Colonel Matthews had not provided the answers she had hoped for and she was not prepared to tell Emily what she had learned without being able to supply a reason for Father Lound's actions. She was hoping for an answer that was kinder to his memory than that he was simply out for money or believed the Germans should win. In any case, she had not resolved what had become of him, and there were those bones in Belgium that troubled her.

Clara sent a message to Emily to let her know that there was now no choice, Clara needed to go to Belgium to continue her case. Emily wrote back, enclosing an open ticket for a steamer to the Continent. It appeared she had purchased it in advance, expecting Clara to need it sooner rather than later. There was nothing left to do but buy tickets for Tommy and Annie.

"Colonel Brandt has said he would like to come with me," Clara told Tommy the day she was going to get the tickets. "He hopes he might be of use. That means you do not need to come, if you so wish."

Tommy had hesitated long enough to indicate to Clara that he was tempted by the offer, then he sighed.

"Got to be done," he muttered under his breath, then louder to Clara. "Buy us a ticket, old girl."

The following day, with the sun shining down upon them, they headed for the steamer. Colonel Brandt was dressed in his best tweed suit and had a stylish new walking cane. He seemed quite jolly about the whole thing. Tommy was quiet and his silence became more noticeable the closer they came to the steamer. Annie took his hand and squeezed it.

"I haven't ever been abroad before," she said with a twinge of nerves. "What are foreign people like?"

Tommy was nudged out of his doldrums by her agitation.

"They are just like us, Annie," he promised. "They just speak a different language."

"I saw this article once, in one of my magazines, about gangs of thieves and murderers who roam the countryside in foreign countries. I hadn't thought about that until right now."

"The Belgians are very civilised," Tommy promised her. "I wouldn't pay much heed to that article, at all."

"Well, as long as I am not going to get murdered in my bed," Annie gave an awkward laugh, then she became serious. "I'm not going to get murdered in my bed, am I?"

Clara was not paying attention to the ongoing discussion between her brother and Annie. She was only vaguely aware that Tommy was attempting to convinced Annie that they were not about to go to Belgium and be murdered. Clara had other matters on her mind, namely the papers she had brought in an attaché case. She had gone through Gerald Priggins file once again and added to it from the loose papers in the box Emily had supplied. She now had all the relevant items in her case and at her disposal should she need them. She could not help wondering what she was going to find in Belgium.

She came to a pause at the foot of the walkway up to the steamer. Glancing behind she realised she was alone. Annie and Tommy were intensely conversing about survival abroad, while Colonel Brandt was busy organising the careful stowing of his travelling trunk. Clara almost smiled to herself. Funny how always on a case, eventually she had to go it alone. There seemed a certain significance to the fact that she would be striding up the gangplank on her own. The burden of discovery was always on her shoulders and no one else's.

Still, onwards and upwards. She had a mystery to solve.

Safely in the steamer's comfortable saloon, with the sea softly lapping at the sides of the boat and audible through the open windows, Clara took out the file on Father Lound once more. As she had done a dozen times before, she picked up her transcript concerning the bones found in the forest and read through it. Each time she thought she might find something more in the words, some detail she had missed. Each time she was disappointed.

Annie brought over a cup of tea she had purchased at the saloon bar. She was struggling to find her sea legs and the cups wobbled in her hands somewhat alarmingly as she approached Clara.

"I don't know why I am doing this," she muttered as she put the cups on the table. "I feel all a dither. I could have stayed at home, in my own kitchen."

"I thought you were hoping to get some new cake recipes?" Clara reminded her.

"I said that to Tommy, mainly I am here for him. Ohhh," Annie had glanced out of the window at the sea and was looking alarmed. "What if we sink Clara?"

"That is highly unlikely," Clara replied. "Do you want one of the seasickness pills I brought along? They are very good."

"I don't feel sick, I feel worried," Annie responded, finding it hard to pull her eyes off the grey ocean. "Ships sink all the time and lives are lost. There was that mine that nearly blew you up at New Year's on the Mary Jane, what if we hit a mine?"

"The sea lanes are heavily used Annie, there are no mines left here," Clara promised.

"I imagine that is what everyone was thinking at New Year's, yet suddenly there was a mine!"

"Annie, you are going to be perfectly all right," Clara reassured her friend. "We are only at sea a couple of hours, in any case."

Annie took a deep breath, then shut her eyes and braced her hands on the edge of the table.

"I am doing this for Tommy," she told herself firmly. "I can do this."

"Shush, he is coming," Clara said hastily.

Tommy and Colonel Brandt had been walking the deck in the sunshine. Clara wondered what they had been discussing, as Tommy had a smile on his face and looked far more cheery than he had done when they set out on this adventure.

"The captain says the crossing will be speedy as the weather is so fine," Colonel Brandt observed, sitting down next to Clara.

Tommy sat beside Annie.

"Now, before we land, I wanted to ask what your plan of action was Clara," Brandt said. "How can I be of best use to you?"

"I have a list of people to interview," Clara said. "Including the Belgium police and the local doctor who was involved in examining a skeleton that was found in the woods which might be that of Father Lound."

"He's dead then?" Tommy asked.

"Maybe," Clara offered him the transcript.

Tommy whistled through his teeth.

"Someone murdered this poor fellow, for whatever reason," Tommy put down the paper. "Finding out who did that seems likely impossible."

"I specialise in impossible," Clara winked at him. "In any case, we shall have to work separately to cover as much ground as we can. Tommy and Annie, you two stick together. Tommy can speak French, even if he is a little rusty. Colonel Brandt…"

"May I suggest I stay at your side?" Brandt interrupted her. "I have contacts who may be of use and my French is extremely good, not that I am questioning your language skills, but I may be able to open doors for you?"

Clara hesitated. She had intended to send Colonel

Brandt off in one direction, while she went in another. Working together had not been her plan. She didn't like to admit that pride played a part as well. She didn't want the locals to think she was incapable of conducting this case alone or, worse, that she was Colonel Brandt's assistant.

"I am quite happy working alone," Clara explained as diplomatically as she could. "There may be hesitancy from some people to speak to me if they are aware a British colonel is by my side. This is a case of treason, after all, and these people will be uneasy around the military."

"I did not mean to imply you were incapable of working independently," Brandt said with a smile to indicate he was not offended. "I merely wish to be of as much use as possible."

"And you shall," Clara observed. "There are many people to interview and to locate."

"Perhaps a better partnership would be for me and the colonel to work together, while you and Annie team up?" Tommy suggested. "Brandt and I shall attack the official side of things, while you and Annie can look to the civilians who may be uneasy speaking to former soldiers."

Clara frowned, she had the impression that Brandt and Tommy had been talking and had agreed that she should not be left to roam any part of Belgium alone. She was starting to feel annoyed. Then she glanced at Annie, who was looking most uneasy and came to a decision. Brandt was clearly having a positive effect on Tommy and Annie was now the one who needed to be distracted from her worries. If Clara could not escape her friends' insistence she not work alone, at least she could team up with another woman.

"All right, Annie, you shall join me. You are good at talking to people."

"I don't speak French," Annie mumbled.

"That's fine, my dear, a lot of Belgians speak jolly good English," Colonel Brandt smiled. "Now that is all settled, can I interest anyone in a game of cards to pass the time?"

~~~*~~~

They arrived in France in the early afternoon and it was then necessary to find a coach to take them into Belgium. The journey was uneventful, but long, and it was nightfall by the time they arrived at the little town where seven years ago Albion Hope was founded. There were still signs of the hardship the place had gone through. Several buildings stood in ruins, abandoned by their former occupants who were presumably either dead or long gone from this place. Roads were still being repaired from the damage caused by the heavy artillery carted along them, and from stray German shells that had crashed into the ground.

There were odd things that reminded you that this place had once been a war zone; scraps of barbed wire, empty artillery shells purloined to use for mundane tasks, such as water buckets, a German helmet sitting on a windowsill and gathering dust.

The people, however, were cheerful and greeted the new arrivals with smiles. It soon became plain that the town was a hotspot for tourists. There was a little spa nearby that was serviced by a local spring, the water of which was said to have great curative properties. Clara and her friends found they were among a dozen souls heading for the same place. Some were heading on to the spa, others were making a pilgrimage to a local saint's shrine, while others were stopping at the town as it was near to a British military cemetery where they had relatives buried. Tourism appeared to be the lifeblood of this place, and it did not take long for Clara to find a suitable hotel to make her base of operations.

It was too late to begin interviewing people, but their host seemed talkative, so Clara decided to chat to him and see what he recalled of Albion Hope and Father Lound when they went down to dinner. It was a quiet evening for the hotel owner as it was mid-week and he only had Clara's party and a couple of others to attend to. He was more than willing, after dinner had been digested, to chat with Clara and her friends in the hotel's saloon.

Clara began the conversation by explaining they had come to see the place where Albion Hope had once existed.

"You mean the old Vernon chateau," their host, Monsieur Janssen, replied. "Back in 1915 old Monsieur Vernon became very unwell and it was suggested he go to the spa to recuperate. In the meantime, some British priests were looking for a place to begin this rest home of theirs. Monsieur Vernon said they could use his property, gifted it to them for the duration of the war. He subsequently passed away, but not without making provision in his will for them. They could use his old chateau for as long as there were British soldiers needing its solace, then it must revert to the possession of his daughter, his only heir.

"That happened in 1919. His daughter came to town, for she did not live here, took one look at the chateau and decided to sell it. Now it belongs to the Coppens family, who have spent a great deal of time making it liveable again. The shelling made a lot of houses unsettled, you know, um, that is not quite the English word?"

"Unstable?" Clara suggested.

"Maybe that is it. Anyway, the shells, they shook the buildings badly and everything became cracked and wanted to fall down," Janssen made a whistling noise and brought his hand down on the top of the bar. "The good Fathers, they did not really understand this and they did not make repairs. I think the attic was so bad it was remarkable the floor had not fallen in, and there was a crack big enough to fit your fist in at the rear of the building. It ran up to the second floor!

"This very hotel, you would not know it now, but the whole back wall collapsed. Yes, yes it did. I see you look surprised, but I worked hard to have it fixed. We don't blame the Fathers, of course, for letting their house get so bad. They were men of God, not of bricks and mortar."

"Did they play a big role in the town?" Tommy asked when Janssen paused for breath.

"A big part! Monsieur, they were the biggest! Why, they came and brought back our hope. We were so close to just abandoning all this, we thought we had lost. You cannot appreciate our despair," Janssen tutted to himself. "All was in ruins, so many people homeless, and the Germans seemed to get closer and closer. You have heard about our little shrine to St Helena outside the town? She is the town's saint. It is said she turned back an army of the English in the days when our peoples could not always agree. That would be many centuries past.

"Every child in the town is raised believing St Helena will give them protection from the enemy. And then, in the last war, it seemed as if she had abandoned us. Our own priest prayed daily to her, but we feared the worst. And then these men of God appear and say they are opening a house of rest for the English troops at the Front and we knew, just knew, that Helena had saved us! For God would not build such a house to see it overrun by Germans!"

Monsieur Janssen beamed with delight.

"There were three priests involved in the project, I believe," Clara said. "Father Howard, Father Stevens and one other?"

"Father Lound," Janssen said automatically. "A very nice young man, I liked him a lot. He performed a very moving funeral service for our late mayor."

"It is remarkable that none of this has been written about," Colonel Brandt was drinking a glass of brandy as he spoke. "I mean, what an extraordinary thing. Someone should take the time to record all this. It should not just be forgotten."

"But you are curious?" Janssen said. "Maybe you could write such a book?"

"I am not a writer," Clara smiled. "But, you are right, I am curious. Ever since I learned about Albion Hope I have wanted to know more."

That was not a lie, though her exact motives were slightly different.

"I wish more English would come to learn about Albion

Hope. It was such a marvellous thing. It did not just help the soldiers, though that was its first goal, it helped us too. That is what made it so fantastical!"

Janssen was somewhat dramatic in his praise, but his point was genuine. Albion Hope had done what its name had suggested, it had brought hope to the people in the town. It had given them the strength to carry on.

"I was thinking of placing a sign near the chateau," Monsieur Janssen scratched at his chin. "To say this is where Albion Hope was. I think that would be good, yes?"

"Better than seeing it forgotten," Brandt agreed.

Janssen took a better look at the old colonel.

"Did you serve in the war, Monsieur?"

"Too old," Brandt snorted. "I was in the military, but my days were long past when this last conflict came."

Janssen's eyes strayed to Tommy. They hinted at the same question, but Janssen was diplomatic enough not to ask aloud. Tommy frowned.

"I was in the war," he said.

He had become depressed again after their arrival in the town. He seemed almost pained. Janssen picked up a glass from behind the bar and filled it with brandy. He passed it to Tommy.

"On the house, monsieur, any drink you have here will be on the house. I owe you my gratitude."

Tommy looked at the glass, mildly stunned. Then he looked at Janssen. Conflicting emotions played on his face, then he accepted the drink.

"Merci," he said. "Merci."

Janssen smiled.

"I am very glad the English came," he continued. "Very glad. Look, I show you something."

Janssen hooked his finger and motioned that they ought to follow him. He came out from behind the bar and walked to the wall near his entrance door. Between the wall and the large window next to it he pointed to a mark in the plasterwork.

"This hole, it goes right through," he pressed his finger

into the hole and wriggled it around. "This is the mark left by a German rifleman. The Germans managed to get into our village just the once, they were here but a few hours and then, glory to St Helena, the English came and pushed them back. But here is where a German rifleman tried to shoot my cat. My cat! Poor creature went white overnight from the horror."

Janssen seemed rather proud of the hole, even if it could have been caused by anything. Clara had her doubts about the cat turning white after the incident, however.

"I leave this hole as a reminder of what happened. I never want to forget the madness this world fell into," Janssen pressed a hand to his chest and became solemn. "I will never support war and I shall never allow a German to set foot in my hotel. We must never forget what they did."

Tommy became sombre. Clara decided it was time to move on to a different topic.

"Tell me more about Albion Hope," she said, hoping to lure Janssen back to his bar.

The ruse worked. He was more than glad to speak of the place which, according to him, had saved his town from complete despair and abandonment.

"Such good men, such good friends," he purred, pouring himself a glass of some golden spirit. "Father Howard used to come and have a drink with me most days. He spent a lot of time in the trenches helping men find solace in themselves and in God. He carried such a burden with him for the sake of his work. When the war was done, he said he was going to retire to a place called No-Fun-Bear-Land. I thought it a very odd sounding place. Why are the bears allowed no fun there?"

"Northumberland," Clara interpreted. "It has nothing to do with bears. Is Father Howard still there?"

"Maybe," Janssen shrugged. "He sends me Christmas cards, but he always forgets to enclose his address, so I can't send one back."

"What about Father Stevens? What was he like?"

"Serious," Janssen pulled a stern face to mimic the priest. "He never smiled. He arranged all the official side of Albion Hope, all the administration. He didn't deal with the people who came there. He never had a drink with me."

This, apparently, was a serious crime to Janssen's way of thinking.

"He was not a bad man, he just could not bring himself to be happy while a war was raging. He stayed in town after the war, to help people return to their old ways and rebuild their lives. That was a great kindness, and he was good at fundraising. Anyway, he moved to France a year or so ago."

Clara was disappointed. She doubted she would be able to track the man easily if that were the case.

"Then there was Father Lound," Janssen kept talking happily. "Father Lound seemed so young. I know the girls in the town were fond of him. He was charming, a little handsome too. He preached a good sermon. Not too long or depressing."

"Where did he move to after the war?" Clara asked, feigning innocence about what really happened to Lound.

Janssen's good humour slipped, he almost winced as he spoke.

"That is a little odd. One day Father Lound just disappeared. No one could say where he went or why. It was a very big mystery," Janssen hesitated. "There was gossip, rumours."

"Oh dear," Clara said, hoping Janssen would elaborate.

"Many people thought he ran off with a woman," Janssen drummed his fingers on the bar. "That is a pretty bad thing to say of a priest, you know?"

"If they said he had run off with a woman, does that mean a lady from the town was missing too?" Colonel Brandt postulated.

Janssen's frown deepened.

"That is the oddest thing, there was a lady missing. Madame Deveraux. She was a respected widow. At one time her family had been wealthy, her husband left her a lot of money, but when the Germans came into town they attacked her home, robbed her of everything. She had her husband's money in a bank, but the Germans raided that too and took all their reserve. There was nothing left," Janssen clicked his tongue, saddened by the actions of the enemy. "Madame Devereaux became poor overnight, and with four children to support it was very hard, very hard indeed. Her neighbours could only offer her a little help, they too had been hit hard. Madame Devereaux, for the first time in her life, began to work. She could sew a bit and she was prepared to do manual labour on the local farms. Her son was a blessing. Ramon worked hard for the family, he was often doing odd jobs at Albion Hope.

"Madame Devereaux hoped to send her three daughters away to live with an aunt, but it was impossible to arrange the travel. The eldest girl started to keep dubious company. That was what upset people so much. She saw that soldiers on leave had money and would spend it on a pretty girl. Well, we all know where that leads.

"It was all getting very bad. There were suspicions the girl was pregnant. Then, one morning, the Devereauxs were gone. The suspicion was they had disappeared to avoid the shame of the girl's misfortune. Maybe gone to that aunt they had spoken of. Only later was it realised that Father Lound was missing too."

"And people put two and two together," Colonel Brandt nodded.

"That was the strangest part. Everyone said Father Lound must have run off with a woman, but if the woman were Madame Devereaux it seemed very unusual. You see, Madame Deveraux had married late and had her children even later. She had just turned fifty and, though a respectable widow, she was not very attractive. She had lost a lot of weight and looked quite scrawny and haggard. She had the face of a much older woman and could never be described as handsome, let alone pretty. It was sad, but no one could see what a good-looking young priest would be doing with her."

"Maybe it was the daughter that caught his eye?" Clara suggested.

"Mademoiselle Devereaux was certainly pretty, but I know Father Lound disapproved of her lifestyle and she was often very, very rude to him. I have seen her say horrible things to him when he questioned what she was doing. She disliked what he stood for and hated that he criticised her choices," Janssen shook his head. "I cannot see that Father Lound would run off with her. I feel sure the girl distrusted him and despised him. In any case, you don't elope with an entire family in tow."

"That is true," Clara agreed.

"What became of the Devereauxs?" Colonel Brandt asked.

"Who can say?" Janssen shrugged his shoulders. "They never came back. They must have gone to live with that aunt."

None of this made sense. Why would Father Lound run away with the family? Where would they go? Perhaps the two events were mere coincidences? Father Lound had papers in his possession that indicated he was passing secrets to the Germans. If he was returned to England and found guilty of treason, that was an offence that carried the death sentence and he had to think of his family. His actions would tarnish them too. Maybe he disappeared to avoid trouble. The obvious answer could be the right one. For some reason Father Lound had taken those papers, he could not prevent them from being found in his office. His only real choice after that was to flee when he got the chance.

"You know, there was something else," Janssen had poured himself another glass of the golden spirit and was talkative. "It was about a year later. Little Ernst and Pietro were playing in the woods, looking for the things little boys consider treasures among the fallen leaves, and they came across what they first thought was an animal skull. They pulled it from the ground and realised it was a person's skull and ran for help.

"The gendarmes came and dug out all these bones. It was a full skeleton. Someone had been killed and buried in the woods. The skeleton was still clutching a rosary and was wearing a crucifix. Here in the town, we were convinced that this was Father Lound."

"Murdered?" Colonel Brandt did a good impression of being surprised despite already knowing this part of the tale.

"Shot in the back of the head," Janssen shook his own head sadly. "That is how people are executed, yes?"

"It is the way villains execute people," Tommy interjected.

"Someone killed Father Lound," Janssen continued. "Maybe he never ran away at all? The place he was found is not far from the path that leads to St Helena's shrine. I think he was walking there to pray, and a criminal surprised him and shot him."

"What for?" Clara asked. "He was still wearing his crucifix. They can't have wished to rob him."

Janssen looked confused by her reasoning and hesitated, then a new determination came to his eyes.

"Must have been a German. They killed people all the time for no reason."

Janssen had had several drinks by now and was starting to sound a little slurred. The night was drawing on and they were moving beyond the realms of genuine information and into speculation. It was time to call it a night.

"Thank you Monsieur Janssen for being so generous with your time," Clara said to the man.

"No bother," Janssen slurred. "Did I show you the bullet hole in my wall? Germans took a shot at my cat!"

"You did," Tommy assured him.

"I think we are all ready for our beds," Clara explained, politely removing herself from the bar.

"Breakfast is at nine o'clock," Janssen quickly added. "It is very good, all the eggs are fresh!"

"We shall be sure to attend," Clara promised, making a

concerted effort to retreat now.

The others were following, heading for the stairs that would lead up to their rooms. Janssen was clearing up their glasses and continuing to mutter about the Germans.

They were on the stairs before Annie spoke. She had been quiet through the evening, content to just listen.

"I think poor Father Lound has had a very raw deal," she declared. "I'm not sure the man was a traitor and I am certain he did not deserve to be murdered in the woods."

Clara was rather inclined to agree with her.

Chapter Twelve

After breakfast the next day, they split up; Brandt and Tommy went to speak to the local police and see what they could learn about the body in the woods, while Clara and Annie went to the former Albion Hope house.

Juliet and Claude Coppens had transformed the chateau from a dangerously unstable shell, into a beautiful family home. The shutters on the windows were painted a duck-egg blue and at each window sill there was a box of flowers. The air was alive with bees buzzing from box to box, overflowing with industry. The chateau was level with the street, and the door opened straight onto the pavement. There was a garden at the back, swinging around to one side of the property. A brick wall ran around the entire grounds, but Clara could just make out apple trees over the top. It looked a very respectable and very comfortable town house.

Clara used the lion's head door knocker to announce her presence at the front of the house and then waited patiently for a response. Annie was looking around her slightly uneasily, as if she feared that Belgian citizens might bite.

A young woman answered the door. She was in a blue smock-type dress and her dark hair was pulled back in a soft braid that hung down her back. She looked at Clara with some surprise. Clara imagined that the town was small enough to mean Madame Coppens rarely answered the door to anyone she did not know. Speaking in French,

Clara explained herself.

"Madame, I am Clara Fitzgerald. I have come to learn more about Albion Hope and the men who founded it. Might I ask you about your home?"

Juliet Coppens looked uncertain, then she held out her hands in a gesture of 'what would it matter?'

"Please come in," she said. "I don't know if I can help you much about when the house was used by Albion Hope, but you are welcome to have a look around."

Juliet showed them in and took them upstairs to a room at the front of the house which was arranged as a sunny parlour.

"I shall fetch my husband. He knows much more about the history of the house," Juliet said, before departing from her guests.

Annie made a short circuit of the room, taking in its generous proportions, pale green walls and Rococo furniture. There was a big, ornate mirror hanging over the fireplace, something you would never see in an English parlour, at least, not in a townhouse parlour. There were also several dark paintings of sombre looking Belgians, who appeared to frown down at the guests.

"Do you think you can sit on the sofas, or are they just for show?" Annie asked, tentatively poking the arm of one of the chairs in question.

It had very fancifully carved legs and arms; they appeared to be constructed of leaves and acorns covered in gold. The fabric of the sofa was cream with a pale red pattern of more leaves scrolling across it. It was fatly stuffed and dimpled deeply when Annie prodded it with a finger.

"I am sure we can sit," Clara said, though she wasn't really sure at all.

They were distracted by the arrival of a man. He was in a brown suit, very tall and lean, with a small head that perched on his neck. He wore tiny black rimmed glasses and had a thin moustache. He observed the two women for a moment, then introduced himself.

"Monsieur Coppens, at your service. Ladies, do please sit."

Clara translated this for Annie, who was obviously relieved to have been instructed to use the furniture. She still sat down with great care, fearing that at any moment this insubstantial looking seat would collapse beneath her.

"My wife says you are interested about when this chateau was the home of Albion Hope?" Monsieur Coppens began.

"We are indeed," Clara replied. "I am particularly interested in Father Lound, who served here."

Monsieur Coppens nodded.

"I have something that may interest you," he rose and went to a bureau at the side of the room. He opened a drawer and retrieved a small box. Bringing it back to Clara, he explained. "When we took on the house, we discovered that much had been left behind. This room, for instance, had been an office. I believe, from the contents of the office, that it had been used by Father Lound. We found a number of papers and photographs, also books, belonging to him. I saved them, though the roof had developed a leak and some were beyond salvaging. If you are interested, I can get the other papers for you. These are the photographs we found."

Clara almost gasped at this news. She had not expected such a windfall, or to be sitting in the very room where Father Lound's world had come crashing down around him. Somewhere in this space had stood his desk and on it had been those damning papers. She was in the room where Colonel Matthews had accused him of treason and he had maintained his silence. Was it here also that he decided to disappear for good?

Clara took the box of treasures and started to explore the contents. The photographs were of people she did not know, though several showed a young priest who she guessed was Father Lound. There was a picture of him at a Christmas party, stood at the head of a table. Down either side of the table, ranging in age, were children. Boys and girls all wearing homemade party hats and with expressions of uncertain merriment on their faces, as if they feared something would happen to spoil the fun. On the back of the picture was scrawled in pencil 'Christmas 1916.' Another picture was of Father Lound and several lads in the garden collecting apples from the trees. Another was of three priests stood together. Father Lound was on the right of the trio, the older two must have been Father Howard and Father Stevens, though it was hard to know which was which. Clara surmised, from what Janssen had said, that the smiling man was Father Howard, which meant the solemn man was Father Stevens.

Another picture showed a funeral procession. There were several images of this occasion, which had clearly been deemed important for the photographer to capture it. Clara guessed this was the funeral of the town mayor. One picture showed four young men shouldering the mayor's coffin into the church. Clara assumed one of the four was Ramon Devereaux, the problem was that only two men had been captured in the photo, the other two were hidden behind the coffin. The two that were visible were older than Ramon.

"Do you know who any of these people are?" Clara asked Monsieur Coppens as she flicked through the images.

Coppens bent forward and peered at the images.

"I know most of them, is there anyone you wish me to pick out in particular?"

"Ramon Devereaux," Clara answered.

A strange look crossed Coppens' face, then he obeyed and picked out several pictures from the box. In each he pointed out a young man as Ramon. The individual was rather serious-looking and rarely smiled at the camera. Clara had imagined Ramon to be different, not this grim-looking young man. He was almost as tall as Father Lound and appeared to have fair hair. His face still had the soft lines of youth, even when he was scowling. He never seemed entirely engaged in the activity he was performing, as if his mind was always elsewhere. In the apple-picking picture, while the other lads were laughing at something that had been said, Ramon was a little apart, concentrating on a basket of apples and seemingly lost in thought.

"Why do you want to know about Ramon Devereaux?" Coppens asked.

Clara softly smiled. She had never planned on keeping her intentions secret.

"I am a private detective from England," She explained to Coppens. "Father Lound's sister has asked me to look into his disappearance. I am not sure, but I have to consider there may be a connection between him vanishing and the dramatic departure of the Devereaux family at the same time. I am aware that Father Lound had a great deal of contact with Ramon through Albion Hope and, thus, I surmise with his family."

Coppens became serious.

"I had hoped, vainly perhaps, that Father Lound had made it back to England safely or that at least his family knew of his whereabouts. I am sorry to hear that was not the case. Especially as it throws a new, tragic light on the remains found in the woods."

"You must have heard the rumours concerning the Father?"

"Oh yes," Coppens nodded. "My wife and I spent the war with my wife's parents. We returned to this town to find our old home destroyed. Luckily, we had a little money put by and we were able to buy this property. Of course, we were told of the history of Albion Hope and of those who worked here."

"And the rumours?" Clara persisted.

Coppens was solemn a moment.

"This house holds secrets," he said, finding it hard to meet Clara's eyes. "Not physical secrets, just memories in the walls. People gossip, but no one really knows what happened here in that October of 1917. Maybe Father Howard and Father Stevens knew, but they certainly did not say. Still, I feel it sometimes, a weight of…"

Coppens glanced around the room they were sitting in,

his brows crinkling over his eyes as he tried to put into words what he was thinking.

"It is like he is still here. I walk into this room sometimes and it seems as if he just left a moment ahead of me. I never feel like this is my front parlour, it is always his office," Coppens shook his head. "My wife does not feel it, she thinks I am a little mad. I can't help it though, it's like he never really went away."

"You make it sound like a ghost story," Clara said softly.

"Maybe it is," Coppens responded. "You know, no one ever saw him leave. That has to be the most peculiar part of it all. You would think someone would have noticed him packing or leaving the house. He didn't disappear in the middle of the night. He was missed at supper time. He vanished in the afternoon, taking just his small suitcase. Why did no one see him walking away? Why was he not spotted?"

Clara had to admit that was curious, but a wily man could have eluded attention by using roads he knew would be quiet. The town was emptier back then, and there were lots of abandoned buildings he could slip into and hide in, waiting until dark before leaving completely.

"Would you like to take the photographs and papers?" Coppens asked. "I do not need them. They may offer you some clue."

"I would be glad of them," Clara agreed promptly. "Did you happen to know the Devereauxs before the war?"

"I did," Coppens nodded. "We were acquaintances, though not really friends. Monsieur Devereaux was something of a character, very jolly. But a very good businessman, until his sad death."

"What happened to him?"

"He went overboard travelling on a ferry. Ramon saw it all, he was, I suppose, twelve or thirteen. His father was at the rail talking to another man, when this gentleman suddenly became irate and grappled with Monsieur Devereaux and pushed him over the side. Ramon raised the alarm, but they never found his father. Nor could the gentleman who pushed him be identified. Ramon never saw his face," Coppens pulled a grimace to indicate how tragic this all was. "Everyone was most saddened, it was an awful thing to happen. No one could explain it either. There was nothing in Monsieur Devereaux's papers to explain why he had been killed."

"What an awful thing to occur," Clara said, thinking of poor Ramon watching his father being flung to his death. It was starting to appear as if there were far more mysteries in this case than just the one. "My understanding is that Madame Devereaux was left well off by her husband, but lost it all to the Germans in the war?"

"Yes," Coppens agreed. "Much of the Devereaux wealth was tied up in property and antiques. Well, the Germans overran the former in the war, occupying the land so it could not be rented or sold, and the latter they stole. Just to add insult to injury, Madame Devereaux's bank was also occupied by the Germans, and all their reserves stolen. Many of the bank's customers were made bankrupt overnight."

"That must have been very hard for the family."

"It was," Coppens said. "I was not here at that point, but we had friends who wrote to my wife and I and told us all this. Poor Madame Devereaux took on work wherever she could just to survive. She was not a woman used to hard labour and I don't suppose she had the skills that might be expected of a woman who has worked all her life. It must have brought her great shame to have to work the fields. Her eldest daughter decided to follow another path, and that is really not spoken about."

"I have heard she found the British soldiers who came to the town very friendly," Clara said coyly.

Coppens nodded, a bleak look on his face.

"Everyone thought it most awful and wondered what her father would have thought. Ramon tried his best to fill his father's boots, but the only work he could find was doing odd-jobs for people. He worked here a lot, when this house was Albion Hope. I found a book of accounts and there were regular small payments to R. Devereaux for work he had completed about the place."

"They must have been very bitter about everything," Clara observed. "That sort of destruction of one's life can be extremely damaging."

"I cannot say," Coppens replied.

"Can you think of someone who could?" Clara asked. "I can't say for certain if the Devereaux disappearance is linked to that of Father Lound, but it seems extremely likely. If I could learn more about the Devereauxs, I might be able to find out what happened to the priest."

Coppens paused for a second, thinking to himself.

"Please, just a moment," he raised a hand to emphasise his words then went to the door of the room.

Coppens called for his wife and when she appeared they had a hasty and hushed conversation in French. Then she departed and he returned to Clara.

"My wife knew better than I did," he gave an embarrassed smile. "There is an old woman who was the neighbour of the Devereauxs. She now lives in a home for the elderly up the hill. Her name is Madame Smet. I can give you the address. She may be able to help you."

"Thank you, that would be most useful."

Clara and Annie departed the Coppens' home with a parcel of documents and photographs wrapped in brown paper, and more questions than answers. Clara felt as if her head was spinning with information, but none of it seemed relevant just yet. There was still much to discover, still a lot more secrets this town was clutching onto.

After a quick check of the time and a map Annie had bought in a shop, they set off for their next stop. Maybe Madame Smet could offer them some fresh ideas.

Chapter Thirteen

Colonel Brandt and Tommy arrived at the local police station and asked if it would be possible to see the person in charge. Colonel Brandt used his rank to press home their request, also hinting that they were investigating a military matter from during the war. Lound's supposed treachery was certainly something the military were interested in, so the suggestion did not seem unreasonable.

After a short wait, they were introduced to the Belgium police force's equivalent of a Chief Inspector. He was a man by the name of Peeters, and he invited Brandt and Tommy into his office.

"What is this matter that concerns you so?" He asked once they were all seated.

"Five years ago, a man disappeared from this town, his name was Father Lound and he was suspected of being a traitor to the British," Tommy explained. "He was never located and we have been asked to investigate the matter further and to determine whether he was guilty of treason, or whether his good name has been unfairly sullied."

"As you may appreciate, it has taken several years post-war to catch up with all these affairs," Colonel Brandt added, acting like the good military official he had once been. "Father Lound's case was fairly low on our case list, we have only just got around to it."

"I understand," Peeters answered. He was a young man for his role, probably only just reaching his late thirties. He had very dark hair and an elegant moustache. He seemed quite serious, but was also most polite and proper. He was easily old enough to remember Father Lound's disappearance. "I will be glad to help settle this matter for the British. I did not realise Father Lound's loyalty was still under investigation."

"It has been kept very quiet," Colonel Brandt elaborated. "For the sake of the family. There was not enough evidence at the time to prove for certain the father was a spy, and it would be a terrible thing to label him a traitor without good cause. The damage to his family would be simply unbearable. Father Lound vanished before a proper investigation could be carried out and there was not the time nor the resources in 1917 to pursue him. It was thought best to let the matter drop. Now we have the time and, perhaps more to the point, the interest, to discover the truth."

"I only knew of Father Lound vaguely," Peeters continued. "I was an inspector back then. I was always very busy, but not directly with Albion Hope. That place caused us no problems. No, I seemed to always be running about after thieves in those days. People thought they could rob some of the abandoned houses, and the not so abandoned ones too. Then there were the minor crimes, fist fights, quarrels gone too far, occasional trespassing or vandalism. Nothing serious, usually."

"Was Father Lound's disappearance reported to the police?" Tommy asked.

Peeters leaned back in his chair, making it creak slightly.

"It was. By a priest," Peeters tried to drag the man's name from his memory with visible effort. "I am sorry, the details do not spring to mind, but there will be a case file. I do recall the inspectors were sent out to search for the man. There was a great concern as it was very out of character for the father to simply disappear. The fact his suitcase was gone suggested he had runaway for some reason. I believe it was loosely linked to the disappearance of another family in the town. The Devereauxs."

"Yes, that is what we heard," Tommy concurred. "Father Lound knew the family, especially Ramon Devereaux who worked at Albion Hope from time to time."

Peeters' eyes sparkled and he leaned forward to speak to them as if they were conspirators.

"Now, Ramon Devereaux I knew. His was a name every inspector had heard of at some point."

That attracted Tommy and Brandt's attention.

"Why was that?" Tommy asked keenly.

"The boy could not stay out of trouble, simply put," Peeters' shrugged his shoulders. "I understand that the family were in dire straits, but Ramon tried to handle the situation in a way that was unacceptable. He would break into houses and steal money, we caught him red-handed once or twice, but sympathy for the family's situation made us generous. He was given a warning on both occasions and the house-breaking did stop, as far as we knew, at least.

"His other problem was his temper. He had a bad one. He was often getting into fights with soldiers, usually because of his sister. She consorted with the soldiers and was prostituting herself. We turned a blind eye, again because of the family's situation, though we had warned her once or twice. Ramon would accost any soldier he saw talking to his sister and this usually resulted in a fight."

Tommy was intrigued. Very little had been said about Ramon Devereaux before, Janssen had only referred to him vaguely, almost as if he was irrelevant. That had given the impression that he was quiet and unassuming, someone who got on with their life without causing much of a ripple. Now they were learning this was far from true.

"What about the Devereauxs' disappearance?" Tommy asked.

"Happened at the same time the priest vanished," Peeters recalled. "No one reported it at first, though we were all aware of the gossip. Then an old woman called and said her neighbours had gone in the night without warning. Seeing as the whole family had gone and they had taken their belongings, there seemed no reason to think there was anything particularly sinister about it. We did investigate, but there was no sign of a crime taking place. There was a rumour the eldest girl was pregnant and we unofficially suspected this was the cause of their departure. The mother was very self-conscious about the family's fall from grace, so to speak. She probably could not bear the shame of the daughter bearing a child out of wedlock in a town where she was known."

"You never discovered where they had gone?" Tommy asked.

"We never looked that hard," Peeters admitted, though he did not seem abashed by this revelation. "We were shorthanded and with a lot else going on. There was no reason to pursue them as far as we could tell and, I confess, it was a relief to have Ramon out of our hair."

"What about the skeleton found in the woods about a year later?" Tommy pressed on. "Was that linked to the disappearances?"

"Ah, yes, the bones!" Peeters became more enthusiastic. Murder was a rare thing in the town, and it was something more interesting than housebreaking and brawls. "I was a Candidate Chief Inspector by then. I remember the investigation well. The bones had not been disturbed by animals, which was fortunate, though we never found all the finger and toe bones. They are very small and easily lost in the ground.

"The grave was unexpectedly deep for a hasty burial, usually these things are shallow due to the time it takes to dig them. That did make us speculate that more than one individual was involved in the crime. Heavy rain had revealed the corpse. The grave was on a slope and the rain had washed a large chunk of the top soil down. Enough, at least, to reveal the skull. This was at the shallowest point of the grave. We worked out that the victim had been buried in a sitting position. It seems the grave was deep but not long, and the body had to be folded up, with the head nearest the top.

"There was no real evidence of who the victim was, aside from a gold necklace, which later proved to be a crucifix, and a rosary. The body was also wearing the remains of shoes, but the acidity of the soil had eaten away any other clothes. If you want to know more I can put you in touch with the surgeon who examined the bones for us."

"That would be helpful," Tommy nodded. "Did you link the body to Father Lound at all?"

"It crossed our minds," Peeters admitted. "A priest goes missing and then we find a skeleton with religious items. We couldn't prove it was him, however. And, of course, there was the bullet hole in the back of the skull. That made us stop and think. Someone killed that man. If it was Lound, he was probably dead before we were even alerted to him being missing."

Colonel Brandt was growing restless and clearly wanted to speak.

"There was no indication of the murderer?" He said.

"None," Peeters answered smartly. "Of course, things like footprints would have been washed away long before. There was no gun, or anything like that. Truly a mystery. We did what we could, but there was nothing to work with. If it was Father Lound, no one could suggest a reason someone would want to kill him."

"Did you think it was significant he was buried near the path to the shrine of St Helena?" Brandt asked.

Peeters folded his hands on his desk.

"Maybe. There was the obvious link between the religious trappings of the skeleton and St Helena's shrine. That made it seem even more likely the body was of the priest. However, Lound supposedly took his suitcase with him and that has never been found," Peeters seemed to consider this important. "The shrine was also a popular meeting point for secret rendezvous in the war. It was a good place to stake out if we were looking for someone dabbling in black market goods. If the statue in that shrine could speak, she would have all manner of tales to tell about people meeting there. I'm not sure if anyone actually ever went to pray at the shrine."

Peeters found this amusing and smirked.

"Could we see the files?" Tommy asked.

Peeters only now hesitated.

"They are supposed to be sealed until the case is either solved or so much time has passed that they can cause no harm to anyone living who is mentioned in them. I cannot just show them to civilians."

"They may be the key to proving or disproving Father Lound was a traitor, surely that is reason enough to make an exception?" Brandt suggested, somehow managing to sound even more 'military' than before. "It is important to wrap up this case for the sake of the family. I could ask for some sort of official authorisation from the military, if you would like?"

Peeters did not speak at once. It was plain he was torn. Brandt's demeanour and obvious military links were making him think twice about denying them access to the files. But there was still police procedure to consider. He scratched at his head.

"Father Lound may have sold secrets to the Germans in the war," Brandt pushed him. "Or he may have been a victim of a misunderstanding, it is important we learn the truth. The war left us with many loose ends and it would be preferable if this was not to remain one of them."

"The British government desires this?" Peeters asked uneasily.

"The British military desires this," Colonel Brandt said, in the understanding that he was part of the British military, despite being retired, and thus his statement could not be considered a lie. "It is part of their post-war work. There are many stories like this, as you may appreciate."

Peeters came to a decision.

"I'll let you look at the files, but only here at the station. Also, I cannot let you make transcripts, understood?"

"That is very reasonable," Colonel Brandt assured him. "I truly hope we can bring peace to the family of Father

Lound by learning what really happened to him, and what he was doing during the war."

Peeters did not seem convinced, but he was willing to give them the benefit of the doubt.

"I'll need to have the files pulled from our archive. Could I ask you to return this afternoon?"

"That would be fine," Tommy promised. "Thank you."

Peeters showed them out of the office and they found themselves on the street with a couple of hours to spare. Brandt pulled out his old pocket watch and assessed the time.

"Maybe we could find something to eat?" He suggested.

Tommy was agreeable to this. They walked along, looking for a café.

"I think Father Lound was the man in that grave," Tommy said suddenly. "I don't think he disappeared of his own accord. I think someone murdered him."

"Who, and why?" Brandt asked.

"I don't entirely trust that Colonel Matthews," Tommy said sinisterly. "In times of war, even officers do strange and awful things. He might have thought he could not prove the case of Lound being a traitor, or maybe he just thought it was quicker and simpler to be rid of him. If he really had committed treason, he was going to be executed anyway."

"Matthews was my subordinate and a man I respected," Brandt said carefully, and with a slightly reproving look directed at Tommy. "I don't believe him a cold-blooded murderer."

"You weren't here during the war," Tommy countered. "You don't know the way things were. No one started out as a cold-blooded murderer, but this place changed them, changed us. The war made you think differently and act out-of-character. I think it is possible."

Tommy looked about the town, his face suddenly grim.

"Just being here brings back thoughts I have not had in years. I start to feel the hate bubbling again. The hate for anything German, the hate for anyone who would not do their duty, the hate for someone who would betray us." Tommy came to a halt, his mouth was dry, a sensation of deep and painful emotion creeping up his throat and threatening to choke him. "I would have done it. I would have killed a man I thought was a traitor."

"I don't think you would have, Tommy," Brandt said gently.

"I would have," Tommy contradicted him. "I would have done it. Given the chance. And I wouldn't have regretted it, either."

Chapter Fourteen

The home was at the top of a steep hill, which Clara felt was slightly ironic considering its clientele were all elderly or infirm. She noticed a nurse valiantly pushing an old man in a wheelchair up the hill and pointed her out to Annie.

"Shall we help?"

The two ladies went over and Clara asked in French if they could be of assistance. The nurse started to hesitate and then accepted. They pushed the chair together up the remainder of the slope.

"Quite a hike!" Clara declared as they finally reached the top and the ground levelled off.

"Oui, it gets no better," the nurse laughed, patting the shoulder of the old man in the chair. "But monsieur must have his daily air."

The old man made a mumbled murmur, whether it was relevant to what the nurse had said was difficult to tell.

"We have come to see if we might visit with one of your residents, Madame Smet," Clara explained as they walked with the nurse to the door of the house.

"You have never been before," the nurse said, taking a good look at Clara. "You are English?"

"Is it the accent?" Clara asked.

"I spent time in England," the nurse smiled. "Before the war, when I was just a girl."

"Well, you are right, we have never been here before. I am Clara Fitzgerald, I work in England as a private detective. I am looking into the case of an Englishman who went missing in Belgium during the war."

"A solider?" The nurse became crestfallen. She knew as well as anyone else that many young men went missing during the fighting, never to be found. Somewhere in the Belgium soil their bones lay, waiting to be discovered once more.

"Not a soldier," Clara said. "He was a priest in this town. Father Lound."

The nurse didn't recognise the name.

"I only came here after the war," she said. "I am not local. Maybe I have heard the name in passing, but, no, it doesn't ring a bell."

"Father Lound had a connection with the Devereaux family who lived in this town, they also left. Madame Smet used to be their neighbour and I hoped she would be able to tell me more about the family."

The nurse glanced towards the house. It was a large chateau with beautifully kept gardens. Probably it could house eight or ten residents in luxurious comfort. It was the sort of place that straddled the line between hospital and hotel. The patients had all their medical needs attended to, while surrounded by doting staff who served fine meals, made sure the rooms were tidy and that the residents had all they could desire to make them happy.

"Madame Smet is not keen on visitors," the nurse said at last. "I can ask her for you, of course."

"That would be most kind," Clara agreed. "I realise she might not care to speak with us. But, please explain that I am trying to help Father Lound's sister to discover what became of him."

The nurse nodded.

"Just let me sort out…" she tipped her head to the old man in the wheelchair who was now making odd humming sounds to himself and sucking his lips in.

They followed the nurse into the hall of the house and she disappeared with her charge. Annie glanced around the interior with an approving look.

"Very clean," she said. "It seems all right."

"What did you expect?" Clara asked.

"I wasn't sure," Annie replied. "I guess I was remembering the old workhouse that used to be near Brighton. Do you remember that place?"

"I never went there."

"When I was a girl, I sometimes went over with my father to help with the pigs the workhouse kept. I remember going inside and it was so bleak, and there were children my age in there. I shuddered looking at them. That place is closed now, but I saw all the old people who had nowhere else to go dumped there. They were cold and hungry, and miserable."

"Poor souls," Clara said, feeling genuinely sorry for anyone who ended up in such a situation. "This is the sort of place you go to when you are old and wealthy."

"How the other half live," Annie whistled.

A man, who looked like a porter, approached Clara and asked if he could help them. Clara suddenly realised she had not learned the nurse's name and could not state who exactly she was waiting for. She politely told him that they were being looked after and hoped the porter would not ask her for further details. He seemed satisfied and walked away. Perhaps he just assumed they were mad Englishwomen wanting a tour of the home. The Belgians seemed very accepting of the quirky ways of the English tourists in their town.

Clara and Annie had to wait for nearly half an hour before the nurse returned.

"My apologies for the delay. I had to make sure my charge was settled and then went to speak to Madame Smet," she said as she approached them. "You are in luck. She wants to see you. She said no at first, until I mentioned Father Lound's sister and the Devereauxs. Will you come this way?"

The nurse led them through the hall and into a large dining room, turning right they came to a large staircase with a lift running up through the centre where the stairs looped around. Annie eyed the metal cage of the lift with foreboding and gave an audible sigh of relief when the nurse headed for the stairs instead.

"Madame Smet is nearly one hundred," the nurse explained as they followed her. "She is a widow and had no children, her nearest relative is a great niece in Bruges. Not many people call on her these days. She has outlived most of her friends. That being said, she participates in all our social activities and is very cheery. I really didn't think she would agree to speak to you, but the names you mentioned sparked her interest."

They reached the first floor and the nurse led them along a corridor. There was a door marked with M. Smet. The nurse paused, knocked and then showed them in.

"I'll have to come back in about an hour, as it will be dinner time," she informed Clara and Annie, before she went to attend to her other duties.

Madame Smet was sat in a wheelchair by a floor-to-ceiling window. She had probably always been a small woman, but she had shrunk considerably with age and almost appeared to have curled up into a tiny ball in her seat. She wore a shawl that did not quite cover her extremely thin arms. Her face was so wrinkled it was rather like a very badly creased sheet, and it was only when she smiled that Clara could tell where the deep furrows ended and her mouth began. She had bright brown eyes that sparkled with great intelligence and Clara sensed that here was a woman with a strong mind, a woman who had seen and knew things. She was starting to feel hopeful.

"Madame Smet, I am Clara Fitzgerald and this is my friend Annie. We have come from England to try to discover what happened to Father Lound back in 1917."

"He disappeared," the old woman said, her voice steady despite her age. "That is what happened."

"I think you know as well as I do, that that is not the answer his sister is looking for. Why did he vanish? Where did he go? Is he still alive somewhere? These are the questions I must answer."

Madame Smet listened keenly, her smile growing.

"The nurse says you are a private detective?"

"I am," Clara said.

"I like to see a woman doing something so… manly," Madame Smet's smile broke into a grin. "How delightful. Do you have a lot of trouble from men over it?"

"On occasion," Clara admitted. "I have to prove myself each case afresh, but I chose this road."

"Good for you," Madame Smet lifted a bony arm. "Please be seated."

Clara and Annie sat on a blue sofa opposite Madame Smet. It was much like the one in the Coppens' house, with spindly legs that troubled Annie a lot.

"Your friend is very quiet," Madame Smet said.

"She doesn't speak French," Clara explained.

"Ah," Madame Smet responded, then she switched languages. "Then I shall speak in English."

Annie looked surprised, then remembered her manners.

"Thank you, madame. I wish I could speak French, but I never learned it."

Madame Smet seemed amused.

"I can speak English, Italian and a little Spanish. You should learn a language, young lady. Learning keeps your mind alert. Never stop seeking out new things."

"I'll try," Annie promised.

Madame Smet turned her attention back to Clara.

"I think you are intelligent enough to know that Father Lound must be dead," she said bluntly.

"That seems most likely," Clara replied. "Though I have to keep my mind open to the possibility he lives, just in case."

"Naturally," Madame Smet nodded. "But in reality, he has been dead a long time. Maybe since that day in October 1917. You know about the bones in the woods?"

"I do."

"Has to be him," Madame Smet gave a sigh. "You know, I find most men boring and pompous. I never used to. I was very fond of men as a young woman, but then I married and I realised that men really are overrated. My husband was good enough, I can't fault him for that. He had no real spark, however. I like spark. Father Lound had a spark."

"Really?" Clara was surprised to hear such a description of a priest.

"Oh yes," Madame Smet was smiling again. "He shouldn't have been a priest, he was far too radical in his thoughts. He would come over to my house quite often and we would have very enlightened conversations. He had a lot of views on the war, he didn't like how things were going. He felt the ordinary men were being used as cannon fodder. It made him very angry."

This was news to Clara and it made her start to wonder if Father Lound could have been a pacifist traitor after all. She was returning to that idea proposed by Father Dobson, that betrayal could be motivated by a sense of greater good rather than by financial or political considerations.

"He was friendly with the Devereaux family?" Clara asked.

"Yes. The boy, Ramon, had gone to Albion Hope to ask for work. Father Lound must have learned through him about the problems the family was experiencing. He came to the house first with some clothes for the younger girls, and then with food and other items. He started to get to know Beatrice. That woman was so burdened by life, my heart broke for her."

"I have heard the family was impoverished," Clara nodded.

"It was the shame of it all," Madame Smet explained. "Her having to work for a living after being so wealthy. She was a proud woman and I think she felt the town was looking down on her, maybe even laughing at her. She had lovely hands, you know? The softest, finest hands, and they were ruined by the work she had to take on.

"Eh, but some will say that is how it is. That other women must work and ruin their hands, why not her? Just because she was born into money and married more of it. No one really understands that a woman like Beatrice has no understanding of work, she is not raised to it, she does not have the skills for it. She has been trained to live in luxury and that is all she knows. It makes it a burden to begin to work hard.

"And then there was the elder girl, Elena. A beautiful thing, but so very vain and spoiled. She was not going to work on the land, she would not ruin herself that way. I think she started innocently enough with the men. Accepting their gifts when she walked out with them. Then, I suppose, she realised she could earn more money by offering her body as well as her time."

Madame Smet shrugged her shoulders, as if it was all very logical, a very expected way of things.

"I never liked Elena. She had a clever mind, but no inclination to use it. Do you know what a waste that is? I hate waste."

"You knew the family well? You were friends?"

"We were," Madame Smet agreed. "In happier times we would invite each other over for meals. Beatrice was not native to the town, her husband was. When she came here I must have already seemed old to her, but we became friends. Our houses were next to each other and it was good to have someone to talk to after I lost my husband. I knew the children from the day they were born. I watched them grow up."

"You must have heard the talk that Father Lound was romantically involved with Beatrice, then?"

Madame Smet gave a loud laugh.

"Oh yes, I heard that! People really do say stupid things!" The old woman chuckled to herself. "Beatrice was far too old for the priest, anyone with a drop of sense could see that. I know men can be attracted to older women, but usually they are still glamorous, or have some other attractions, such as wealth, to draw the men in. Beatrice had neither. Four children had wrecked her figure and she was never very pretty.

"Now, if people had suggested he was interested in Elena it might make more sense. She was pretty and not so far different in age to him. But there was nothing between them. In fact, Elena hated Father Lound because he kept trying to persuade her to stop running around with soldiers. He had sided with her mother on that and she despised him."

Madame Smet's eyes gave a dangerous twinkle. She knew something and was getting ready to impart it.

"Not that there was no truth to the rumours, mind. Just everyone was looking at the wrong women."

This was news to Clara and she grew excited.

"There was a young woman in Father Lound's life?"

"Lina Peeters, the younger sister of the town's Chief Inspector," Madame Smet stated. "Oh, those two were very close. The good father felt miserable about his feelings for Lina, he told me as much. It was against his vows, but his heart was pulling him. I told him all this celibacy stuff was nonsense anyway. God didn't invent that, it was some repressed, sexless church official who wanted to make himself feel better. I told him to run away with her. He told me I really was a crazy old woman. I said, age makes you realise you can't miss an opportunity.

"He never got the chance. Maybe he would have done, given enough time. I think he was veering that way. Events overtook him and something happened to him. I suppose that is why I think he is dead. I don't think he would have left Lina, not like that. If he had decided to break away from her, he would have been honest about it. He held a lot of store in his honour and doing the right thing."

Clara wasn't sure how to respond. The revelation threw a whole new light on the situation. There were so many pieces to this puzzle now, and none seemed to quite fit. Father Lound's life in Belgium was proving a lot more complicated than she had expected.

"Madame Smet, it is the belief of Father Lound's parents, due to information they were sent by a colonel in the British army, that their son was a traitor to his country. His sister is certain this is untrue, but desperately needs me to prove it. The belief of the army colonel is that Father

Lound was passing information he had learned from idly talking soldiers to the Germans."

"No, never!" Madame Smet declared fiercely, her eyes blazing with outrage. "Where is this colonel? I will speak with him myself and tell him what I think!"

"A trap was set. Fake secret papers were left in a place where a spy could access them. These papers were taken and then found in Father Lound's office. He would not say how they got there. Shortly after he disappeared, further suggesting his guilt."

"What rot!" Madame Smet snorted. "Father Lound would never betray his country!"

"What if he thought it would help the men in the trenches? The men he felt were being let down by the army?"

"You don't betray men to help them," Madame Smet snapped. "Father Lound was intelligent, did I not make that plain? He understood that every action has multiple consequences, most of them unforeseeable. He would not be so rash as to pass on information, in case it hurt those very men who he worried about. What was in these fake secret papers?"

"The details of British gun emplacements."

"There you go!" Madame Smet smiled, vindicated. "If he passed those on, the Germans would have targeted the guns and killed everyone near them. All those ordinary men Father Lound cared about. Anyway, he did not want the Germans to win this war, he believed that would be a disaster for all of us. He feared what would happen if this town was overrun. He was not trying to end the war sooner by helping the Germans. What stupidity!"

The old woman's certainty was reassuring. Clara found herself smiling, it was a relief to hear someone else stating that Father Lound could not be a traitor.

"That is all well and good," Annie spoke up at last. "But, if Father Lound was not a traitor, why did he leave so abruptly?"

"He may have been protecting someone," Clara said.

"Or, something awful happened to him," Madame Smet's smile had gone, replaced by a bleak grimace. "I believe he was murdered. I don't know why, or by whom, but I think that is what happened."

Clara was starting to fear that was the case too. She was going to say something, when the nurse knocked on the door and declared it was dinner time. The interview was over, but at least Clara had gained some useful insights. What she really needed now was cold, hard proof that Father Lound was not a traitor. What worried her was that that proof might come in the form of bones.

Chapter Fifteen

Lunch had been pleasant. Tommy could not fault the service or the food. Colonel Brandt had been good company, opting to talk about things other than the case, which had been a welcome distraction. Despite all that, and for a reason Tommy could not explain, he felt utterly bleak and depressed. He looked about the streets, at the people getting on with their lives and something overwhelmed him, made him feel like he was trying to scream.

He was attempting to understand the despair overtaking him, trying to unravel the emotions churning within, but to no avail. He didn't know why he felt this way, or why everything seemed to be fading into the background all around him, leaving only the darkness within, the sense of utter desolation. All through lunch he had struggled to follow Colonel Brandt's conversation, instead becoming lost inside himself. He had not felt this way in over a year and he was scared by the suddenness of it all. He was scared he was losing himself again.

He felt a bit better when they started to walk back to the police station. Brandt was still talking and Tommy tried to concentrate on what he was saying. He was watching the people walking by, telling himself to forget the troubles of the past, to instead focus on the here and now. Slowly it seemed to work and by the time they reached the police station, the gloom over Tommy's heart had lifted and he felt better.

Peeters was waiting for them in his office. He had two case files before him. The first was that concerning Father Lound's disappearance, the second concerned the body in the woods.

"I've looked through them again," Peeters said. "I don't see anything new. But you are welcome to read them. There is an empty office next door you can use."

Tommy and Brandt took a folder each and settled to work. Tommy had opted to look at the file on Lound's disappearance first. The top sheet was the report that had been made by Father Howard. It was quite detailed. Howard said he had last seen Father Lound at four o'clock that afternoon. Lound was in the garden, overseeing a project to strengthen the back wall of the house, which was slowly collapsing due to the vibrations of the German shells. To try and stabilise the foundations, deep trenches had been dug under sections of the wall and backfilled with concrete and rubble. A number of local lads, including Ramon Devereaux, had been present and Lound was directing the operation. Howard had not spoken to him, Lound was too absorbed with his task. The project was hazardous and props and boards had been inserted beneath the walls to prevent them collapsing while the trench was dug.

Howard expected Lound to be busy with the work all afternoon and was surprised to walk past the same spot only a half hour later and discover everyone gone. Little did he know that he had seen Father Lound for the last time. He went looking for the absent priest to find out why the work had been put on hold, considering the perilous nature of the situation. There was no sign of him.

Father Howard was annoyed, but not alarmed. Father Lound was also absent from dinner, which was curious, but not deeply troubling. It was when he failed to turn up for mass that Father Howard became concerned. Lound never missed mass, at least not without leaving a message to explain why. No one seemed to know where he was, or where he might have gone. Father Howard and Father

125

Stevens felt his behaviour was odd enough to warrant looking for him. They checked the whole of Albion Hope and that was when they noticed that Father Lound's suitcase was missing from his bedroom. Some clothes were gone from his wardrobe, along with his crucifix and rosary, but oddly his Bible remained in the drawer of his bedside cabinet. Father Howard made an essential point of this, believing Lound would go nowhere without it. The bible had been given to him by his sister when he was ordained as a priest, it not only bore an inscription from her, but numerous notes Lound had made for fast reference to certain texts he found inspiring or useful.

Truly worried by now, the two priests went outside to see if they could find their colleague. They located Ramon Devereaux and another boy, Louis Maes, backfilling the trench beneath the wall and asked them if they had seen Father Lound. Ramon said they had, just a little while before, and he had asked them to finish the work at the trench, but they had no idea where he had gone after that. Father Howard and Father Stevens walked the streets looking for their brother. Father Howard hinted that he thought Ramon had been lying. He suspected Ramon had been supposed to backfill the trench earlier in the afternoon and had abandoned his work for some reason. Ramon could be like that. He felt the lad had realised he would be in trouble for failing to complete the work and had gone back later to finish the job. He probably lied about seeing Father Lound to cover the fact he had neglected his work earlier.

Speaking to the other lads who had been in the garden seemed to confirm this idea. Not long after Howard had last seen his friend, Ramon had gotten into a squabble with another boy and Father Lound had pulled him to one side to talk. Ramon's temper had not cooled and he stormed off, Lound had gone to follow him. The other lads had waited for them to return, when they did not, they had decided to leave. The lad Ramon had fought with wanted to go home and his friends decided to go with him.

Over and over again, Father Howard insisted that the

last time anyone had seen Father Lound was around four o'clock in the garden. After that, he had just vanished into thin air.

Under normal circumstances, the disappearance of a grown man would not have caused the police to act at once, especially as his suitcase was missing. But war was not normal and the police were conscious that it was a dangerous thing to ignore sudden disappearances. A search was begun and all the lads in the garden re-interviewed. Ramon Devereaux was surly with the police, but did eventually admit he had lied about seeing Father Lound later in the day. He had regretted storming off and was concerned he would not be paid for the work he had already done. When Father Howard saw him, he had made up some fiction about Father Lound telling him to do the work there and then to cover up the fact he had walked off.

The last time Ramon Devereaux saw Father Lound was when he had pulled him aside for fighting. Ramon had to get away from everyone. He had hastily walked away and headed into the woods where he raged for a while, threw stones at trees and generally let out his anger in harmless ways. He never saw Father Lound and did not know the priest had tried to follow him.

Louis Maes confirmed Ramon's story. Ramon had told him he had to finish filling in a trench or he would not get paid. Louis was not the brightest of buttons and he followed Ramon like a sheep. When Ramon asked him to help, Louis agreed, even though he was not being paid for the task. He also went along with Ramon when he told Father Howard he had seen Lound mere moments before.

The problem was, Louis said whatever Ramon wanted him to say. There was no way to know if the boy was telling the truth.

The police very rapidly discovered that the trail had gone dry. There was no clue to where Father Lound had gone, no witness to him leaving the town. After doing their best to search the area, the police had to admit defeat. Father Lound was just… gone.

The failure stung, but there was nothing to be done about it. After a while, Father Howard stopped asking the police if there was any news and everyone came to accept that Father Lound was not coming back. Whether he was dead or living somewhere in secret, no one knew. The disappearance of the Devereauxs the same night was treated as coincidence at first, then there was talk that Father Lound's friendship with the family meant that he had run off with them. Everything after that was pure speculation, and the police had wisely avoided noting it in their file. They had to conclude that this was a case they could not solve.

Tommy read every piece of paper in the file, going back to some a couple of times to ensure he had missed nothing. At last he closed the cover and rolled the tension out of his shoulders.

"I can't say there is much here," he told Colonel Brandt. "I'll make some notes for Clara, however. She may see something I can't."

"You've done better than me," Brandt sighed. "As you know I have a medical background, with my father being a doctor, but these autopsy notes and findings are defying my understanding. Maybe the terms are unique to Belgium, but even when I translate them they don't make sense. I think we need to talk to the surgeon who looked at them in the first place, Monsieur Jacobs. He should be able to provide better insight."

"Is there anything in the file of use?" Tommy asked.

"Only what we already know. The skeleton was found in a grave near the side of the road that leads to the shrine of St Helena. There was no physical evidence at the scene to suggest who was responsible. The impression I get from the file is that the police thought the victim was most likely Father Lound."

"I don't blame them," Tommy nodded. "He did vanish mysteriously. No trace of his suitcase, I suppose? His suitcase was missing from his room."

"No sign of that," Colonel Brandt answered.

"Right, well let's track down this surgeon and see what he can tell us. Maybe there was more to those bones than met the eye."

They returned the files to Peeters in his office and explained they wanted to speak to Dr Jacobs, the local surgeon who had been called upon to look at the bones. With war still raging in the background, it was difficult in 1918 to transport bodies to the larger laboratories for examination. The next best thing was to get a local surgeon to look at them. Luckily, Dr Jacobs had experience with such things as he had been an anatomist. It was felt his analysis of the bones would be as good as anyone else's.

Peeters not only gave them Dr Jacobs' address, but directions to his home.

"He'll talk your ears off," he said with a groan. "Don't expect to get away with just a brief conversation."

Tommy and Brandt thanked Peeters and headed off to make the acquaintance of the surgeon. There was still plenty of time left in the afternoon, and they aimed to make good use of it.

Chapter Sixteen

Clara believed in striking while the iron was hot. Madame Smet had told them about Lina Peeters' relationship with Father Lound and Clara wanted to speak to the girl in person and learn what she knew about his disappearance. Maybe she knew nothing, but she must have had her suspicions. It was only natural to wonder what had happened to someone you cared about deeply.

They were able to find out where Lina lived from the helpful nurse they had met before. She had not even hesitated to tell them where to go. The house was not far, even with the two women taking a couple of wrong turns along the way. They arrived just after dinner, a little hungry as they had not eaten. Annie was complaining mildly that they had not been invited to dine at the old people's home. As a guest of Madame Smet, they might have been offered just a little something. She thought it was bad manners. Clara promised they would eat heartily that evening to make up for it.

Lina Peeters lived in a pretty chateau with roses in the garden and a small lily pond. She had yet to marry and functioned as a housekeeper for her brother. The nurse had hinted that the locals thought Lina would never marry. She was already thirty and seemed disinterested in the menfolk of the town. Madame Smet had overheard this and commented that she had always deemed Lina a sensible lady. Besides, she had added, once you have lost your true love it is hard to go for second best.

The nurse had not understood, but Clara did. If Madame Smet was correct, then Father Lound had broken the girl's heart and left her unable to move on with her life.

They knocked at the door of the chateau and it was only a moment before a pretty woman opened the door to them. Lina Peeters was not quite as tall as Clara, with glossy brown hair and vivid green eyes. She looked sad, that struck Clara at once. It was not that she just looked sombre at that moment in time, there was a sense about her that she was never happy, that joy had left her life never to return. Unlike Madame Coppens, she did not show any surprise at strangers on her doorstep, she barely showed any interest.

"Madame Peeters? I am Clara Fitzgerald, I have come from England to investigate the disappearance of Father Lound on behalf of his sister. I have been told you might be able to help me?"

Lina stared at her dully for a moment, then she nodded.

"I guess I might be able to help," she sighed. "Emily, that was his sister's name, yes?"

"Yes," Clara agreed. "She is desperate to know what became of her brother."

"Aren't we all?" Lina said.

She backed away from the door and let them in. Despite her appearance of unhappiness and ambivalence to life, Lina was a good hostess. She settled them in her front room and offered them coffee and cake, the latter most welcome to Annie who was famished.

"I think about Christian every day," Lina said when her guests were comfortable. "Who told you to come to me?"

"Madame Smet," Clara admitted.

Lina smiled softly to herself.

"Madame Smet knew about Christian and I. We were fond of one another, but he never betrayed his vows to the Church," Lina gave a small moan as she lowered herself into a chair. "I prayed night after night for something to happen, to change our relationship. I prayed that God would let my Christian go free. I never thought my prayers would be answered in such a way."

"I don't think this was God's work," Clara said gently. "Not that I am a believer, but I think whatever happened to Father Lound had the hand of man behind it."

Lina became thoughtful, focusing on Clara.

"You know about the bones?"

"Yes."

"It isn't Christian," Lina said bluntly. "I know."

"How?" Clara asked, wondering if the girl had information as to where Father Lound had gone.

"I went to look at them," Lina said. "My brother is the Chief Inspector, I had him pull some strings. I had to look at them, so I would know for sure. As soon as I touched that skull I knew it was not Christian. My heart told me."

Clara's hopes for a physical clue were dashed. Instinct was all very well, but it could be wrong.

"Are you willing to tell me about your relationship with Father Lound?" Clara asked instead.

Lina smiled, for a moment there was a sparkle to her face that brought her alive and made her not just pretty, but truly beautiful. Some people have an aura around them, Lina was one of those people. When her energy was strong, so she glowed from within. It was a glow that Clara felt was rare these days.

"Christian and I were kindred spirits. I know people say these things, but it is true," Lina touched near her eye as if she had sensed tears about to fall. "He was a good friend and I loved him. I know he loved me back. But, his calling was a barrier between us. I am not Catholic, that made it hard to understand how his vows could prevent him from being happy."

Lina bit her lower lip and her head sunk a little.

"We lied to ourselves, pretended we were not in love. It was torture. My brother thought I was insane, told me to forget about Christian and move on with my life, but I could not. Even when we were apart I thought of him constantly. I longed for him. There was nothing unholy or sinful about my feelings, I am sure of this," Lina took a trembling breath. "As our feelings grew, so Christian became more and more torn. We would meet sometimes and talk about everything, about all the possibilities before us. He was considering leaving the priesthood. He hinted at it. The problem was, I think that would have broken him a little. He was so honourable, so loyal. He took his vows incredibly seriously, yet he also took his duty towards me, his love for me, seriously. I knew there would be no simple answer for us.

"Some people say he left because of me, because of his feelings. He left rather than break his vows. They don't know Christian like I do, or rather, did. To just run away without explaining himself to me would have been too cowardly a thing to do. Christian could not have lived with himself. If he intended to disappeared, he would have told me why. I know this. I know it in my heart.

"You don't have to believe me, but I will always trust that Christian did not leave this town of his own free will. He was forced to go, and there was no time to speak to me, no time to even write."

Lina stopped. Her breathing had become rapid and she was clearly pained by what she was saying.

"All these things tell me he is dead," she said at last. "Otherwise, he would have tried to let me know. Those first few months I kidded myself, I told myself a letter would come, and when it did not come, I said that it had gone astray. Eventually, I knew it was never coming. That's when I realised Christian was dead."

"Then surely the bones…"

"No," Lina interrupted Clara firmly. "The skeleton in the woods was not Christian. I know this. I know it here."

Lina pressed a hand to her chest, pressing it over her heart.

"Do you have any idea what became of him then?" Clara asked.

Lina folded her hands in her lap. The glow had disappeared. She looked vulnerable suddenly.

"I have many theories. You know that the Devereauxs disappeared the same night?"

"Yes," Clara nodded. "And some say he ran off with them."

Lina gave a weak laugh.

"People are stupid, Christian disliked the Devereauxs."

"I thought he was friends with them?" Clara said, suddenly surprised.

"He was helping them, because it was his duty as a man of God, but he didn't like them. He felt they were all so full of sin. As Christian put it, God did not make certain things sinful to spoil our fun, no, he recognised these things as being harmful to us, and so he made it plain we should not do them. Christian knew that the Church had added to the list, but that was different, he was talking about the original seven deadly sins. He saw that the Devereauxs were riddled with sin and he desperately wanted to help them so they could improve their lives.

"Madame Devereaux was incredibly proud. Her pride made her vulnerable in a way she did not wish to believe. She hurt herself by this pride, making enemies instead of friends and placing herself in a position where she was tied up in knots by her proud manner. Then there was Elena. She was with a different man every day of the week and was paid for her services. Christian tried to get her decent work, but she would have none of it. She thought it was clever to use her body to earn a living.

"Until she fell pregnant, that is. Then there was Ramon, whose temper and loose morals had caused his family much grief. He stole from people and he hurt those who stood against him. Christian was trying to impress upon him what it was to be a good man, trying to be a father-figure to him, which was very hard.

"No. He was trying to make them better, trying to help them, but to call it a friendship as such is to go too far. I think at times they detested him."

Though it was not what many others had told her, Clara did not doubt Lina's insight. She would have been in a position to know all this. Madame Smet had hinted at the same. She had mentioned how Elena had despised the priest, how he was always trying to persuade her to give up her life of prostitution.

"I found a letter Father Lound had sent to his sister. It appeared that he had attempted to erase a name from it. I thought the name might have been Beatrice, as in Beatrice Devereaux?" Clara said, deciding to test Lina's theory.

"And you thought that implied he was trying to mask his relationship with her?" Lina shrugged her shoulders. "Maybe it was just an error? He wrote the wrong name and could not be bothered to write out the whole letter again? Maybe he thought his sister would read something more into his words than he wanted? I don't know, there could be a dozen reasons, but I can assure you, Christian was no more than a good servant to those people. He did too much for them. It was like they were his project. Don't read too much into it. That is what everyone here does."

Clara felt she had a point. One letter did not constitute an affair. It had seemed a tantalising insight at one time, but the more she learned, the more Clara was inclined to think it was just an innocuous quirk, a minor incident that meant nothing. Father Lound was annoyed at having made an error and decided to take the time to correct it. That could be all it was.

"When did you last see him?" She changed the subject.

"At lunchtime, on the day he vanished. I went to Albion Hope to return a book I had borrowed. There were always many books there and I can read English, even if I can't speak it. Christian helped me pick out a new book."

"How did he seem?"

Lina tilted her head and contemplated the question.

"Do you know how often I have gone over those last few hours in my mind, asking myself the exact same question?" She said. "I have spent sleepless nights questioning what I saw and what I failed to see. I could tell you a lot of things but, to be quite frank, I have thought and thought about this for so long that I am no longer sure what I actually witnessed that day and what I have imagined I witnessed since."

"I understand," Clara replied. "I suppose, if you had felt worried about Christian, you would have considered it more at the time?"

"Yes," Lina nodded keenly, trying to emphasise that, had she known, she would have done everything in her power to change what happened next. "I was not worried. I didn't even know he was missing until my brother told me. I was stunned. I still am stunned."

"Did you ever hear the talk that Father Lound was suspected of being a German spy?" Clara said without thinking, then she corrected herself. "I apologise, that was rather blunt."

"Please," Lina raised a hand to indicate she did not require an apology, "Christian has been gone too long for us to pussy-foot around. To answer your question, I was not aware of that. Why would anyone think such a thing?"

Clara gave her a full outline of Colonel Matthews' ploy to reveal the enemy agent. Lina began to frown.

"What an odd thing. I can say with utter confidence that Christian would never have betrayed us. But then why did he have those papers? Why would he not explain himself?" Lina considered her own questions. "I see why a person who did not know Christian would think it suspicious. However, I also know that Christian would never run away from his responsibilities. Whatever his reason for taking those papers, he would have been prepared to face the judgement and punishment of the British army for his actions. He was not a coward."

"What if he was protecting someone?" Clara asked. "After all, the military were certain there was a spy in this town, and if it was not Father Lound, then we have to ask ourselves who was it really?"

"I can't help you. Other than to say it was not me. If it had been me, I would not have allowed Christian to sacrifice himself for me," a tear escaped Lina's self-control and trickled down her cheek. "I have never met another man like him, I don't think I ever will. He was my true love and I would have laid down my life for him. I shall forever be broken from his loss."

Lina took out a handkerchief from her pocket and hastily held it to her mouth as a sob escaped her lips.

"I'll never be free of this grief, never. Whoever stole Christian from me, whatever the reason... I can't do this anymore. I just can't..."

Chapter Seventeen

Dr Jacobs lived in a chalet-style house. It looked newly built and the garden was still at that stage of development when everything looks undergrown and plain. A polite handwritten notice on the garden path asked visitors not to step on the grass as it had only just been laid. Since the path was not very wide, Tommy and Colonel Brandt walked up it in single-file.

The door to the house was on the left-hand side, not in the middle, and the right-hand wall was split by two large windows. They bulged outwards, giving a good view of the garden. An older gentleman was sitting in one of these windows, reading a book and smoking a large pipe. He spotted his visitors before they were halfway down the path and rose to greet them. Tommy reached the door before Dr Jacobs and wondered if he should knock or not. It seemed the polite thing to do, but was also rather redundant as they had been spotted. His quandary was resolved by Dr Jacobs opening the door before he could reach a decision.

"Good afternoon," the doctor appeared curious, but also concerned.

Tommy imagined the man was asked to help with medical emergencies on occasion. He was a surgeon, after all, and would probably be summoned to deal with any injuries and urgent operations in the town.

"Tommy Fitzgerald," Tommy introduced himself. "And

this is Colonel Brandt. Sorry to intrude, but we wondered if you could spare us a moment of your time? We are looking into the disappearance of Father Lound in 1917 on behalf of his family."

Dr Jacobs relaxed a little as he realised no one was sick or dying. He smiled.

"Come in," he said. "I think I understand why you are here."

He led them into the chalet, which appeared to be a sort of shrine to an active, outdoor life. Tommy had never seen so many pairs of skis in his life, they were hanging on the walls, propped up in corners – one pair was even being used as a coat rack. At the end of the slender entrance hall were several sleds, tilted against a wall and laying one atop the other like playing cards. Further in there were pairs of skates hanging from hooks and black and white photographs of a man Tommy guessed was Dr Jacobs in action. He appeared to have won a lot of prizes for winter sports.

The sitting room where they had first spotted the surgeon was also decorated with a great number of photographs. More than Tommy had ever seen in one place at a time. Photography was still something of a novelty, and mainly left to professionals. Tommy was absolutely certain there were not this many photographs in the whole of his house at Brighton, let alone on one wall. They were fighting for room with a large bookcase that dominated the back wall and seemed to be filled with a mix of titles on medicine and outdoor pursuits. Just to finish off the eclectic nature of the arrangement there were more than a dozen glass display cases containing a variety of animal and bird skeletons. These were presumably from Dr Jacobs' days as an anatomist. Two of the cases contained human bones; one was a carefully laid out skeletal hand, showing every bone, down to the smallest, in the correct place. The other was a human skull which stared at them with empty eye sockets.

Tommy was not sure how anyone could relax in a room with that particular item present.

"Would you like coffee? I shall make some," Dr Jacobs ushered his guests to chairs and then went away to the kitchen at the back of the house.

Colonel Brandt didn't sit down, his natural curiosity took him straight to the human skull. He examined it carefully for a while, before taking a seat.

"Anyone you know?" Tommy asked him.

"I just wondered, what with those bones in the woods being unidentified…" Brandt did not finish his hypothesis that Dr Jacobs had somehow acquired the skull of the murder victim found near the shrine of St Helena. "But it is not. There is no sign of a bullet wound."

Dr Jacobs returned with the coffee on a tray. He set it down, smiling at his guests.

"You are English?" He asked. "I heard you talking together."

"We are," Tommy nodded. "From Brighton, actually."

"I don't know the place," Dr Jacobs shrugged. "I have never been to England. I must one day."

He poured coffee and offered them cream and sugar, before taking up his now cold pipe and relighting it.

"I smoke too much," he said with a grin. "Now, I think you are here about the bones in the woods, yes?"

"Yes," Tommy smiled back. "Chief Inspector Peeters has been helping us. He said you were the surgeon who examined the bones. We've read the case file on them, but some of the medical details confused us."

Dr Jacobs' grin broadened.

"Medical jargon," he said. "I can explain whatever you want. You want to know if the body could be that of Father Lound?"

The man was certainly astute.

"Yes," Tommy continued. "There was never a formal identification of the body."

"No, that was not possible," Dr Jacobs became thoughtful. "Bones can tell you an awful lot, but not necessarily a man's name. For instance, see that skull I keep on the sideboard? What does that tell you about the person it came from, hmm?

"It tells me that the person was in their forties or early fifties when they died. The teeth were worn badly at the back and suggest a rough diet involving a lot of hard food that needed heavy chewing. There are also several missing teeth and one that had a long-term abscess beneath it. There is wear to the teeth on the left that suggests a pipe smoker."

Dr Jacobs flicked his nail at his own pipe, making a sharp noise.

"I shall have the same groove. I can look at the lines on the top of the skull, the fissure lines, and assess age by how well they have fused. I can tell all these physical things. I can say the man suffered with his teeth and was from a poor background who had a rough diet, but can I tell you a name? What his profession was? Whether he liked fish or beef? Whether he was married? No, none of this. He remains an anonymous specimen. In fact, I cannot really say if he was a man or a woman. I think the skull has masculine features, and the circumstances of how it was found suggests a man, but I could be wrong."

"Where did it come from?" Colonel Brandt's fascination was obvious.

"Some boys found it in a field, about five miles from here. The fighting got that close to us, you know?" Dr Jacobs looked unsettled for a moment, uneasy memories returning. "The fields often turn up relics from the war. The ploughs pull up unexploded shells, which are pretty scary to find. Very occasionally we find bones. They must be from men who died and sank in the mud before their comrades could retrieve their corpses."

Tommy had grown silent. The talk was bringing back a painful memory of a time he had lain on a battlefield, badly wounded, the mud seeming to be eating him slowly. He had not sure been if he would die from exposure, thirst, drowning in the mud, or an unlucky shell blast. The hours had been torture, his nerves had been wrung out and there was no going back. He had been found, by some miracle, but the damage was done.

The skull on Dr Jacob's cabinet had taken on a whole new meaning. Here was a man who had lain in the mud, maybe he had been lucky and died instantly, maybe he had not. Maybe he had bled to death in the mud, or frozen to death, or met his end in a dozen unpleasant ways. Only for his skull to be found years later and placed on display.

Dr Jacobs had been watching Tommy. He seemed to know the thoughts going through his mind.

"The boys saw something in the soil of the field and found our friend over there," he said, his tone serious. "Beneath the skull was a battered German helmet. I was summoned and the area was examined for further bones, but to no avail. No one was sure what to do next. There were protests about burying the fellow in the local graveyard. There is a great bitterness towards Germans here, I imagine it is the same in many places in Belgium. A few people wanted to smash the skull to pieces. In the end, I said I would take the head and use it as a medical specimen. It meant it was saved from destruction. One day I like to think I will work out who he was and restore him to his family. Until then, he sits here, safe.

"I hope you can understand that? Better than sitting in a field or being destroyed."

Tommy felt as though the world had taken a step back, as if he was wrapped up inside himself and everything else was not real. The room was not real. Dr Jacobs was not real. And the skull… Everything was like a dream.

His hands had tensed in his lap, knotted into tight fists. He was trying to control the rage and hurt that boiled within him. It was not rage at Dr Jacobs, or at the presence of the German skull, it was an unfathomable sensation. A rage he could not fix on any one thing, but which seemed to dwell within and try to explode every now and then. He was struggling to take a deep breath and restore his own sense of calm.

This was the reason he had feared coming to Belgium. He was terrified of his inner emotions; they were too raw, too violent. They seemed to want to control him and take him over. Rationality lost its grip and he became something else, some creature driven by instincts and a self-destructive will. He hated this side of himself and had suppressed it hard, only for it to now spring forth and knock down all the barriers he had built up.

"My friend, are you all right?" Dr Jacobs asked him gently.

Tommy could not answer, he was gritting his teeth so hard his jaw hurt. As if from another room he heard Colonel Brandt speaking.

"Tommy served in the war. He was badly injured. Being back here…"

"I understand," Dr Jacobs' said, and his tone did sound sympathetic. "Let us not sit here anymore, let me take you for a walk. I think we should get some fresh air and meet a nice lady who might be able to help your friend."

Tommy couldn't move. He felt fixed rigid. Dr Jacobs rose and placed a hand firmly on Tommy's shoulder.

"Tommy Fitzgerald, sitting here will not chase away the demons that haunt you. Come with me, please."

Tommy wasn't sure his legs would work. They felt numb. He had been shot in his legs, that was how he ended up lying in French mud. For years after the war he thought he was permanently crippled, until a good doctor convinced him his injury was a mental one, not a physical one. He had learned to walk again, breaking down a blockade he had built in his own mind. Now, suddenly, that block had resurfaced and he didn't know how to remove it.

"I…" he wasn't sure how to explain, he seemed frozen, his muscles refusing to respond. He didn't want to say he couldn't move, but he was not sure how else to articulate his thoughts.

"Tommy…" Colonel Brandt had started to speak when there was the sound of a door being brashly opened and a young voice echoed through the house.

"Grandpapa!" A young girl burst into the room. She was about ten and had pigtails tied with red ribbons and a floral dress. "Grandpapa, I have fresh bread and cake. Mama said to bring it!"

The girl had rushed forward saying all this, only to suddenly realise her grandfather had guests.

"Oops!" She declared loudly, and then darted back to the kitchen chuckling to herself.

Dr Jacobs shook his head and sighed indulgently.

"Oh, the enthusiasm of youth! My friend, I apologise for the interruption."

Tommy, however, was thinking how fortuitous the child's arrival had been. Her sudden sharp voice, so alive and bold had cut straight through his own anxieties and mental block. Her arrival had brought the world sharply back into focus, just as if a photographer had turned the lens of his camera and magically made an image come into view. Tommy's demons receded. He twitched his leg. He could still feel them. He let out a long breath, his chest still tight and his teeth sore from the clenching of his jaws.

"Don't apologise," he said, getting his mouth to work again. "She reminded me that I am still alive."

He rose stiffly from the chair, relieved that his legs still knew how to bear his weight. That had been a frightening moment.

"I think we should still go for a walk," Dr Jacobs was smiling again. "I always walk in the afternoon, it is good for the blood."

He ushered his guests into the kitchen, where his granddaughter was putting away the things she had brought. She turned to Tommy and lowered her eyes.

"Sorry monsieur."

"Come for a walk, Olivia," Dr Jacobs said. "We are going to the woods. These men are from England. Our friend here was a soldier in the war and deserves our great thanks."

Olivia's eyes widened.

"A real soldier?" She asked Tommy.

He found he was smiling as he nodded. Olivia gave him a very long look, as if she was not sure he was entirely real.

"You look awfully young to be a soldier."

"Olivia, really!" Dr Jacobs laughed.

"He does look young grandpapa! He is not as old as mother or father. I always thought soldiers were old people!"

Tommy started to laugh, he couldn't help it. The child was so brazen. Behind him Colonel Brandt snorted.

"Well, my dear, what about me? I was a soldier too."

Olivia looked at him, her eyes full of mischief.

"I think you tease me, monsieur."

"Aren't I old enough?" Brandt smirked.

"Oh, but you are too old!" Olivia laughed. "You must be the same age as grandpapa!"

"And I, apparently, am ancient," Dr Jacobs rolled his eyes. "Come on Olivia, show us the way."

Olivia bounced out the door, followed by her grandfather and the two Englishmen.

"A few more years and the boys of this town are going to be in trouble," Tommy said to the doctor as they left the house.

Dr Jacobs groaned

"Yes, that is what I fear."

Chapter Eighteen

They walked into the woods that bordered the town. Dr Jacobs explained that once they had been more extensive, but the heavy shelling during the war had reduced them dramatically. Tommy recalled the stunted forests he had come across in those days. Trees stripped of every leaf and branch, many fallen or burned to ruin. The landscape was recovering, but it would take a long time. It was good, however, to hear the birds singing. To know that they were returning and carrying on with life as normal. Tommy remembered the momentary peace hearing a bird singing during a break in the shelling could bring. It was as if the madness had stopped just for an instant.

The path they took through the woods had been well-tended by someone. Olivia skipped ahead, occasionally pausing to watch a bird or squirrel in the trees. She seemed to be full of energy.

"I feared for her during the war," Dr Jacobs confided. "She was so young. I thought the horrors of it all might leave their mark. Maybe they did, maybe it is why she is so resolved to live every moment to the utmost."

"Youth is surprisingly resilient," Colonel Brandt observed.

"I hope you are right," Dr Jacobs said. "Our friend here has that on his side."

Tommy had been watching a sparrow high up in the trees and jerked his head back when he heard this comment.

"It is not far to the shrine," Dr Jacobs smiled at him. "I recommend everyone to come here just once. There is something indefinable about the place. There is a peace to it that was preserved even during the war. Call me an old fool, but I believe a certain spiritual magic lingers here.

"Our friend, back at my house, I brought him here. I placed his skull before St Helena and asked that his soul might have peace. I promised I would look after his bones. I believe that was the right thing to do."

"Most of the doctors I know could care less about religion," Tommy said. "They consider it wrong for a man of science to even consider such things."

"Oh, but this is not about religion," Dr Jacobs grinned. "I told you, this is magic."

Up ahead the trees were falling back, and a clearing was emerging. Olivia was collecting up wildflowers. When she had a suitable bunch, she took them over to a stone structure that looked rather like an ancient Roman temple in miniature, raised up on a plinth. Inside was a wooden statue, painted in lifelike detail, though being out in the elements had worn some of the paint away. Olivia, with respectful care, placed the flowers at the feet the statue. Then she hopped over to Tommy and took his hand.

"This way, monsieur. I want you to meet a friend, her name is Helena and she will make you better."

She led Tommy to the aging statue. The figure was of a young woman wearing biblical clothes and with her head tilted down perhaps in meditation or benediction. Her hands were clasped before her in prayer. Tommy felt uneasy.

"I'm not Catholic."

"That doesn't matter. St Helena hears all hearts," Dr Jacobs appeared at his shoulder.

Olivia pressed a flower into his hand.

"You should kneel," she instructed solemnly.

Tommy hesitated, but the serious look on the child's face somehow made him feel like he should obey. He crouched down, somewhat stiffly as his legs were never going to be fully healed from his injuries. Everyone had gone very quiet.

"Now what?" Tommy asked.

"Just ask St Helena for her blessing," Dr Jacobs said softly. "It doesn't have to be a formal prayer, just speak with your heart. We will give you a moment."

Olivia was ushered away by her grandfather and Tommy heard Colonel Brandt leaving too. He was alone before the statue his thoughts running wild.

Tommy had retained his spirituality throughout the war. He was not sure why, when so many others had lost God, he had found him. But that was how it had been. That wasn't to say he was particularly religious. He did not attend church on Sundays or regularly say his prayers, but he did believe there was a higher power at work in the world. It was a complicated feeling, one he found hard to put into words.

Kneeling before St Helena he felt foolish. He glanced up at the statue. Someone had taken great care over its creation; though the paint was fading and, in places, had fallen away, the statue was still a work of art as much as a religious icon. Tommy had never heard of this saint and was not even certain she was recognised by the Catholic church. She was perhaps purely the work of the people in this town. Did that matter?

He stared at the softly painted face, with its gentle smile and beseeching eyes. It felt like she wanted him to say something. Tommy closed his own eyes and dipped his head, clasping his hands together to pray. Sometimes you had to take a chance. Clara would say this was all nonsense, but did she really know that or did she just find it too incredible to accept it as reality? What harm would it do anyway? Tommy was reaching a stage where anything that could vanquish his demons and prevent them from resurfacing at random moments was attractive. In any case, it was not as though it would do any harm to pray to the statue. As long as Clara never heard about it.

Tommy formed a simple message in his mind and, still feeling awkward, mentally spoke the words to St Helena. He asked for her blessing, apologising in the process that he was not Catholic, and maybe shouldn't really be asking, but, oh well… The demons were bad, he said. Worse than they had been in years. It was coming back to Belgium, of course it was, but he was afraid that now he had stirred the darkness within himself it would stay for good. He hoped she might help him, but he didn't expect anything, not really. She probably had better things to do, and he never went to church…

His thoughts trailed off. He lifted his eyes and looked at the statue again. Was he expecting some sort of change in its demeanour? The statue was still a statue. He started to feel stupid. Tommy rose stiffly and wandered back to find the others.

Colonel Brandt spotted him first and called out from the trees. Tommy turned off the main path to the shrine and walked just a few paces into the woods, to a spot marked with a large rock. Dr Jacobs was quizzing Olivia on the names of the wildflowers around them as he approached.

"Ah, my friend! This is the place where the bones were found."

Tommy noticed that the ground sloped slightly and the soil was very soft. It would have been easy to dig a grave quickly here, but it was also clear how a little heavy rain could wash the soil down the slope. Some of the trees had their roots exposed where the soil had eroded.

"His head was where you are standing," Dr Jacobs had picked up a fallen branch and pointed to Tommy's feet. "He was curled up in a foetal position and placed upright in the grave. I suspected he had been tied up in that position to make it easier to get the body into the small grave. There was no trace of rope, however. I did postulate that he might have been made to kneel in the grave where he was killed, that would explain why he was upright with his knees bent, but more likely he was placed that way afterwards."

Dr Jacobs didn't seem to have any qualms about saying

all this as Olivia wove a garland of wildflowers on the grass beside him. The little girl seemed oblivious to the discussion, or perhaps she was used to her grandfather talking about his work.

"What can you tell us about the victim?" Tommy asked. "I know he was holding a rosary and wearing a crucifix, was there anything else in the grave."

"Scraps of material," Dr Jacobs frowned. "This soil is very acidic, it eats anything organic. There was no clothing left, except for small pieces of leather near the feet that appeared to be from a pair of boots. As you say, he was wearing a crucifix and carrying a rosary. The crucifix was made of gold and I would have thought worth quite a bit. That it was not taken seems to suggest he was not killed for his valuables. The rosary was made of various materials. Some of the beads were amber, others coral and some just wood. It was wrapped up in the finger bones, suggesting he was clutching it in his last moments. I had the impression he was praying as he was killed.

"He was shot in the back of the head. The bullet was still in the skull remarkably. I did not have the expertise to analyse it myself, so I sent it away. A preliminary report suggested it was a bullet from a low calibre revolver, not military issue, but probably German."

"German!" Brandt almost coughed on the word. "Are we saying the man was killed by enemy troops?"

"It raises the possibility," Dr Jacobs agreed. "However, the revolver could have been bought before the war or have been stolen from a German soldier. It was not something the German army issued to its men."

"Another clue that proves useless on its own," Tommy sighed. "Is there anything else the bones told you which might have helped identify the man?"

"He was tall, about six foot. Still quite young. Remember what I said about the fissures on the skull? They were still fusing and were very visible, they virtually disappear in older people," Dr Jacobs casually drew a squiggle in the soft soil, which may have been a representation of a skull fissure. "I doubt the man was more than twenty years old, though he could have been about twenty-four or twenty-five.

"He was in good health, at least from what the bones could tell me. The only noticeable defect was that he had broken his arm at some point. It would not have been that long ago as the new bone growth was quite fresh. I would guess maybe two or three years before he died. Otherwise there was nothing remarkable. I must emphasise that while it is not possible to be absolutely certain the victim was a man, certain skeletal features were very masculine. I doubt it was a tall woman."

Tommy found himself staring at the ground before his feet, as if he could stare into the soil and see something that would explain who had been buried there. He noticed that Colonel Brandt was doing the same.

"Do you suppose the man in the grave was Father Lound?" Tommy asked.

Dr Jacobs gave a soft sigh.

"It is what the police believed. There was no way of formally identifying him. We thought about writing to the family, but the war was still raging and things got in the way. It sounds awful, but as soon as things became difficult we pushed the case to one side to work on other, more urgent things. I never did write to the family. Maybe that is just as well. I don't like distressing people for no reason. I could not prove this was Father Lound and the family could not possibly identify him from a skeleton," Dr Jacobs shrugged his shoulders. "The broken arm was interesting. I thought about chasing down Father Lound's medical records, and then I didn't."

"If you are right, Father Lound must have broken his arm not long before he came to Belgium. There must be someone who can confirm that for us," Tommy pulled a face. "And, if he never broke his arm, then we have a new question. Who was in the grave?"

"It is a real riddle," Dr Jacobs nodded. "No one recalls any suspicious activity in the woods around the time the body must have been buried. I have speculated over all this many nights. It was his right arm that was broken, halfway between the wrist and elbow."

"I don't suppose…" Tommy stopped himself, considering what he was about to say, then looked at Dr Jacobs. "Did you know of anyone else in the town, of the right age and height, who had broken their arm in the past?"

"That is where things get curious," Dr Jacobs gave a strange smile. "I do know of one."

"Who?" Tommy asked.

"Ramon Devereaux," Dr Jacobs said. "But, you see, it cannot have been him in the grave."

"Why not?" Tommy asked, thinking that Ramon had vanished at the same time as Father Lound, and that he fitted the description of the body, except for the crucifix and the rosary. "Why can't it be him?"

"Well, because I know that Ramon is alive," Dr Jacobs grinned. "I know what became of the Devereauxs and where they are now."

Chapter Nineteen

Annie and Clara returned to the hotel their minds overflowing with information. Clara had written down a lot of notes, but much more she had consigned to her memory and hoped she didn't forget it. Her scribbles were more aids to her recollection than anything else.

"Welcome back mademoiselles," Janssen greeted them with delight. "I have a most excellent meal cooking for tonight. It is a lovely beef casserole with Belgium dumplings. I am sure you will like it a lot. But you look so tired! Might I get you a drink?"

"Soda water would be nice," Clara said and Annie concurred.

The girls settled themselves into a pair of comfy chairs in the hotel lounge to await the return to Brandt and Tommy.

"I am confused," Annie admitted.

"Why is that?" Clara had closed her eyes, feeling very tired.

"Nothing makes sense. Was Father Lound a traitor or not? Was he murdered or not? Was he friends with the Devereauxs or not? Did he love Lina or not? I can't see how you can untangle all this."

"It's what I do," Clara smiled. "At some point all the random pieces will begin to form a pattern. You just have to find the key to it all."

"I think I shall stick to baking," Annie said glumly.

"Recipes makes sense… usually."

Tommy and Colonel Brandt appeared in the hotel foyer and the girls waved to them. They walked over looking as exhausted as Clara felt.

"Anything?" She asked.

"No one saw Father Lound leave the town," Tommy said. "I made lots of notes from the case file for you."

Tommy removed a bundle of papers from his pocket and handed them to Clara.

"The most interesting thing is that we talked to the surgeon who examined the bones from the wood. The victim had broken their arm a couple of years before they died. If we could learn whether Father Lound ever broke his arm we could prove or disprove if the body was his."

"There is one other thing, we felt this was very important," Colonel Brandt added as Tommy finished. "Dr Jacobs knows where the Devereauxs are living."

Clara became excited enough that her weariness briefly evaporated.

"He does? Who is Dr Jacobs?"

"The surgeon who helped the police with the bones in the woods," Tommy took up the discussion. "He was contacted by Madame Devereaux around the time the bones in the woods were discovered. She needed to acquire the family medical records and hoped Dr Jacobs could assist her. One of her daughters was unwell with a complaint she had had before, and the doctor who was currently treating her wanted to see her past records. She requested all the family's records, to save her having to ask again in the future, including those for Ramon Devereaux."

"That means the body in the woods can't be Ramon," Colonel Brandt explained.

"Hold up," Clara stopped them. "When did the body in the woods become Ramon?"

"Ramon was the only other young man in the town who was missing and who had broken his arm in the past. If the body in the grave was not Father Lound's, it could have been his, except Ramon is alive and well in a little town called…" Tommy dragged a piece of paper from his pocket and screwed up his eyes as he read from it. "Lugrule. No idea how you pronounce that."

"Well then, we now have two more avenues to explore. I shall telegram Emily Priggins and ask if her brother ever broke his arm and we seek out the Devereauxs and see if their disappearance had anything to do with Father Lound's," Clara was elated, at last she had a way forward. "There are still many questions to answer, but we are getting there, that is for sure."

"What about all this traitor business?" Colonel Brandt interrupted. "It has been worrying me a great deal. Someone in this town was selling information to the Germans. Was it Father Lound?"

"Those who knew him best don't think so," Annie spoke up. "I don't think he did it."

"Then there was someone else?" Colonel Brandt raised the question. "Who?"

They were all silent again. The possibilities were slender. There was no doubting that the treachery ceased after Father Lound disappeared. It could be that the spy simply decided it was best to stop his activities after the sting at Albion Hope, but it was also very tempting to imagine the end to the problem was due to the spy taking his leave of the town. That made for a very short list of suspects.

"I'm going to send that telegram," Clara rose. "I'll be back for dinner. I am famished."

She was nearly out of the hotel, when she heard quick footsteps behind her and realised Colonel Brandt was following.

"Mind if I join you?" He asked, looking anxious.

Clara shrugged to indicate she did not mind. They fell into step side-by-side.

"It's this treachery business that has me agitated," Colonel Brandt spoke in a low voice. "Maybe it is the old soldier within me, but I can't stop thinking about it. I know it is not what you were tasked with, but I really think you need to determine who the traitor was, Clara. They should face justice. They did not just betray our troops, they betrayed the people in this town. It is wrong that they should get away with it."

Colonel Brandt's usually cheery face had drooped into a frown and he did indeed look very upset.

"You don't believe it was Father Lound then?"

"Everything I hear about his last few hours in this town do not sound like those of a traitor who has been found out. He did not appear to be in any hurry to leave, which you would think he would be having been discovered with those papers," Brandt shook his head. "You know, it almost seems to me that he was not intending to leave at all. He was getting on with projects at Albion Hope as if nothing was happening."

"Might have all been an act."

"What for? Why hang around? He could have left the instant Colonel Matthews was gone. There was no need to waste time," Colonel Brandt paused for a second. "I know you feel Matthews jumped the gun on this one, and possibly he did, but he is a sensible man. If he suspected someone was betraying information to the Germans, then I think he was right. That he failed to see that Father Lound was probably not the guilty party is another matter."

They walked on for a while, Clara mulling over everything that had been said.

"How would someone do it?" She asked at last. "How do you sell secrets to the enemy?"

"Depends on the circumstances," Brandt said. "First you make contact with the enemy somehow. That is perhaps the hardest part. You have to convince them you are willing to help and have good information to supply. You might go to an enemy camp or outpost, depends if it is a one-off effort, or a long-term arrangement. For instance, a soldier contemplating treason might allow himself to be captured and then reveal what he knew."

"I would be curious to know how near to this town the

German line was," Clara mused. "And how easy it would be for someone to reach them regularly in 1917."

"There could have been an intermediary," Colonel Brandt said. "The traitor may not have had to go direct to those they were selling information to."

"But the intermediary still had to get through the British lines to reach the Germans, assuming they communicated face-to-face."

"There are other ways," Colonel Brandt nodded. "We had 'stay-behind' agents, who would quite literally stay behind when the enemy moved forward and allow themselves to be overtaken. Once behind the enemy line they would start learning what information they could and would then find ways to send it to the British. One method was messenger pigeons, but that required regular drops over enemy territory of fresh birds. Another method was to have a safe box where something could be left for another agent to collect. That would be at a place where the lines were close, or even a neutral point.

"It was also possible to communicate by telephone, but it was unreliable as the wires were often cut. Other methods involved coded messages being signalled at night. Really, there are probably so many ways it is impossible to imagine them all."

"I wonder if there is anyone local who knew about the military movements around the town," Clara thought aloud. "They could give an insight into how contact was made."

"I would be happy to telegram Colonel Matthews for his knowledge on the subject," Colonel Brandt suggested. "He must have considered that problem too. This town was in something of a No Man's Land, from what I recall. The Germans were on the doorstep more than once. It would be entirely possible for them to have left 'stay-behind' agents when they were pushed back. There are plenty of woods and abandoned houses for them to have hidden in. Easy enough for a local to have made contact with them, given information to them, and then for the agents to worry about passing it on."

"Anyone in the town could have been behind it?"

"Anyone who was in contact with the British soldiers who came here and had access to Albion Hope."

Clara winced at the scope of the problem, and in the middle of it all was Father Lound. She had no real proof he was not a traitor, and the circumstances Colonel Brandt had just described would have worked to his advantage if he had wanted to sell secrets.

"There is one other thing," Colonel Brandt said, his whole demeanour grave. "Whoever did this had no qualms and no conscience. I don't think that sounds like Father Lound and, personally, had I been here rather than Colonel Matthews, I would have considered him a red herring. Maybe he was protecting someone, or maybe he just did not know what to say when the papers were found in his office. Either way, I don't think it was him.

"Whoever did this, they were evil and they need to be found and punished."

They made their way to the Post Office and discovered the staff extremely fluent in English – they routinely sent messages home for British tourists and had Clara and Colonel Brandt's respective telegrams dealt with speedily and efficiently. There was plenty of time to get back to the hotel for dinner.

Janssen had prepared something involving chicken and turnips. It tasted more appealing than its contents suggested. There were lots of potatoes in a creamy sauce and fresh bread. Everyone had generous servings. When dessert arrived Clara broached the topic she was most curious about with their host.

"Where is the town of Lugrule?" She asked Janssen.

"Several miles away," Janssen shrugged carelessly. "I never go there. The people are…"

He paused for a considerable time to contemplate just the right word for the residents of Lugrule.

"Crude," he concluded. "If you are already bored with our town, I would suggest a ride out to a lovely little village a couple of miles from here."

"We are certainly not bored with your town," Clara told him warmly. "It is just I have had word that a friend is in Lugrule and I thought about visiting them."

"Poor soul, if you do visit them, tell them to come and spend the rest of their holiday here," Janssen replied and his condolences seemed genuine, rather than the spite of prejudice.

"Why do you consider Lugrule such a bad place?" Colonel Brandt asked their host.

Janssen raised his hands in a gesture that indicated he had quite a list of reasons for his assertion.

"Lugrule was built up during the rise of industry in Belgium, it was once very famous for its ironworks. There were great factories employing many hundreds of people. But its wealth could not stop the place being a blot on the landscape," Janssen clicked his tongue as he reflected on the past. "It always used to be said the winter snows were black instead of white in Lugrule, and in the summer the trees were coated in soot. The rivers were fouled along with the ground. Soon it was realised that the town was killing the local wildlife, polluting the landscape and ruining the soil for miles around. Farmer after farmer had to abandon his home for the crops would not grow well and the cattle would not thrive. Something had to be done.

"Eventually the government had to step in. Efforts had been made locally to no effect. The men in charge of Lugrule refused to see the problem and were wealthy enough to make light work of any fines that were imposed on the town. When the government said that Lugrule was a hazard to human life and all production must stop, there were protests from the workers and residents who relied on the ironworks. But, ultimately, it could not be allowed to continue. A ban was imposed on the purchase of goods from Lugrule by Belgium firms, and they were not allowed to export their products. Very soon their trade withered to nothing."

"How very awful for those who relied on the iron for

their livelihood," Clara frowned.

"What of the farmer's whose livelihood the factories had ruined? What of the children who sickened and died before they could grow up? What of the men who were dead before they were forty from the work? Everyone suffered," Janssen shook his head. "The factory owners were to blame, of course. They had been pushed for years to better regulate their waste products and to improve the conditions of the factories, but it was cheaper to keep poisoning the land. In the end, you could not drink any of the local water, not if you wanted to live to a ripe old age. All the residents of Lugrule were suffering from lead poisoning at varying degrees of severity. There was also arsenic in the water. It was awful."

It didn't sound like much of a place to live, and not somewhere you would want to move to after living in the pleasant surroundings of Janssen's town. Not, unless, you had no choice.

"Do many people live there now?" Clara asked.

"A few. Most had to leave," Janssen seemed to think this was not such a bad thing. "Those that remain scavenge off the remains of the ironworks. The factories produced tonnes of waste and much of it contained fragments of iron or other minerals that can be collected and sold for a small pittance. Some people live in Lugrule and walk three or four miles each day to reach a farm or somewhere else they can work. Only the very poor exist there, and those who try to help them."

"It does sound pretty grim," Tommy observed. "Why would anyone choose to go there?"

"Exactly," Janssen was satisfied he had made his point. "I have heard some of the farms that were on the very outskirts are being returned to use. The water is still poisoned, but not so badly. Actually, I believe some of the old waste is full of nitrates which can be sold to make fertiliser. But it is very bad to collect and kills people faster than anything else if it gets into the lungs."

Clara thought it sounded awful, but that was the place

she had to go if she was to confront the Devereauxs and hear their side of the story. They had disappeared for a reason, whether it was linked to Father Lound's death or not.

Janssen had other guests to attend to and made his excuses. Clara and her companions sat and finished their puddings, musing on the information Janssen had just imparted. The mystery of the Devereauxs had deepened. Why had they chosen such a hellhole to escape to? Could it really all be due to the eldest girl's pregnancy, or was it due to something else? Clara was thinking about Ramon's links to Father Lound. How far would the Father go for that family? Would he consider risking his own reputation, his own life to protect Ramon? For Clara could not help thinking that if there was anyone who might have acted as a traitor to his town, Ramon Devereaux was it.

Chapter Twenty

Night was never Tommy's friend. Over the years he had learned to accept its dark embrace and to endure it, but he was never entirely easy when the sun set and the world was enveloped in black nothingness.

Part of the problem was that night involved sleeping and Tommy's sleep had never been the same since the war. The doctors at the first hospital he had been confined in had told him the nightmares would ease with time. They were wrong. They did not ease, but they became familiar and Tommy could largely cope with them. He didn't wake up screaming these days, instead he would jerk awake, his body caked in sweat and the dregs of some awful dream lingering at the corners of his mind. Sometimes his heart was pounding as if he had just run a mile.

He had developed tricks for coping. He found there was solace in the quiet act of pouring a glass of water and sipping it slowly, so there was always a jug of water and a glass by his bed at night. With each sip of water, he could feel his heart calming and he could start to focus on relaxing again. The Fitzgeralds' dog, Bramble, was also a huge comfort. He slept on Tommy's bed and would cuddle up to his master when he awoke from his dreams. The dog would press into him as hard as it could, as if he knew something was wrong.

Time had also healed over some of the scars the war had left inside Tommy. He was able to put distance between himself and that terrible period of his life. Occasionally, he could almost pretend it was not even real, that it was something he had read about in a strange book.

Until he came to Belgium.

Tommy could not articulate to Clara, Annie or anyone else, just how crippling those old memories were, and how much he feared that going back to the place where they were created would somehow spark them back into life. He didn't know how to speak about such things, no one had taught him how, and the prevailing attitude among the army doctors was that he ought to really push them out of his mind, forget about them altogether, and if he couldn't... well, he would just have to try harder.

Tommy had tried hard; really hard. But the memories did not go away entirely, they just faded a little. He knew they were always there at the periphery of his thoughts, like a savage tiger waiting to pounce the moment he grew unwary. He had been scared that coming to Belgium would give that tiger just what it needed to strike.

At first, much to his relief, that had not been the case. He had suffered no noticeable increase in his nightmares, if anything, the initial night in the hotel he had been so exhausted he had slept well. It was the following night that was the problem.

Maybe it was that strange episode at Dr Jacobs' house that had triggered it all. Or maybe it was that his brain had now had time to absorb the fact that Tommy was back in the country where his life had changed. All he knew was that something had been nudged awake.

That night he had the worst nightmare he had suffered in a long time. The images were fragmentary, but that only made them worse. He saw friends who had perished a long time ago, die all over again before his eyes. He saw a lot of blood and a lot of gore. He physically felt the grief and horror this all caused, along with the pain in his leg as he was shot down on that fateful day and lay in the battlefield mud. That was not the worst part, the terrible bit came always at the end of the nightmare. He would dream he was lying in the mud and that he was sinking, the mud seeping up and over him. He would try to push himself up, to rise from the ground, but he could not fight hard enough to escape the terrible suction as he was drawn deeper and deeper. He could feel the mud flowing over his arms until he was paralysed, he could not pull them away anymore, and then the mud was flooding over his face and he would feel it pouring into his mouth and causing him to struggle to breathe.

Just as suffocation seemed inevitable, he would awaken violently.

That night he woke with a muffled scream and nearly fell out of bed. He found that his blanket seemed to have tangled about him and restrained him like a rope. He gasped painfully for air, uncertain if he was capable of breathing or not, his thoughts so muddled and disjointed. For a few seconds there was only blinding panic and no sense of rationality.

Tommy could not remember where he was and his fear heightened. He didn't recognise the room and his mind seemed unable to help him. When he wrestled the blanket free he was cold and scared. His legs ached like they were on fire and he reached for them, rubbing at the flesh, trying to stop the terrible pain. He was shaking from head to foot, the violence of the sensation so strong he was amazed the bed was not rattling as well. His teeth chattered in his head and he felt sick to his stomach. The tears finally fell from his eyes; almost an after-thought, but falling nonetheless.

Every ounce of grief and terror he had ever experienced during the war, every drop of horror and fury, hit him again. Smacking into his chest like an iron bar and knocking the wind from him. He wanted to run away, and yet he also wanted to fight, only there was nothing to fight. The war was done.

He was done.

Tommy somehow managed to stumble from the room and made his way downstairs. Colonel Brandt was sharing the room with him, but had not stirred from his deep slumber. Tommy left him to his snoring, angry that the man could sleep so contentedly when he was suffering like this.

Tommy found the hotel door was locked, but the key was close to hand and he made it outside, heading into the night, his feet finding a route to the nearest bridge in town. Tommy was still in a daze, he was aching inside and out. His legs still hurt and felt numb, that he could walk at all was a sort of miracle. But Tommy wasn't thinking of miracles right then. He was thinking dark thoughts that had not disturbed him for many years. The last time he had suffered them, he had not been in a position to act upon them as his legs had not been functioning. Now he could walk and he walked to a bridge with a quietly babbling river running beneath it.

He was not connecting thoughts in a rational sense. He was operating out of desperation. In his head he could hear the cries of his friends; poor old Bobby Roper calling for his mother as his guts spilled out into a trench; desperate Freddie Lyons clinging to an arm that was no longer connected to his body and bleeding to death as he sobbed; anguished Archie Holmes, telling Tommy over and over again he could not die as his young wife was pregnant, even while he slowly faded from a gunshot to the chest.

They were long gone, and yet they were also forever at the back of Tommy's mind, calling to him, reminding him that he lived when they did not. How was that? What had made him lucky?

Tommy stumbled. There was a loose stone on the bridge and for a second the pain in his toe snapped him back to himself. He clenched his fists. He had been so stupid. When Dr Jacobs had insisted he pray before St. Helena, he had actually believed that there was something in it! He had thought he would be healed. More fool him! He had just had the worst nightmare of his life and he could not go on any longer, not like this. He could not bear the pain inside. No one understood that.

Tommy leaned on the rail of the bridge and stared down

at the water. He never wanted to dream again, he never wanted to think again. He rocked forward a little. He had tried, he told himself, he had attempted to get better. No would could argue with that. There had been doctors and there had been prayers and helpful friends, and Clara and Annie, of course. None of it had made a difference. He could no longer endure. He could no longer smile bravely and cope.

He put his feet up on the bottom of the barrier, so he could push himself over. He wasn't sure how deep the water was. He didn't really care. Maybe he would crack his head open rather than drown, would that matter? He rocked forward again, one more push and it would be over. He would be glad to be out of this life and all the traumas it brought him.

Footsteps near the bridge made him freeze. His hands clenched tight around the rail, so he didn't think he could pull his hands away even if he wanted to. He was breathing hard, not wanting to be seen like this. Shame replaced terror and the tears fell again. Then a breeze fluttered by him and he shivered from the cold. He thought someone was walking towards him. His feet came down from the barrier and back onto the bridge. He tried to right himself, to make it looked like he was just out for a walk. He took a breath, composed himself. Finally, he let go of the rail, his knuckles white and stiff as he turned to face the only other person out this late at night. He was expecting to get asked what he was doing, it must look odd, a man in pyjamas on the bridge. He wasn't expecting to turn around to an empty space.

He hesitated. Tommy was sure he had heard footsteps. They had sounded as if they were coming towards him. He was even sure he had felt that odd sensation of a person walking up behind him, like when someone comes into a room you are in. Apparently, he had been wrong.

The roads near the bridge were all open and easy to see, if someone had walked past he should still be able to spot them. They would have come from behind, walked past the bridge and then into his eyeline. There was no one.

Tommy started to feel a little strange. He had always believed he had an acute sense of hearing, and a ready instinct for knowing someone was about. He had been credited for just that during the war on multiple occasions. His 'sixth sense' had enabled him to spot snipers and prevent his working party from stumbling into enemy troops more than once. It was perhaps the reason he had lasted the entire war, when so many could not last a month.

Yet, for once, his senses had let him down. There had been no one near the bridge. The footsteps must have been in his mind.

Tommy shivered again, he was very cold now. He had walked out bare-foot and the night was not that warm. The dregs of his nightmare were lifting as the reality of the situation was slowly restored. He glanced at the bridge rail and felt guilty at what had nearly transpired. Rubbing a hand over his face, he felt terrible; had he gone through with what he had intended he would have been letting down his sister and Annie. Suddenly, all he could think about was how horrible it would have been for them to wake up and discover him missing, then to learn he had drowned himself. He would have caused them such pain.

"Stupid man!" He scolded himself angrily.

The cold breeze seemed to scuttle around him again. It tugged at his legs this time, like little fingers pulling him away from the rail of the bridge. Unconsciously he moved forward and his naked foot stepped on something soft.

Tommy automatically bent down and picked up what had become stuck to his foot. He walked off the bridge, the item in the palm of his hand until he reached one of the public bins that dotted the pathways, right by a lit street lamp. Opening his hand to place the scrap in with the other rubbish he stopped. The thing that he had stepped on was a wildflower. Tommy didn't know its name, but he did recognise it as one of the flowers that Dr Jacobs' granddaughter had collected into a bunch and presented to St. Helena. It seemed remarkable that such a delicate flower would have blown all the way into town.

Tommy felt rather odd. He didn't put the flower into the bin. Instead he carried it back to the hotel. He let himself back in through the unlocked door, turned the key and replaced it where he had found it. Then he went up to his room where Colonel Brandt still snored away.

The blankets were on the floor and had to be replaced on the bed, then Tommy could climb in and begin to warm back up. The terrible thoughts and feelings had dispersed, now just a mild echo in the back of his mind. He took another look at the flower he had found.

What a peculiar night. He had clearly still been dreaming when he walked to the bridge, some sort of sleepwalking. The footsteps he heard were a part of that dream, just before he came sharply to his senses. Tommy scratched at his head. He supposed that was it, anyway. What a relief the nightmare had let go of him just in time!

Tommy put the flower, now a little squashed, onto the cabinet beside his bed and then slipped beneath the blanket. He didn't want to think about what had so nearly happened. He was tired, and his eyes drifted shut. His body relaxed and this time when he slept, it was the deep, dreamless sleep he so craved. No more nightmares. No more midnight walks that almost ended in doom. Tommy finally got the rest he needed.

When he awoke the next morning, the sun coming through the window and Colonel Brandt yawning as he sat on the edge of his bed, everything seemed like a very weird dream. He was not so sure he had left the hotel at all. Maybe it had all been part of the nightmare? However, his feet were filthy, clear evidence he had walked the roads.

Tommy looked for the wildflower he had carefully brought back with him.

It was nowhere to be found.

Chapter Twenty-one

They agreed to split up once again. Colonel Brandt and Tommy would follow up on the treachery side of the case, while Clara and Annie would travel to Lugrule and locate the Devereauxs. The first stop, however, was the Post Office, to see if a reply had come for the telegrams sent the day before.

"I don't like the sound of this place we are going to," Annie grumbled as they walked along. "I shan't eat a thing, I won't dare."

"We will ask Janssen to pack us some provisions," Clara told her merrily, she was unconcerned about poisoned water or air pollution, instead she was excited about the prospect of tracking down the Devereauxs. They had a lot of questions to answer.

Clara glanced at her brother. He seemed very bright and happy that morning, it was not an unpleasant thing to see, but she wondered what had caused the change in him. He had returned to the hotel yesterday evening withdrawn and with a frown on his face. Colonel Brandt had mentioned the incident at the doctor's house and Clara had been worried. Yet, today Tommy looked quite content and his normal self. Clara shrugged off her anxieties. He seemed fine.

It turned out that Emily had been very prompt in responding to Clara's telegram and a reply was waiting for her. It stated all she needed to know.

NEVER BROKE ARM – STOP

The body in the woods was not Father Lound's. Clara had begun to suspect as much, but then who on earth could it be? Ramon Devereaux she would see later today, ruling him out and there was no one else missing from the town. Could it possibly be that a stranger had been killed in the woods? She supposed that was not unlikely considering the activities that had been going on during those years. Probably they would never know who the poor soul was in the grave. There was one last thing she could do, however.

"Can you go back to Peeters and ask if he ever had the rosary and the cross looked at to determine who they belonged to?" She said to her brother. "We now know Father Lound was not in that grave, but if they were his possessions, he must have had contact with whoever was."

Tommy agreed. Colonel Brandt was disappointed that his own telegram had not been answered. He seemed to take the delay very personally. Clara guessed Colonel Matthews was already sick of this affair and was not going to rush to respond, not when he was doing his best to ignore the problem. She didn't say anything, however.

They parted company outside the Post Office. Clara had obtained directions to a gentleman with a horse and trap, who often took tourists out and about. He would probably transport them to Lugrule. She headed off with Annie.

"I have been thinking," Annie said as they walked, "Supposing something happened to Father Lound, an accident, and he lost all his memories like Captain O'Harris did. Then he wouldn't know who he was or who to contact, and he could be still alive but missing."

"The possibility is always there until we prove otherwise," Clara concurred. "But I think it unlikely. He was in the town on the last day he was ever seen. Any accident would have occurred here, where people knew him. If he had lost all his memories, he would still have been with people who could direct him back to his family. And we have to think about his missing luggage."

"Oh yes, that," Annie sighed. "Unless, he was travelling

somewhere completely innocently and had an accident and lost his memory."

"We'll bear it in mind," Clara told her, smiling at her optimism.

The gentleman with the pony and trap was called Hermann and he greeted the ladies warmly. His whole business involved ferrying tourists about the countryside, taking them to popular views and the famous nearby spa. He even produced a small catalogue which suggested the best places to visit for those who were not sure where they wanted to go. He was somewhat astonished when Clara explained that she wanted to go to Lugrule.

"There is nothing there, mademoiselle, just the ruins of the factories and very, very poor folk. I never take anyone there."

"I have a friend in the town I wish to see," Clara explained.

Hermann still looked perplexed, but he agreed to take them, it was after all their money. He settled them in the trap, with its red leather seats and a canopy should the weather turn bad. His pony was a chestnut brown with white socks and she was called Louvain.

"After the unfortunate town," Hermann explained. "My mother came from Louvain, I remember."

They set off with the lively pony trotting fast. Hermann felt the need to act as their tour guide and insisted on pointing out sites which they could have been visiting rather than Lugrule. He motioned to the road that would have taken them to the spa and seemed most put out he was not to take them there. Annie was becoming interested in everything around her.

"What is that place, monsieur?" She asked as they passed a grand house with an extensive garden.

"That was once the home of a very famous Belgium opera singer," Hermann explained with a good deal of pride. "It was badly damaged during the war, but the singer's daughter has spent much time restoring it and it is now a museum to her mother. You can arrange an

171

appointment to visit. I think it very worthwhile, there is one room that escaped the worst damage and it has some very handsome plasterwork."

"When this case is over, Annie, we shall spend some time exploring all these places," Clara promised her friend.

Annie looked embarrassed that her interest had been so noticeable.

"That isn't necessary."

"This is your first time outside of England, I think it is very necessary," Clara smiled.

Hermann had been listening in to their conversation.

"I shall conduct you on a special tour of all the best places," he insisted. "You will enjoy them a good deal."

He spent the rest of the journey outlining the places he would take Annie and Clara, telling them all about the history of the area (carefully missing out the war years) and altogether getting more excited about the arrangement than Annie herself. Clara wondered how much he was plotting to charge them for his services.

Their arrival in Lugrule curbed his enthusiasm. They drove in down a wide road, the houses on either side no more than piles of rubble. Skeletal iron frames rose over the town, all that remained of the great foundries and factories that had desolated the area. For every house that appeared inhabited, there were two or three that were clearly deserted.

"During the early years of the war, this area became a battleground," Hermann explained, his voice no longer excited. "The factories made good gun emplacements, until they were wrecked by shelling. A lot of the houses were used as hideouts by soldiers. The local inhabitants hid in the woods, well, what was left of them, until the fighting was done. There was nowhere else they could go. By the end of 1916, the British line had moved forward and beyond this town. People returned, but look at it. Nothing has been done. There are still the shell holes unfilled, still the piles of rubble from the destruction."

Hermann was right. All along the roadway there were

deep holes now filled with water, which had clearly been made by high explosives. There were many homes that were ruins, the roofs, windows, doors and much of the walls gone. Piles of broken bricks and wood had never been cleared and were being gradually covered with grass, forming rugged mounds that had the appearance of cairns. Clara felt a shudder run down her spine as she looked at this place that had never moved on from those horrific war years.

"Who is your friend?" Hermann asked. "Why are they here?"

It was a good question. Why would anyone choose to live here?

"Actually, I am looking for Madame Devereaux," Clara explained. "I was told she moved here."

Hermann's interest returned.

"This is where the Devereauxs went to? Well, I never!" He looked around at the ruined buildings and seemed to be taking everything in with fresh eyes. "Now that is a big fall from grace! My father worked for Monsieur Devereaux when he was alive. He was his coachman, drove him everywhere. Even drove the funeral carriage when he died. My father will be horrified when he learns where the family ended up."

Clara could not deny his words. For a woman who had grown up in luxurious wealth, had lived in a grand house and never had to work, the transformation to living in Lugrule must have been devastating. It was a place no one would choose to live if they could help it. Clara could only imagine that severe circumstances had pushed the Devereauxs in this direction. Circumstances beyond a child conceived out of wedlock.

"Any idea of an address?" Hermann asked over his shoulder.

Clara had the address Colonel Brandt had obtained off the good doctor. Hermann did not know the district well enough to be able to take them directly there, so they had to stop and ask an old man where to go. They crawled down dusty and almost impassable roads. The shells had not avoided the thoroughfares and great holes gaped in the ground, forcing Hermann to guide his pony onto a verge and very gingerly creep around the devastation. This was not a town that saw many wheeled vehicles, and no one had bothered to repair the roadway. Clara wondered how long it would be before this place was abandoned completely. There was only so long this wreckage could sustain life if nothing was done to improve it.

They eventually came to a long low cottage sitting alone on the roadside. The houses either side were nothing more than shells. A grey cat slunk about the empty walls and disappeared from view. Hermann narrowed his eyes at the house.

"Is this it?"

Clara could not answer him. The house appeared occupied, but there was no sign of the tenants. Scrappy curtains hung at the windows and some effort had been made to grow flowers in the strip of ground that separated the road from the front of the house.

Clara dropped from the trap and walked to the door, then she hesitated. She had a feeling the Devereauxs had fled to this unsavoury place to avoid people. The odds were against her presence being welcomed.

"Do you want me to wait?" Hermann asked.

Clara felt like asking him what he expected her to do if he didn't. She would be abandoned here in this town with no means of getting back to her hotel. But the question had to be asked.

"Yes, please wait."

Hermann looked about him uneasily, as if bandits would emerge from the ruins any moment and attack him. Clara doubted that any of the locals would be interested in the trap and the only use they would probably have for the pony would be to eat it.

"I hopefully won't be long."

"Take your time, I'll admire the view," Hermann said with a grimace.

Annie had dropped down from the trap and joined Clara. It was now or never. Clara knocked on the front door of the house, the sound seeming very hollow as it echoed inside. It was always possible no one was home.

"Why would anyone live here?" Annie whispered in a hushed tone of horror.

"Desperation," Clara replied.

Someone came to the door. It popped open a crack and half a face was visible through the gap. Clara thought it was an older woman's face. She eyed her visitors and then noticed the pony and trap and jumped in surprised. It was possible that Madame Devereaux recognised the son of her husband's former driver. Even if she did not, the sight of the vehicle in this town must have been unexpected.

"I am looking for Madame Devereaux," Clara said politely, at which point the door was shut firmly in her face and there was the sound of a bolt being drawn across.

Hermann glanced down from his driver's seat.

"Rather rude," he observed.

Clara frowned. Obviously the woman in the house did not want to talk to them, now what was she going to do? Clara resolved herself to knocking on the door again. Annie drifted to the side of the house to see if there was another way in or out. No one responded to Clara's banging.

"Any suggestions?" Clara asked Hermann.

Their driver scratched at his head, then he dropped from his seat and knocked at the door.

"Madame Devereaux, its Hermann van Hartt, you remember my father?"

There was no response from inside.

"We've been wondering about you all these years. My father has been worried. He thought a lot of your husband, he would have done anything for your family," Hermann paused to listen and see if anyone replied. There was still nothing. "He will be upset to know you are living here. He always hoped you would come to him if you needed anything. He would always offer his help. I would too."

"Madame Devereaux, I am not here to cause trouble," Clara added. "I am here because I have been asked to try and trace Father Christian Lound. His sister has tasked me with this. She wants to know what happened to him. I only came because I thought you might have information."

The house could have been empty for all the response they were receiving. Clara sighed. It was not often she failed to speak to someone in a case, but there were odd occasions when a person would completely refuse to acknowledge her queries. When that happened, you had to accept the situation and either try to persuade them or move on.

"She isn't going to speak to us," Clara frowned. "For some reason she is determined to hide away."

Hermann looked apologetic, as if he felt bad he had not been able to persuade his former employer to speak to them. They all walked back to the pony and trap.

A gentleman had appeared near Louvain. He had seemingly emerged from the rubble and his presence took Clara by surprise. Hermann eyed him suspiciously, perhaps thinking he would steal the horse.

"You want to know about the Devereauxs?" The man asked, his eyes glinting like dark, jet beads.

"I do," Clara said, anticipating what was to come.

"I can tell you all about them," the man said keenly. "As long as you have the money to pay me for the effort."

Chapter Twenty-two

"I really thought he would have taken the time to respond," Colonel Brandt complained as he walked with Tommy towards the police station. "I thought Matthews would have the decency to realise that this was important."

Tommy wasn't sure how to reply. In his experience, colonels had only a vague idea of what was urgent or important.

"Maybe the telegram arrived after he left his office," he said, though he was doing it more to console Brandt than to defend Matthews. From what he had heard about the colonel, he didn't think the man was worth his time.

"I know he is unhappy with me," Brandt continued, sounding mournful now. "He feels that I have undermined him, questioned his decision. No one likes to feel like that."

"We all make mistakes," Tommy observed. "We have to be big enough to accept that and to not be silly about it."

"I suppose he feels I have stuck my oar into things that don't concern me. I am long retired, after all," Brandt looked miserable. "And I am interfering in something that I know so little about. I wasn't there, I didn't even serve in the war."

"We are all agreed that Father Lound was not the traitor in this equation," Tommy pointed out. "Therefore, someone got away with betraying the British, and any colonel worth his salt would not let that rest."

Colonel Brandt smiled a little.

"That is true," he agreed. "Do you think I might be worth my salt?"

"A lot more than Colonel Matthews," Tommy nodded. "Now, let's see what Peeters has to say."

Chief Inspector Peeters was not entirely happy to see the return of the Englishmen. He refused to see them at first and made them wait around for an hour, before he finally decided he would talk to them.

"Did you not get all you needed from the files?" He asked tetchily when they were in his office.

"Just a couple more questions," Tommy answered. "We wondered if you ever had anyone identify the rosary and crucifix?"

Peeters snorted.

"Naturally we did," he said. "At least I think we did."

Suddenly Peeters did not look so confident.

"I was only Candidate Chief Inspector then," he added hastily. "I don't recall every detail. Maybe there was an oversight. We were in the middle of a war and everything was a little rushed."

"It was not mentioned in the case file," Colonel Brandt said as gently as he could.

Peeters' shoulders sagged.

"Then we must have forgotten to do so. We could have asked the priests at Albion Hope. Oh," Peeters' earlier annoyance at a second disturbance was gone. "This is very bad. Had we identified the rosary and crucifix as belonging to a specific person that would have given us a clue to the person in the grave. It would not have been conclusive alone, you can't be conclusive about these things unless you can tie the bones to a person, but it would have made us pretty confident."

"How many people in the town might carry such things?" Brandt asked.

"We have a few Catholics," Peeters said. "Though, to be honest, only one had disappeared that we knew of. I imagine that was why things got pushed to one side, it rather seemed obvious that the skeleton must be that of

Father Lound. Only, we could not prove it or say what happened to him, so we never passed the news to England.

"I know that looks bad, but please appreciate the period in which this all occurred. We were struggling, we had little in the way of resources. We did not know then that the war would be over soon. Our main concern was helping the living."

"The body in the woods could not have been Father Lound," Tommy said coolly. As much as he did appreciate the difficulties war had placed the police in, that was no excuse for failing to do something as simple as asking Father Howard or Stevens about the rosary and crucifix. That would have taken little time and cost no money. "Dr Jacobs explained that the skeleton belonged to an individual who had once broken their arm. We have had it confirmed by Father Lound's sister that he had never done such a thing. The body was not his."

Chief Inspector Peeters looked uneasy. All these years he had worked under the assumption the body was that of Father Lound and while it had rankled that the case had not been solved, he could at least console himself with feeling the mystery of the priest's disappearance was somewhat resolved. Now he had an unidentified skeleton and a missing priest, everything was suddenly very messy again.

"This… this is not good," he admitted. "There was never anyone else suggested for the body. We are not missing any other priests."

"Something bad was happening here during the war," Colonel Brandt interjected. "Treachery was afoot. If the skeleton was not connected with that I would be heartily surprised. Someone was making money by betraying the British and I want to know who it was and to bring them to justice."

"Father Lound…" Peeters began but Tommy cut him off.

"Father Lound's disappearance does look suspicious, but we cannot rule out anyone in this town. In fact, the

Father's behaviour rather suggests he was not guilty. Something happened to him too."

"But there is no evidence, nothing. Only scraps of information that make no sense," Peeters protested.

"We start with what we have," Tommy countered. "And that is the rosary and crucifix. Let's find out who they belonged to, that may identify our corpse or offer a clue."

"What if they belonged to Father Lound?" Peeters said. "And yet he is not the skeleton, so if they are his…"

The policeman's eyes widened.

"If they are his then the person in the grave took them from him. They were either willingly given, which seems unlikely as such things are very personal to a priest, or they were taken, stolen. In which case, the person in that grave may have been the last person to see Father Lound before he vanished," Peeters shook his head. "And that leads us nowhere, because we don't know who that man in the grave was!"

Chief Inspector Peeters stood up and started to pace about the room. He was clearly finding this all very frustrating. His earlier desire to help the British was now overshadowed by doubts that they could resolve this issue at all. He could be left with an impossible mess, a blot on his career. Not only had a priest vanished without a trace (having first been accused of treason), but a stranger had been murdered in the nearby woods. It had been much easier when Peeters had thought those bones were Father Lound's. It had wrapped everything up so nicely.

"I am afraid I have no more time for this," Peeters suddenly snapped. "I have a meeting soon and need to prepare."

"About the rosary and crucifix?" Tommy said.

"I shall consider them again when I have time," Peeters wasn't meeting his eye. "And I shall let you know the outcome. I did promise to help the British, after all, I must uphold that promise."

Tommy gave Colonel Brandt a look that implied what he thought of Peeters' promise of help. Then they both rose to leave.

"One last thing," Peeters barked, "tell your friends to leave my sister out of this. She was very upset when I went home last night. She has suffered enough, I won't have her upset like this again. Do you understand?"

Tommy gave him a smile and then left with Brandt.

"At least we know why he was in such a bad mood," Tommy remarked as they headed back to the street.

"He seemed so accommodating at first, very disappointing," Brandt muttered. "Oh well, shall we be extra disappointed and return to the Post Office to see if Colonel Matthews has responded to my telegram?"

The woman at the Post Office recognised Colonel Brandt when he entered, and her smile indicated that he was not about to be disappointed again. She handed over a slip of paper, remarking on his perfect timing; the telegram had arrived just a few minutes earlier.

Colonel Matthews had been predictably succinct in his response to Brandt's request. There was no one British left in the area he could talk to, but a Belgium army captain, who had served in the Army Group Flanders, had been involved in the investigation of treachery in the town. He was local to the area and still lived only a few miles away. He had been the liaison between the British military and the local population. He might recall something useful.

Matthews finished by remarking that he had known there were German agents living like outlaws in the area and someone in the town was communicating with them. These agents were never caught, as far as he knew, though there was every chance they had been discovered and shot without anything official being reported. In any case, after Father Lound disappeared the problem of information leaking from the town ended. Matthews did not have the resources or time to chase phantom agents who could take months to locate, not when they were no longer a risk to his operations.

"He manages to imply in the span of three lines that he still considers Father Lound the culprit," Brandt almost chuckled at the indignation that steamed from the letters of the telegram.

"Can I speak with you, monsieur?" The Post Office clerk motioned to Brandt.

"Oh, did I not pay the right money?"

"No, no, monsieur, that is fine," the woman glanced to her right, where her assistant was serving the only other customer. "I would like to speak to you about the contents of your telegram. I must apologise first for reading it, but it is very hard when I receive the telegram to avoid doing so. As hard as you try, you tend to pick things out."

Brandt and Tommy came closer to the counter.

"Madame, I completely understand. Telegrams are far from the most secret of communications, requiring as they do a third person to send and receive them."

The woman still looked ashamed that she had noticed the contents.

"It was when I saw the word 'treachery' that I startled," the woman continued. "You know, I heard the rumours that ran about the town back then. One of my friends, she said she saw some strange men lurking at the edge of town. They were not soldiers. She reported them to the police, but I don't think anything was done."

"Does your friend still live in the town?" Colonel Brandt asked.

"No, monsieur, she moved to Bruges a long time ago. But she told me about these men, she told several people, so we could look out for them. The Germans did horrible things in the war, monsieur, and we were scared these men would hurt us."

"Can you tell me about them?" Brandt was now even more curious.

"There were two of them. Both with dark hair and moustaches, one was taller than the other. They were in their thirties and they loitered in the shadows at the edge of town. My friend said they did not look like refugees or runaways from the army. They did not look worried about being seen. She thought they were waiting for someone."

"Where was this that she saw them?"

"In the woods, by the shrine of St. Helena," the woman explained, "where that skeleton was found the next year. I always wondered if the body was of one of those men. The bones were never identified."

The woman had not apparently made the connection between Father Lound and the skeleton, or perhaps she had and then dismissed the idea.

"My friend often collected mushrooms in the autumn in those woods. We all gathered what we could to supplement our limited food," the woman continued. "That is how she saw the men, she saw them more than once. And, on one occasion, as she was heading back into town, she stumbled into Ramon Devereaux."

The woman's eyes grew big.

"You know about him?" She asked.

"We have heard his name mentioned," Brandt agreed.

"Ramon was dangerous. He had a nasty temper. I was so glad when the family left the town. They were too generous to him at Albion Hope. They offered him work and food, maybe they thought they could help make him a better person. He would never be a good person, never," the woman took a shaky breath. "We all said at the time, if ever there was a person who would gladly betray his people, it was Ramon Devereaux. And we started to think about the connections; the strangers in the woods, Ramon being seen nearby and then the family's sudden departure after the British army came to town. The more I think about it, the more I am sure. Ramon Devereaux was the traitor."

The woman finished her statement dramatically, thudding her hands on the counter and looking convinced that she had solved the mystery. Tommy had to admit it was a very odd set of coincidences.

"Thank you, madame, for being so forthright with us," Colonel Brandt said kindly. "Might you also be able to give us directions to the gentleman mentioned in the telegram, Captain Mercier?"

The woman said she could, and she even found them a map to help them traverse the countryside. She suggested they hire horses from a local stable and gave them directions for that too. They finally left the Post Office slightly overwhelmed by information.

"Ramon Devereaux," Tommy mused. "You do have to wonder about him. Everyone seems to think he was trouble, and presumably he still is in Lugrule. Doesn't explain Father Lound, though."

"I am more concerned with the fact that the traitor is still alive," Colonel Brandt's usually mild expression had clouded over. He looked angry, and Tommy found it slightly disturbing to know that his gentle friend had such darkness within him. "He can be brought to justice for his crimes."

Tommy did not know what to say to that. He found himself mulling over exactly how many crimes Ramon had dabbled in during his teenage years. Had he rapidly progressed from housebreaking to treason? Could he also have stretched to murder? Ramon was the last person to see Father Lound alive. They had argued and Lound had followed him. It only took a small leap of imagination to think that argument had been about the stealing of information from soldiers visiting Albion Hope.

"Could Father Lound have been protecting Ramon?" Tommy said aloud. "Perhaps thinking the lad was foolish, or that his family needed him and so he ought not to be shot as a traitor?"

"Stupid man," Colonel Brandt snorted. "You don't give a traitor any quarter. They are men without morals."

But, supposing…"

"There is no supposing," Brandt cut him off. "That young man was a rogue who could have cost many men their lives. I'll see to it that he is punished for his crimes. On that I swear!"

Colonel Brandt stalked off. Tommy hesitated a moment before following. Brandt was right, of course, a man could not escape punishment for his crimes. Ramon Devereaux was soon going to find his past catching up with him, and it was not going to be a pleasant experience.

Chapter Twenty-three

The man would only tell them his first name. He was Lars and he had lived in Lugrule all his life, except for the unpleasant year when the Germans had taken it over and there had been a lot of fighting. Then the British had occupied it and no one thought they would ever return. But they did.

Lars made no comment on the condition of his hometown. He would not be drawn on his life history or how he made a living. Any question Clara put to him that he did not deem relevant to the facts at hand he ignored.

Clara surmised he was in his late thirties, though he looked a good deal older. He was black with the filth that shrouded the whole town, everything from his clothes to his skin was covered in a sooty layer. At one point he had a coughing fit and spat out a wad of phlegm that was as black as the grime on his clothes. Clara thought that did not bode well for his future health.

Lars wanted to negotiate for talking with them, but first he indicated they should retreat to his house where they would not be disturbed. Hermann looked unhappy about this and was clearly itching to escape the town. There was something about Lugrule that made you feel more and more oppressed the longer you remained. Hermann was clearly succumbing to this and so seemed his pony. They could not leave just yet, however, and Hermann reluctantly agreed to join them at Lars' home.

The house was squalid. The top floor must have been hit by a shell, or debris. It no longer existed, except for a few bricks marking where the walls once rose up. An effort had been made to weather proof the remains of the wooden floor above, creating a roof for the rooms below. There were two in the lower storey; one served as Lars' kitchen and parlour, while the back room was his bedroom. Everything was dark, the walls grey and blackened by damp, the floor so filthy that even Annie's best efforts with a scrubbing brush could not have restored it. Lars' possessions consisted of an old stove that was falling to pieces, a ramshackle table and various items of crockery, all of which were chipped and cracked. He did not offer them any refreshments when they came into his house, for which Clara was most grateful.

"You can sit," Lars said, somewhat ungraciously.

There were three chairs at the table, the back bars of one had been sawn off, leaving spiky teeth just at the edge. Clara imagined the wood had been used in desperation to heat the stove. The girls took two of the chairs, while Lars took the third. Hermann perched uneasily on the sill of the window. A perpetual draught slipped through the wooden casement and Clara dreaded to think how cold this place must get in the winter.

"I want money before I talk," Lars said, his sharp tone had more than a hint of anxiety about it.

Clara was willing to give him money, though it was not her usual policy of paying for information. Seeing how Lars lived, she almost deemed his fee a charitable donation. She opened her purse and took out a wad of paper notes. Hermann started to fuss when he saw how much she was offering Lars, but Clara was unconcerned. She could easily draw more money from her bank, unlike Lars. She supposed he made his living sifting through the dust piles for mineral cast-offs and selling them for a pittance. It explained his appearance and his ill-health.

Lars' eyes turned into giant saucers as he saw the amount she was offering him. He held out his hand quickly, but Clara put the money on the table and pressed her palm firmly down upon it.

"Half now, and the other half after we have talked," she said gently. She did not really think that Lars would cheat her, but he might be willing to offer a bit more information if she held some of the money back.

Clara carefully counted out half the notes and placed them in Lars' palm. The money seemed so crisp and clean in his grubby hand, as if she had minted it that morning. Lars suppressed a small groan of elation at the sight of the money. He almost lost himself for a moment gazing at it, then he remembered himself. Looking more alive than before, and far friendlier, he spoke.

"You want to know about the Devereauxs?"

"Yes," Clara replied. "How long have they been here?"

"Since 1917. I remember that very clearly. I had only just returned to Lugrule after the British finally left the town. Everything was ruined, but many of the people here could go nowhere else. It was very surprising for us when strangers arrived to set up home. They did not look like workers, either."

"Did they say why they had come here?"

"They spoke to no one," Lars shrugged. "We were not that interested, either. When you have to keep a roof over your head by any means you can, you have very little time for curiosity. The older woman, Madame Devereaux, she tried to offer her services as a seamstress, but no one has money for that here. We mend our own clothes. Eventually she realised she would have to apply herself to the work we all turn to – sifting the dust."

"That is a hard job," Clara said sympathetically.

"It destroys you," Lars agreed, though with no sign of bitterness at the statement. "It killed my father and probably it shall kill me. But it is better than starving to death or dying of the cold."

Lars' eyes went back to the money in his hand and he gave another small sigh of relief. At least he would not be cold that winter.

"Does Madame Devereaux ever speak about her life before she came here?" Clara persisted, thinking that Lars was not going to be able to offer her any information that she did not already know.

"She does speak," Lars said. "When she drinks she gets more talkative. That is how I know she used to be very wealthy. She is very bitter to have been brought to this. She thinks she is better than us. She blames her husband and the Germans, but mainly her husband. And she gets very angry with her eldest girl. The girl won't work the dust piles, she refuses. Instead she will walk for miles to sell her body and earn money that way. It is very sad. We may be filthy and very poor, but we dust workers are at least respectable.

"Besides, the girl looks sicker than any of us. I think she has caught something off one of her clients. She cannot be very old, but her body is a wreck. It is awful. Madame Devereaux has tried many times to stop her, they fight quite violently at times, but there is no hope. Then there are the younger girls. They went to the small school here for a time to finish their education. A lady travels here three days a week to teach the children, in the hopes that they can better themselves and move away from the dust piles."

Lars came to a halt. The endlessness of his own situation, the hopelessness, had struck him hard as he talked. It was the sort of thing that was always there at the back of a man's mind, but which could be almost ignored during the daily struggle for survival. Just every now and then it would pierce through the cloud of forgetfulness and kick a man in the teeth. Lars took a deep breath, which rattled up from his chest and almost brought on another coughing fit, then he shook off his melancholy and returned to the conversation.

"The middle girl, she now works the dust piles with her mother. Such a pretty thing. The teacher- woman said she had potential, that she was very bright and should be sent away to learn more. But there is no money for that and now with the youngest girl so sick, every one of the family must work to pay the doctors' bills.

"Madame Devereaux is in a lot of debt. She has borrowed money for her youngest daughter from very unpleasant people. Now she fears every knock on her door. That is probably why she turned you away."

"I am not a debt collector," Clara promised Lars.

"You don't look like one," Lars grinned. "You are too nice."

Clara was surprised by the flattery, then she remembered that beneath the grime and dust, Lars was a relatively young man talking to two young women.

"Is the youngest girl dangerously ill?" Clara asked.

"Madame Devereaux denies it, but everyone thinks it is consumption. Something to do with the lungs, anyway. The girl cannot leave the house at all and I am not sure she will last this coming winter."

"That is awful," for all that Clara had heard about the Devereauxs, she would not wish such misery upon them.

Lars was more pragmatic.

"Many people die during the winter months here. Many children. It is not a place to raise a family. It is one reason I never married," Lars sighed, this time it was a sigh of great sadness. "I made a decision not to inflict this life on anyone else. Children do not thrive here. It is better I live and die alone."

Lars had lost some of the feral aggression that had first flickered over his face when they met him. He seemed more human all of a sudden. Clara was actually growing to like him. She wished she could do more for him.

"What of the boy, Ramon?" She asked.

"I see him from time to time," Lars nodded. "He seems healthy enough, surprising in a way."

"No one ever comes to see him?" Clara asked.

Lars looked confused.

"Who would?"

That was a good point, the Devereauxs had come here to hide away from the world. Very few knew they lived here.

"Does Madame Devereaux ever talk about a priest called Father Lound?"

"Never," Lars said firmly. "She hates religion. We have a church service here once a month. A vicar travels in. She once spat horrible abuse at him. Madame Devereaux hates God. Maybe she blames him for her own misfortunes? Most of us prefer to think of him as a saviour, as the last resource of hope for us penniless folks. One day I dream of going to Heaven and being free."

Lars closed his eyes and trembled with obvious longing for that moment. When there was no escape from the hellish existence you lived in beyond death, no wonder the thought of an afterlife was so attractive.

"I am not ready to go yet, though," Lars opened his eyes again.

"What does Ramon make of religion?" Clara asked.

Lars gave her an odd look.

"What does any child of five years make of religion?" He said. "I doubt he knows God exists, his mother won't tell him."

"Wait, child?" It was Clara's turn to look confused. "I am talking about Madame Devereaux's son."

"What son?" Lars looked astonished.

"Madame Devereaux had an adult son named Ramon," Clara explained.

Lars shook his head.

"No, she came here only with her daughters and the eldest gave birth to a boy who she named Ramon."

Clara hesitated for a moment, then she came close to smiling. Now it was obvious who was buried in the woods, well, she thought it was pretty obvious. There was always that outside chance that Ramon was alive somewhere but had opted not to live with his family. It seemed more likely, however, that he had never left the town. Someone had killed him and buried him in a grave near the shrine.

Could it be?

Ramon had Father Lound's belongings, what if the

priest had been there and given them to him? What if Father Lound's disappearance was not because he had been murdered, but because he was a murderer?

The revelation was terrible, but it made sense of the circumstances. Ramon had disappeared at the same time as Father Lound and then his family had runaway to this hellish place. Clara had always felt it was a strange coincidence. Surely there was a link between these two events?

Clara placed the rest of the money on the table and pushed it towards Lars.

"Thank you for speaking to us," she said.

She and Annie returned to the town in Hermann's trap. It was a relief to leave behind the grey bones of Lugrule, its residents seemingly a hair's breadth away from utter destitution. Clara thought that only the worst of situations could drive a person to choose to live there. Surely the worst of situations might include the murder of your son?

Yet there were still too many questions. Why would Father Lound kill Ramon Devereaux? Unless he suspected Ramon of being the traitor and felt it was his duty to his country, to the townsfolk, to dispatch the troublemaker? Clara found that a difficult thought, why would Father Lound take justice into his own hands? But who else could have killed Ramon? Who else would have had reason? The men Ramon was feeding information to? Would they have risked murdering an informant?

Clara was growing frustrated. There was a pattern forming, but not clearly enough to explain all this. And so many of the people she needed to speak to were long gone or would not talk to her, leaving her guessing, maybe making wrong assumptions.

It was uncomfortable to imagine Father Lound as a murderer, but that might just explain why he disappeared without a trace. Why he could not tell anyone where he was going. It would explain why he took his hastily packed luggage, forgetting personal items in his haste. It would explain why Ramon had the rosary and crucifix. The rosary was in his hand, as if he had been praying as he died. A last gesture of kindness from Lound? Better he deal with the traitor than the military, who would make the situation very public and shame the entire family.

What had Father Dobson said about a priest's morals not necessarily being the same as that of a secular person's? He had implied that Lound might have committed treason if he had a good reason for it, a reason that made sense from a religious and moral perspective. What about murder?

Clara was confused. There was still something not quite right with the whole picture. She almost felt as if she was looking at things reversed in a mirror. Bits seemed right, but other bits were clearly wrong. Somewhere in this mess was the key to solving this mystery.

What if she could not find it?

Chapter Twenty-four

Captain Mercier lived in a sprawling farmhouse a few miles from the town. Tommy and Colonel Brandt had rented horses to reach it. The farm had been in the Mercier family for several generations and the Captain lived there with his wife, children, parents and grandparents. They raised beef cattle.

The two Englishmen rode down a road with a drainage ditch running either side, that divided two large areas of pasture. A number of young bullocks watched them idly, swishing big black tails at the summer flies. At the end of the road there was a yard lined on three sides by buildings. On the left a feed store, on the right a barn and straight ahead the house. An old tractor was stood in the middle of the yard and three men were hovering around it, deep in discussion. They all turned as Tommy and Brandt approached.

The nearest man, who was only in his late twenties, stepped forward and greeted them.

"Can I help you?"

"Might you be Captain Mercier?" Tommy asked, dropping from the horse.

The man nodded.

"I am, though no one has called me Captain Mercier since the war."

"Captain Thomas Fitzgerald," Tommy introduced himself formally, partly to demonstrate his shared past with Mercier and partly to explain his business there. "This is Colonel Brandt. We wondered if we could speak to you on a military matter."

Captain Mercier looked more than a little surprised. The war had been over for several years and clearly he had put it firmly in his past. However, after a moment to take in what had been said to him, he nodded.

"We can go inside, I just need to tell my father what is happening."

Mercier walked back towards the tractor where the two other men stood. Tommy and Brandt followed at a distance, bringing the horses closer. They could overhear Mercier explaining to an older man that he needed to speak to the military gentlemen who had just arrived. The third man, stood behind the tractor, pulled a face and there was a brief moment of discord before he accepted the inevitable.

Mercier walked back to Tommy and Brandt.

"You can tie up your horses over here," he showed them to the barn, where the horses could be left with some hay out of the sun.

"Buying a tractor?" Brandt asked Mercier as they headed to the farmhouse.

"Maybe," Mercier looked unconvinced about everything. "Its old, but it would do the job. In the winter we have so much feed to move to the fields for the bullocks and cows. We currently use a horse and cart, but the cart gets stuck in the mud and our horse is old. We thought a tractor might be a better investment."

"But you are not sure?" Brandt guessed.

"Tractors come with their own problems. They need fuel and we can only afford a very old one. What if it goes wrong?"

"Same could be said for the horse," Brandt pointed out.

"True," Mercier smiled and shrugged. "Maybe I am clinging too much to the past and how we have always done things. My father is very keen we move with the times."

He showed them indoors and straight to a formal

parlour. It was prettily decorated in shades of pale green and white. There were a lot of wooden items dotted about and a sheepskin rug on the floor. In one corner was a circular wood-burning stove, the sort Tommy had noticed in a lot of Belgium homes. It was unlit as the parlour was warmed by the summer sun.

"I never thought I would be consulted on a military matter," Captain Mercier said, taking a box from a shelf and offering his guests thin cigarettes wrapped in black paper. Tommy declined. Colonel Brandt gladly accepted. "I was only in the army for the duration of the war. I am a civilian now. It was very odd hearing my rank said once again."

Mercier produced a lighter in the form of a wooden bear. When the bear's head was flipped back it revealed the flame. He lit Colonel Brandt's cigarette and then his own.

"Why would the British military be interested in me? You are British?"

"We are," Tommy confirmed. "The accents give us away, don't they?"

"Just a little," Mercier grinned. "Why are you here?"

Tommy looked to Colonel Brandt to give the answer. It seemed better that he speak; he was technically superior to Tommy, even though they had never served together and were now both civilians. He was also their connection with Colonel Matthews.

"We are investigating an incident that took place during the war," Brandt said. "I believe you became involved."

"What incident?" Mercier was looking worried now. "There were quite a few dramatic situations around here, as there were across Belgium. There was the sabotage of the dykes, for instance, which flooded miles of farmland and homes. We believed that was a deliberate German ploy, though some thought it was sheer bad luck that they shelled the dykes, causing the sides to cave in and the water to overflow."

"This is not about the dykes," Brandt told him. "My

colleague, Colonel Matthews, came to this town looking for a traitor who he thought was selling information on allied military movements to the Germans."

Mercier's eyes darkened and he became sombre.

"I remember that," he said, his tone hard and slightly bitter. "We failed to find the culprit. That makes me angry."

"Matthews gave me a very brief outline of the situation," Brandt continued. "I know you were more heavily involved, could you tell me a little more about what was going on back then, from your perspective?"

Mercier sighed.

"I was summoned by your Colonel Matthews and informed of his suspicion that someone was selling information to the Germans. The town was one of the areas popular with British, French and Belgium soldiers when they were not at the Front. There was Albion Hope, the religious house, have you heard of it?"

"Yes," Brandt nodded. "It was thought the traitor was linked to that house?"

"Indeed," Mercier grimaced. "Nothing major had been leaked, not as yet. But the Germans seemed to have been more alert to recent manoeuvres and even things like the transfer of certain officers. There was something more going on than sheer bad luck. Colonel Matthews wanted to test his theory that Albion Hope was harbouring a spy. He ended up setting a trap. The only person who fell into it was a priest by the name of Father Christian Lound. That was quite a surprise."

"Did you think Lound was a potential traitor?" Tommy asked.

Mercier took a long time to reply. He seemed to find it hard to talk about the whole thing.

"I considered it a possibility. You can never rule anyone out. Before Matthews set his trap, I was sent into town to see if I could pick up on anything. I was confident that Albion Hope was where the information was leaking from. The men who visited the house perceived it as a place they could talk freely, a little too freely. I suggested to Matthews that the troops be reminded to be more careful about their talk on military matters. He was upset by this as the men with the most vital information were always officers," Mercier looked apologetic as he explained this. "The officers were talking too freely, not the ordinary soldiers who rarely had anything important to reveal, anyway. I came across a sergeant major and a captain at Albion Hope, who were keenly talking about proposed military plans in the library. There were other men present and civilians."

Colonel Brandt wriggled his moustache, a sure sign that he was upset.

"It beggars belief, but I am hardly surprised. Met enough officers in my time to know they can be the worst for keeping secrets."

"Colonel Matthews was appalled. Honestly, I think if there had just been a crackdown on loose talk then the whole treachery business would have evaporated. It was opportunistic rather than anything especially organised. Colonel Matthews seemed to think it would be easier to catch the traitor then it would be to stop officers gossiping," Mercier started to roll his eyes at this declaration, then caught himself. "The trap was arranged, and it was far from subtle. Though, having seen how the officers had been behaving, it did not seem so odd. Secret papers were put in the pocket of an officer's tunic and then the tunic was left lying about. I was loitering around as part of the operation. I checked the tunic periodically and, eventually, the papers were missing.

"I informed Colonel Matthews at once. He had stationed himself in a nearby empty house. As soon as I alerted him he flew back to Albion Hope and locked the doors, before instigating a search of everyone there."

"The papers could have been long gone," Tommy pointed out. "The traitor should have taken them and run."

"Yes, but Colonel Matthews was banking on two things. First, that the traitor worked at Albion Hope and it would appear odd if they suddenly left. Second, that they had grown cocky and would not fear pocketing the papers and keeping at the house," Mercier shrugged. "Both suppositions were logical. It was not likely to be a visiting soldier, because they came and went regularly and the treachery could be traced back over several months. It had to be someone who would not look out of place inside the house, and who would not attract attention, therefore it would be someone who worked there, or at least who spent a lot of time there.

"Equally, I could offer a time frame of an hour between the last time I checked on the papers and when they went missing. If we could not find the papers, we should be able to narrow down a list of potential suspects by working out who was at the house during that period. If one of the staff or casual workers at the house had departed within that hour, they would come under instant suspicion."

"The search, however, revealed the papers," Colonel Brandt added gloomily.

"It did," Mercier was frowning, even now it was plain he found it hard to believe what they had discovered. "Colonel Matthews had all the doors locked and the staff brought inside to be searched. The priests protested, they thought it was an invasion of their privacy and disrespectful to the character of Albion Hope as a sanctuary for soldiers. Matthews was not interested."

"Hardly surprising, considering the circumstances," Tommy said.

"Colonel Matthews had everyone searched and then went through the rooms one-by-one. I remember Father Stevens being especially upset and demanding to know what right the colonel had to do this," Mercier's look implied that had been a thankless exercise. "Eventually they searched the office where Father Lound worked and the papers were on his desk. That stunned everyone. Even Father Stevens fell silent. Matthews had not revealed a lot about what he was doing, certainly not to the house staff, but the priests were stubborn and insisted on being told what his search was all about. They were indignant when he explained. Father Stevens seemed heartbroken when the papers were on Father Lound's desk.

"Even Colonel Matthews was shocked. He asked Father Lound how they had arrived on his desk and the priest just said that he couldn't say. Not 'I don't know' or 'I didn't put them there', he just said 'I couldn't say how they got on my desk' and that seemed all the more suspect. Colonel Matthews was so surprised that he failed to arrest the priest at once. I think he needed to get away and consider what had just happened. So we all left. Later we learned that Father Lound had vanished. That confirmed in all our minds that he was the traitor."

"You believe Father Lound was stealing intelligence to give to the Germans?" Tommy pressed him. It did all seem very obvious. The papers on Lound's desk, his refusal to explain them, then his sudden disappearance. If Tommy had not read in the police files about Lound's behaviour during the course of the afternoon – how he had seemed in no hurry to depart – he probably would have thought he was the traitor too. There was still that possibility. No one had offered any evidence to prove otherwise, except for hunches and instincts and firm denials that Father Lound would do any such thing.

"I saw the evidence for myself," Captain Mercier replied. "There was no room for doubt. If Father Lound had protested I might have said otherwise, even if he had stayed to face judgement, but he did neither of those things."

Mercier paused and he was lost in thought for a while.

"War is a funny time," he said at last. "Everyone is so stressed and things that you would take time to think about long and hard normally, you rush at recklessly. We all make bad decisions in the heat of the moment. Maybe that was how it was with Father Lound?"

"What if he was protecting someone?" Tommy suggested.

"Why would he protect such a person?" Mercier looked genuinely amazed. "A traitor is a traitor, putting the lives of the soldiers and the people they protect in danger. I cannot see how protecting such a person makes what Father Lound did any better. In fact, I look down upon him just as much for doing such a thing. He was not helping anyone that way."

"People do strange things when emotions are involved," Tommy said, though he was not entirely sure what he was aiming at by attempting to defend Father Lound. He just rather felt he ought to, considering they were there on behalf of Lound's sister.

"No, there is never a good excuse for protecting a criminal," Mercier was adamant. "The traitor should have faced justice. I am sorry he didn't."

Mercier had finished his cigarette and put out the stub in a nearby ashtray. He had become sullen and uneasy. Finally his eyes flicked up to the two men.

"I think it is about time you explained what you are doing here, don't you?"

Chapter Twenty-five

Clara and Annie walked back into the hotel and were greeted by the ever friendly Janssen.

"Ladies, you are in time for a late luncheon," he beamed. "My, you do look dusty!"

Clara glanced at her skirt for the first time and realised it was coated in an inch of grey dust, her shoes were even worse and she suspected the filth had penetrated her stockings and her lower legs would be covered with it. Annie was looking at her own clothes aghast.

"I said not to go to Lugrule," Janssen winked at them. "Did you meet with your friend?"

"Sort of," Clara answered vaguely.

Janssen seemed to assume this was a normal English answer and did not question it further.

"I'll arrange a pot of tea for you both and some sandwiches. Find a seat in the front parlour."

Janssen headed off before Clara could tell him they were going to get changed first. She looked to Annie who shrugged.

"This dust is not going to come off anytime soon," Annie said with the weariness of someone who knows about cleaning clothes. "We might as well get something to eat first."

Feeling as if Annie had rather given her permission to eat in dusty clothes, Clara followed her friend through to the front parlour, which was thankfully deserted.

"You know what I have been thinking?" Annie said as they both sat down by a window.

"Would you like me to guess, or was that rhetorical?" Clara asked.

Annie gave her a look.

"I was thinking, probably what you were thinking, that Ramon was killed by someone who knew him and the location, the timing, and the fact he had Father Lound's rosary in his hands, rather suggests that the good priest was involved."

"I had considered that. It is awful to contemplate that Father Lound was a murderer."

Annie's eyes widened.

"I wasn't thinking that!" She said in astonishment.

"Then, what?" Clara asked.

"I was thinking that maybe Father Lound followed Ramon that night to stop him committing more treachery and they both got themselves killed. Probably by the Germans Ramon was helping. Ramon was a liability after the discovery and Father Lound was a witness to it all."

"But there was only one body in the woods. Ramon's," Clara pointed out.

"There is only one body we know about," Annie corrected her. "Just because one grave was found, doesn't mean another can't be hidden there."

Clara found herself suddenly pausing. Annie's interpretation could be right. Except…

"Father Lound went missing before Ramon," she said. "And his suitcase was gone. He missed mass."

"This is how I see it," Annie explained. "He was planning to get Ramon away from town, knowing that Colonel Matthews was looking for a traitor and that the penalty for treason is death. He had to be discreet to avoid alerting the military. He packed his suitcase and left Albion Hope early, to make it look like he had run away and put everyone off the scent.

"Later that night he tracked Ramon into the woods, meaning to persuade the boy to leave town. He knew he would have to go too, or else be sentenced to death in Ramon's place. He would not betray the boy, but Ramon might have a crisis of conscience and confess. Either way, they both had to go. Only, Father Lound did not realise Ramon was heading into the woods to meet with his contacts and explain that he could no longer bring them information.

"He stumbled on the meeting. The Germans could not risk a witness. They captured him and decided it would be best if both Ramon and Lound disappeared without a trace. They shot Ramon first. Father Lound gave him the crucifix and rosary to hold to bring him comfort in his final moments. Then he was shot. There were two graves dug and the bodies placed in them. Only one was disturbed by heavy rain and discovered."

Clara looked out the window. Truth be told, it was as good a solution to the mystery as any she had postulated. It was certainly better, from Emily's perspective, if her brother was a victim rather than a murderer.

"There is lot of ground to cover in those woods," Clara mused.

"I would hazard a bet they dug each grave close to one another to save time and effort," Annie replied.

Clara smiled at her friend.

"You seem to have suddenly developed a worrying insight into the burial practices of murderers," she teased.

Annie blushed.

"But it is a very sound idea," Clara quickly corrected herself. "One we must surely act upon. We ought to go straight to Chief Inspector Peeters and propose he conduct an exploratory search of the woods."

Clara was beginning to stand, as Janssen appeared in the parlour with a tray of sandwiches and a large pot of tea. The look of longing on Annie's face, and the disappointment that followed when she saw Clara stand, was too much to bear. Clara resumed her seat.

"After luncheon," Clara said. "We'll go after luncheon."

About an hour later they were heading towards the

police station. Neither of them had so far met with Chief Inspector Peeters, but they had heard all about him from Tommy and Colonel Brandt. Clara was hopeful that he would not be difficult to persuade to help them.

The fellow on the front desk hesitated when Clara explained who she was and her purpose. Little did Clara know of the fraught encounter Brandt and Tommy had had that morning with Peeters. But the man on the desk did know and he was uncertain about setting more of these strange English people on his superior. In the end, however, it was plain Clara was not going to leave without seeing him and the man gave in.

Clara reflected that this was remarkably similar to her usual experiences with the Brighton police and almost smirked to herself. Perhaps it was her.

Peeters blustered down the stairs after his subordinate when he heard there were more nosy foreigners in his station. He took a good look at Clara as he appeared. Clara didn't feel it was a friendly look and was beginning to think Tommy had sugar-coated his description of Peeters.

"Chief Inspector," she greeted him warmly, nonetheless, "I apologise for the disturbance. You have been speaking with my friends, I believe?"

"I have," Peeters did not return the warmth. "Are you the woman who spoke to my sister and upset her? Can't you leave all that in the past?"

"Murder is not something easily forgotten," Clara replied firmly. "Your sister may have learned to live with the trauma, but she had certainly not consigned it to the past. Nor will she ever have the chance to attempt to heal when there are so many unanswered questions. Namely, where is Father Lound? You must know, Chief Inspector, that when a person is missing it eats away at those who care for them. Only discovering what became of them, knowing if they are dead or alive, can bring them the peace they need and deserve. While your sister has a small glimmer of hope Father Lound is still alive, she will never be able to truly move on."

Peeters narrowed his eyes.

"She was doing very well, until you showed up."

"Do you really believe that?" Clara asked him. "For I saw a woman whose heart still ached for a man most likely long dead. Do not kid yourself that as she no longer speaks about things she has actually forgotten them. I think your sister is in a very bad place, and without assistance she may get worse."

"Who are you to judge my sister?" Peeters snapped.

"I am judging no one, just offering my observations. I also wish to offer my help. There is another woman who cannot rest and who is struggling to live her life because of what happened here in 1917. Emily Priggins asked me to find out what happened to her brother. She had to defy her father to do so, no easy matter if you knew who her father was," Clara hoped she was appealing to Peeters' sense of moral duty and to his empathy. "She has gone out on a limb, and I owe her a duty to do the same. I am not questioning your policing skills. I am fully aware that trying to trace a missing man in the middle of a war is a thankless task. It's difficult enough in peacetime."

Peeters seemed slightly mollified. He had not lost his frown, however.

"I have done all I can. Allowed your friends to look at the case files and answered all their questions. I even agreed to make enquiries concerning the rosary and crucifix," Peeters paused and looked slightly embarrassed. "I asked my sister. She is certain the items belonged to Father Lound."

"I feared as much," Clara nodded. "If we could bother you for a little longer, my friend Annie has come up with an idea concerning the events of that night when Lound disappeared and I would like you to hear her out. We may be able to resolve this mystery at last."

Peeters glanced at Annie, who was looking uneasy. She did not understand what Clara and Peeters were saying, as it was all in French, but she recognised her name and she blushed even deeper when Clara nodded to her and she realised they were discussing her theory. Peeters' stern look made her want to run away. Annie did not like dealing with the police, she was only just getting used to Inspector Park-Coombs back in Brighton.

"I do have other work," Peeters grumbled to Clara, but he sounded less fierce than before.

"I shall not disturb you for long," Clara promised. "I need not mention that there is also a military matter to consider with this case. And if Annie's theory is right, we shall solve both in one move."

That, at least, appealed to Peeters.

"Let's go to my office," he agreed.

Once upstairs, Clara explained Annie's theory. Annie sat mute during the proceedings, looking mildly worried by everything. Peeters listened patiently and his frown lifted as the theory took root in his mind. It was all very plausible. When Clara had finished, she waited for his response.

"It does seem very likely that Ramon is our skeleton, now you know he never left the town," Peeters said. "And the way he died is very much the way a military agent would execute someone. During the war I was sent to other areas of Belgium when mass graves were uncovered and a large police presence was needed. These graves were the work of German troops who had executed random Belgium citizens as they marched through the country. Many of these victims were shot through the back of the head.

"Ramon would not surprise me as a traitor either. He was always looking to make easy money and was not against breaking the law to do so. I despaired for his future. Somehow, I always thought he would end up dying in some miserable fashion.

"And that brings us back to Father Lound. He did seem to be fond of helping the Devereauxs. He had sympathy for them when no one else did. My sister said it would do him no good. Looks like she was right."

"It is just a theory without proof," Clara pointed out. "I

wouldn't want our idea to be taken as the likeliest solution and prevent other options being explored. I know finding the culprits for this crime is probably never going to happen. If they were not captured and killed during the war, these agents must have made their way back to Germany. We shall never be able to bring them to justice, but we may at least be able to give Ramon and Father Lound proper burials and offer some peace to their friends and family."

"I don't think there is such a thing as peace for the Devereauxs," Peeters said grimly. "Especially in Lugrule. Why have they gone to such a pit?"

"I think they are hiding," Clara answered. "Madame Devereaux knew her son was engaged in criminal activities, maybe she even knew about his treachery. When the British military started to investigate she could have panicked, especially when Ramon vanished. Fearing the consequences for herself and her family, she fled to somewhere she thought no one would come looking."

"Lugrule is certainly a place people go to disappear," Peeters agreed. "It is also the place for the destitute and despondent. Without Ramon, Madame Devereaux would have had little source of income. Lugrule is at least a cheap place to live."

"Now I have outlined our theory, would you be willing to have the woods searched for Father Lound's body?"

Peeters had become side-tracked with thoughts of the Devereauxs' unhappy existence. He suddenly realised he was being asked a question, and one that would require men and resources. His frown returned.

"That is a big operation. I couldn't just recall all my men and march them to the woods. We would need shovels and things."

"What if we asked the townsfolk for help?" Clara suggested. "They would surely turn out to assist?"

Peeters looked wary of the idea, though it would be less of a drain on his own resources and he wouldn't have to pay the townsfolk. He glanced out of the window, looking at the afternoon sun and Clara could almost see him calculating in his head how many hours of daylight they had left to accomplish their task.

"You are not going to leave me alone until I resolve this, are you?" Peeters said.

"You are quite right," Clara smiled at him.

Peeters sighed.

"I shall have a message sent out to ask the townsfolk to help us search the woods. Give us about an hour to gather volunteers and then we can set out. I'll call on Dr Jacobs too, he will need to be there if we find any remains," Peeters became silent for a moment. "You are right, about my sister. She is still suffering. If we find Lound's remains, do you think it will give her peace?"

"Not at once," Clara explained honestly. "But it will stop the questions rolling in her mind. It will bring an end to that period of her life. It will help. I can't guarantee she will suddenly be back to the person she was before, that is very much up to her."

Peeters gave a wry smile.

"I rather thought you would say that."

"You can't cure everything," Clara sighed. "If only we could, but we can make things bearable. It will be better than her imagining Father Lound ran off and abandoned her."

"Will it?" Peeters chuckled humourlessly. "I am not so sure about that."

Chapter Twenty-Six

"What a complicated business," Captain Mercier said after Tommy had finished the lengthy explanation for their being in Belgium. "I knew Father Lound reasonably well. All the military men did. After he vanished and we all assumed that indicated his guilt, we endeavoured to forget about him. It never crossed my mind that there must be people out there who cared about him and wondered what had happened. His sister can't accept he was a traitor?"

"She, and others who knew him well, believe it would have been entirely out of character."

Mercier snorted.

"I heard things like that all the time during the war. When men deserted or committed suicide, or did something more mundane like cheated others out of their money. There was always someone who said that was not like them at all, that they would not possibly have done things like that," Mercier shrugged. "I came to the conclusion that war makes men do things that they never otherwise would have done. How many of the soldiers out there would ever have shot a man in ordinary life? Yet in the trenches it was a regular occurrence. I know I would never have considered myself a murderer before the war, but I soon became one when my life was in the balance."

"That's a difficult ethical question," Tommy said uneasily. "Shooting the enemy is not the same as murdering someone."

"Isn't it?" Mercier asked him sharply. "The law says if you kill a person by a deliberate act of violence, and with the intention of doing so, it is murder. All of those things apply to what we were doing in the trenches. Was it because we had been ordered to do it, or because our comrades were doing the same that it made things easier? Was it because we were protecting our families and our countries that justified it to us? I don't know. But I do know that, dress it up as you like, we all became murderers when we stepped on that battlefield."

Tommy didn't like such talk. He had struggled with a lot of demons after the war, but he had not fought with himself over whether what he had done was self-defence or murder. He had never considered that he had been wrong in shooting the enemy. They would have shot him. The commanding officers and the propaganda they were regularly fed reminded them that the Germans were monsters, quick to kill and maim and rape. They were animals rather than men. You ate that sort of stuff up at the time, as it meant you could sleep at night – well, almost. Tommy had made a conscious effort not to think about those things ever since. He wasn't entirely happy about Mercier bringing the subject up now. After all, what else could he have done?

"That is by-the-by," Colonel Brandt interrupted. "I agree that a loved one saying a person could not possibly have committed a crime is no evidence they did not, however, we do have to always listen to those peoples' concerns, especially when the proof that a person did commit a crime is just as vague."

"Finding stolen papers in a man's office and then him running away is hardly vague," Mercier snapped. He was beginning to dislike the way the Englishmen were trying to defend Father Lound.

"My point is, something very odd happened in the town that day, something that has left a lot of questions in its wake. We only want to answer those questions."

Mercier reluctantly accepted this explanation. Then he

relaxed a fraction.

"If I can do anything more to help, I shall. I am not a heartless man, I appreciate Lound's sister is struggling to understand all this mess and has further questions."

"Thank you," Colonel Brandt replied. "And let me add that as a military man, and a friend of Colonel Matthews, I do not intend to leave Belgium until I know for sure who the traitor was. If it was Lound and he is dead, then so be it. But if it was someone else and they have escaped justice to live their life as if nothing happened, then I intend to hunt them down and expose them to the world. Betrayal does not deserve mercy."

Brandt's words were hard, but he had a point. Treachery could lead to the deaths of innocents and enable a wretched enemy to conquer a neutral country such as Belgium was at the start of the war. It could not be just forgotten.

"What I hoped you could help me with was how treachery might have occurred here? I can understand how information was obtained, but how was it sent to the Germans?" Brandt concluded.

Mercier perked up.

"That is a very valid question and one I investigated diligently at the time. A traitor can only commit his betrayal if he has the ability to communicate with the enemy. In 1917, the town was behind the British front line, therefore direct communication was impossible. We had to look for other methods," Mercier was excited as he explained the problem. "After assessing the situation and determining that there was no means of a local communicating with the enemy directly, my colleagues and I agreed that they must be using an intermediate in the area. Probably enemy agents who were living on the fringes of the community and were passing intelligence from someone in the town to the Germans.

"We had received reports of a pair of unknown men loitering about the area, sometimes stealing from farms. They were unlikely to be refugees as they avoided contact with the locals. We suspected they were agents working for the Germans and had probably persuaded someone in the town to pass information to them. As they had been seen near the shrine of St. Helena a few times, that seemed to make it all the more likely Father Lound was their source of intelligence."

"Did Father Lound often go to the shrine?" Tommy asked.

Mercier seemed put out by the question.

"He was a Catholic priest and it was a saint's shrine," Mercier responded, as if that made it obvious. "In any case, I made it my job to find these men, with the permission of Colonel Matthews. After the disappearance of Father Lound, it was the only link I had to the treachery in town. These man had to be caught and dealt with, before more information was stolen."

Colonel Brandt was sitting forward in his chair, listening keenly.

"Did you capture them?"

Captain Mercier had grown enthused as he talked, now he looked a little embarrassed.

"Not precisely. We searched the countryside and eventually found an abandoned woodsman's hut. Inside there were wicker crates, the sort used for carrier pigeons and a crude wireless set. It could send Morse code messages to the Germans. It was interesting, because one of the reasons we knew we had a leak was because Morse messages had been overheard through our own wireless sets giving vital information to the enemy.

"The pigeons had all been used and it looked like the wireless had been abandoned. Probably the Germans had realised it was pointless as we were overhearing what they were sending and changing our tactics and deployments as a result. Though it was damn annoying! We kept having to alter our plans and that must have delighted the Germans. Inconveniencing us was almost as good as being able to smash our positions.

"We did find paraffin, which we suspected was for use

in a signalling lamp. They must have found a position that was isolated and from which they could signal short messages to their commanders. I hoped we could track the men, as they did not seem to have left long before. It wasn't to be."

Colonel Brandt's face fell.

"They got away?"

"Not entirely. As I said, they had been raiding local farms and stealing food. Unfortunately, they had a habit of visiting the farms in a set order. The farmers worked out this pattern and plotted to all be at the farm they thought would next be hit. The men appeared as expected, the farmers attempted to catch them and they fled. In the chaos that followed both men were shot. One died instantly, the other lingered just long enough for the farmers to work out the pair were German. They buried them in a nearby field," Mercier's tone indicated how disappointing this had all been. "We eventually learned of what had happened and went to the farm. The bodies were exhumed and examined for any papers or clues to their identity. Aside from a book on Morse code and a letter from one fellow's mother, there was little to aid us. We reburied them and promised the farmer there would be no trouble for him. He had shot enemy agents, after all."

Colonel Brandt joined Mercier in looking slightly disappointed. It was, however, understandable. War was a different kettle of fish to peacetime.

"Were you hoping they might still be alive?" Mercier asked.

"I was hopeful you had had the chance to speak with them and learn something about their activities."

"Sorry," Mercier said, without looking particularly apologetic.

Outside, in the corridor, there was a slow scuffle of feet and the older man Tommy had surmised was Mercier's father appeared in the doorway.

"If you are done, Renaud wants to get going," he said in a voice that indicated there was no real rush. "Oh, and a lad has ridden over from the town. He says that the police are asking for all able men to gather near the shrine of St. Helena with shovels, as they are going to begin a search of the place for a second body, like that one they found before."

Tommy glanced at Colonel Brandt and in unison they said.

"Clara!"

"What is this?" Mercier asked them.

"We have colleagues in the town," Tommy explained. "They are pursuing the disappearance of Father Lound from a different angle. Now, we know that the bones in the woods are not those of the priest, but I would guess our friends believe that he may be resting in a similar grave there all the same."

Mercier's eyes twinkled.

"If you found his body, that would be interesting. The shrine was the rendezvous for the spies, we knew that. I always wondered who that skeleton was. I think I shall go over with my shovel and help with the search."

"What about the tractor?" Mercier's father asked in that same, placid tone, as if it really was not all that important and could wait.

Mercier frowned.

"Eh, buy it father, you know you want to."

Mercier's father grinned from ear to ear, then he excused himself and vanished. Mercier shrugged to his guests.

"He loves engines."

A short time later they were back at the woods. Several men were already at work, scouring an area around the shrine where the first skeleton had been found. Peeters was supervising and Dr Jacobs was on hand to identify anything that was brought out of the ground.

Brandt and Tommy noticed Clara and Annie standing near the saint's statue and joined them.

"How did you persuade Peeters to do all this?" Tommy asked his sister, smirking at her.

"Persistence," she winked at him. "Also, it is damn irritating having an Englishwoman twisting your ear for any length of time."

"How long have they been at it?" Colonel Brandt was watching the workers.

"Half an hour or so," Clara was about to say more when a cry went up and they all hurried over to see what was going on.

One of the men had been digging in the area near where the first bones were found and had come across something in the soil. He held it out to Dr Jacobs. It was not a bone, but a very small item. Dr Jacobs carefully brushed dirt from it.

"It is the remains of a bullet casing," he said with a frown. Then he bent down and dug with his fingers in the soil where the casing had been discovered. He was at it several moments before he came across something. Clutching his fingers around the object he wriggled it out of the soil.

It was a revolver. Badly corroded by its time in the soil, but obvious as a gun. The bullet chamber had been broken open before it was buried, allowing the spent bullet casing and several unused bullets to scatter into the earth. Dr Jacobs frowned.

"How very odd. Someone broke open the gun then discarded it."

Captain Mercier walked over and asked to see the gun. He cleaned it as best he could with his fingers, then examined it all over.

"It's not German. The bullets are, but not the gun," he said, clearly surprised. "I think it is a British gun."

Tommy glanced at Clara.

"Father Lound," Clara said to him in a whisper. "I feared he might have been the one to kill Ramon."

Tommy frowned.

"Ramon?"

"Those are his the bones in the grave. He was not in Lugrule, has never been there. I don't know why his mother lied, as she would not speak to me," Clara explained.

"Looks like we now know what killed the man who was buried here," Captain Mercier was saying, having not overheard Clara.

The party continued to dig on. Odd things appeared from the soil and gave brief moments of excitement, only to prove to be something innocent and not worthy of further investigation. The greatest excitement was caused by the discovery of a long rib bone, which Dr Jacobs confidently asserted belonged to a large dog and not a man.

The sun worked its way across the sky and everyone's enthusiasm drooped. There was no sign of another grave and their search area had widened far away from where they had begun. It was becoming plain that no one else was buried here.

"Sorry Annie," Clara said when Peeters called it a day. "It was a good theory."

Annie was frowning.

"I really thought we would find Father Lound. He has to be buried somewhere."

"Maybe he killed Ramon and ran away," Clara suggested. "The gun was British."

"Do you believe that?" Annie asked her.

Clara was not sure. She found it hard to imagine the priest as a killer, just as it had been hard to imagine him as a traitor. There was no real evidence for either accusation, but there was also no body.

They started to walk back into town. Monsieur Coppens joined them.

"Were we looking for Father Lound?" He asked Clara. The diggers had not been told who they were searching for, only to look for bones.

"We were," Clara replied.

"Hmm," Coppens mused. "Well, it got me out of doing a job at home. The corner of the house is sagging again. Shouldn't be with all the rubble and concrete they put under it, but the cracks are definitely returning. We've had a builder come over and he thinks the hole was not packed well enough and a gap has formed."

"The foundations," Clara mumbled to herself, then she glanced up at Monsieur Coppens. "Maybe something that was put in that hole has disintegrated?"

"Yes, that is possible," Coppens nodded. "In any case, we shall have to excavate and refill it, unless we want to lose the corner of the house."

"I think you should dig it out right away, this instant," Clara came to a halt, the other diggers were behind her along with Chief Inspector Peeters. "In fact, I think we should all come along and help you."

"What is this?" Peeters asked moodily.

"Chief Inspector, I think I know where the body of Father Lound was buried. I think I know who killed him and why, and how he disposed of the body. What happened afterwards I am not so sure about, but this, this I know and we must act at once."

Peeters grumbled.

"You've had us on one wild goose chase today already."

"Annie was right, I was right also when I said I thought Father Lound was dead. We just needed to find his grave and if it isn't in the woods, then there is only one logical place for it to be. Chief Inspector, you must trust me on this."

Peeters looked like he would protest again, but with all the townsfolk around him he was hesitant to be rude. He finally sighed and agreed.

"Well then, where must we dig now?"

Chapter Twenty-seven

Madame Coppens made them all coffee. It was a long job, requiring her to boil a lot of water and routinely refill her little coffee pot. Annie helped her. She also helped her cook food for the workers. It was the least the Coppens could do for the men who were now helping them with their subsidence problem, even if the reason for that help was because Clara believed that the unfortunate Father Lound had been buried amid the rubble and concrete used to shore up the Coppens' house footings. It was a hunch, but the more she thought about it, the more certain she was.

Father Lound had not just walked away. He was not that sort of man. To vanish the way he did, meant he must have been dead. And dead men have to be buried somewhere. Clara had not mentioned to anyone yet that the person who had filled in this hole was Ramon Devereaux, and that he was also the last person to see Father Lound alive, and the one who argued with the priest just before he vanished. Not to mention, a prime suspect for being the town's traitor. Everything made sense.

As long as they found the body, of course.

A few of the men went away and fetched sturdy wooden beams, which they could wedge beneath the wall of the house as the ground was excavated beneath it. It was rather like digging a mine shaft, someone explained to Clara, you had to put in joists to support what was above, while you dug out the soil, rubble and lumps of concrete. It was soon plain that the work to improve the foundations had been very slipshod. The rubble had not been packed down and air pockets had been left. The concrete had been made too thick and had not filled the gaps well. Over time, the pressure of the house above had pushed the air from the gaps, allowing the rubble to collapse, with the result the house started to slip again.

There were a dozen men working to dig out the foundations, they had formed a chain with some filling solid baskets with rubble, while others brought it out of the hole and put it in a pile nearby. Others were hacking out the lumps of concrete. There were mutterings about how poor the previous work had been. Coppens was looking a little embarrassed about the mess beneath his house, even if it had nothing to do with him; he had just bought the property.

Chief Inspector Peeters stood to one side smoking a cigarette and looking disinterested about the whole affair. Clara hoped she had not made another bad guess when she suggested they dig here. Peeters would certainly not help her again if that was the case. She accepted a cup of coffee from Madame Coppens, even though she really was not keen on coffee, but because she was desperate for something to distract her. Colonel Brandt and Tommy were being as supportive as they could, but even they looked worried. What had Clara done?

"Hey! Look at this!"

The workers came to an abrupt stop. Clara took a tentative step forward. Peeters had not moved but was looking over. One of the men who had been hacking out concrete had just pulled out a large chunk and discovered a hole in the debris. Within this hole he had spotted an object.

Clara held her breath as he pulled the thing from the small space. It was rectangular, badly squashed by the weight of the stones and broken bricks piled on it, yet still recognisable as a suitcase. Clara hurried forward and took the suitcase from the man. She had to slip into the hollow growing beneath the house to do so, then climb back out. Once she was back above ground, she put the battered case on the grass and tried to open the locks. Unsurprisingly they would not budge. They had clearly been immersed in water for some time – there were pools of water amid the rubble, where it had seeped down through the ground soil – and were bent out of shape.

Peeters walked over and crouched down. He produced a pocket knife with a large blade and wriggled it under the catches. He was able to prise them from the case, the leather covering being so softened by water that the tiny pins that held the catches in place pinged free with ease. Dr Jacobs wandered over and everyone paused and hovered around the discovery as the lid was finally pulled open.

All the objects inside were soaked through. There were a pair of pyjamas, a set of trousers and a shirt, on top of a priest's cassock. Clara breathed a sigh of relief. Here was Father Lound's missing suitcase. It had never left town, which surely meant he had never left either. Captain Mercier moved closer and examined the case. He saw the cassock too and a look of concern crossed his face. Peeters turned around and faced the workers.

"Dig carefully. We are looking for the remains of a person in there."

A new resolve came over the men. They were tired and their muscles ached, but they had a purpose. While they continued to dig, Clara carefully unpacked the suitcase. Captain Mercier loitered at her shoulder to examine the contents. Aside from the clothes, there was a hair brush and shaving kit. What struck Clara, however, was the lack of personal belongings. There were no photographs or letters, no diary, no books, trinkets or tokens, all the little things a person carries with them. This suitcase was full of essentials and nothing else.

"No slippers," Captain Mercier mused as the paltry contents were laid out. "When I pack my suitcase, I always make sure I have my slippers."

"No paper or envelopes for writing to family," Clara

added. "No money or passport. This is not the way a person packs if they intend to leave a place for good, or even just to be gone for a few days. It is the way a person might pack for someone else, a person in haste who wants to make it look like someone has left town in a hurry."

Captain Mercier gave a soft groan, then sat on the ground beside Clara.

"It looks like I may have been wrong about Father Lound," he said glumly.

"If it is any consolation, I think Father Lound was very wrong about the person he was trying to protect," Clara sighed. "He made a mistake and I think it cost him his life."

"Who do you suspect?"

"Ramon Devereaux."

Captain Mercier mused on the name.

"I didn't know him," he said, looking ashamed by the fact.

From the expanding hole in the ground there was another cry and Clara hastened over to see what had been discovered. Dr Jacobs had clambered into the pit and was very gingerly removing a portion of bone from a space in the rubble.

"We need to clear this area very carefully," he said loudly to those nearest him, indicating a space immediately before him. "This is where the bones will be. Take your time, don't let the stones fall and crush anything."

Dr Jacobs took a step back, allowing the workers in, but near to hand to keep an eye on the work. He examined the long bone in his hands.

"It is human?" Clara asked. It had to be, of course it did, but she had been wrong about the woods and now felt she could not risk being wrong again.

Dr Jacobs glanced up at her.

"It is. From an adult male, I would say, by the length and thickness."

Clara did not know whether to be relieved or heartbroken. At last they had located Father Lound, but with it came the knowledge he had been murdered and would never return to his family. How could anyone be happy about that?

More bones emerged from the rubble. Dr Jacobs asked that a large sheet be laid on the grass and he began to reconstruct the skeleton one piece at a time. The leg bone was placed first, followed by a couple of vertebra and then another leg bone. As each piece was placed in its appropriate position on the sheet, it seemed as if the doctor was putting together a gruesome jigsaw puzzle. The rubble was being removed stone by stone now, the process time-consuming, but no one wanted to be responsible for damaging the remains. More vertebra emerged, and then someone spotted tiny bones that had fallen to the soil. These were the bones of the foot, the most delicate of the bones in the body, next to those of the hand.

"It seems our man must have been put in head first," Dr Jacobs said as the remains mounted up.

Clara was restlessly walking about in the Coppens' garden. They had some bones, but no definitive proof, as yet, that this was Father Lound. But it had to be him, didn't it?

On the road just beyond the house, people were gathering. Word was spreading that something was going on. It wasn't long before someone peered over the garden wall and spotted the bones being laid out by Dr Jacobs and reported back to the others. Now there was a ripple of excitement among the crowd.

Peeters prowled on the outskirts of the excavation area, eyeing up the growing crowd of onlookers with a stern expression. No one was going to interfere with police business, not while he was in charge.

"We have a pelvis!" Dr Jacobs called out, he sounded quite excited. "I am now certain this fellow is male and young. No signs of wear and tear on the bones yet that would indicate he was aging."

Peeters was distracted from the crowd for a moment, when he looked back his face fell.

"No, no!"

Lina Peeters had pushed through the crowd and was opening the garden gate to the Coppens' property.

"No one is to enter!" Peeters told his sister fiercely.

She paused with her hand on the gate latch and glowered at him.

"I have not waited all these years, not know whether I should be mourning for a man who was dead or hating him for leaving me, just for you to stop me now," Lina said firmly.

She depressed the latch and entered. Her act of crossing the threshold seemed to spark the rest of the crowd into action and people started to pour into the garden. Peeters ran forward in alarm. Clara called out to Colonel Brandt and Tommy, along with any of the men who were free to run forward and stop the surge.

Lina slipped past her brother, he made little effort to prevent her. But the other spectators were forced back. People pushed and barged, wanting to get a better look at what was going on, but Peeters' authority and the physical barrier of the men with him, stopped them. After a few moments of arguing, the crowd retreated to the street again and Colonel Brandt stationed himself with Tommy at the gate to deter any future attempts to enter.

Lina had made her way to the sheet on the grass and was looking at it as if the bones upon it were something unreal, something alien. Clara stepped near her, trying to offer her as much support as she could.

"I… I don't recognise him," Lina said, tears trickling down her face. "I know that sounds foolish. How would I recognise the bones of the man I loved? But, I thought… I thought I would sense it was him, somehow."

Peeters came up behind his sister and placed an arm around her shoulders.

"I am sorry," he said. "I am so very sorry."

"We have a skull!"

Deep in the hole the men had come across the most important piece of this puzzle. Dr Jacobs took gentle possession of the skull, bringing it to his sheet with an air of reverence. He placed it at the top of the skeleton and then crouched to look closer.

"I was worried this might have been crushed when the body was buried," he said. "However, it is intact, except for this portion over the eye socket."

Clara joined him to examine the skull. It appeared that a sharp object had slammed into the priest's head just above his left eye.

"I would say a stone or similar heavy blunt object did this," Dr Jacobs postulated. "You know, a fragment of bone has sheared off and gone into the brain, and it remains inside the skull. I can see it, just."

"This killed him?" Clara asked.

"I would suspect it did. This does not look to me like something caused by rubble being piled on top of the body," Dr Jacobs was examining the skull further. "No other signs of injury, though he does have a tooth missing and that came out not long before his death."

Lina gave a soft sob.

"That is Christian," her voice trembled as she spoke. "A week before he vanished, he fell down some steps near the river. He was trying to catch an old lady's cat that had escaped her house. The silly man knocked his tooth out in the process."

Lina put her hands over her face and her whole body shook with the terrible realisation of what she was looking at. Her brother tried to pull her to him, to comfort her.

"If this is Christian…" he started to say.

"It is Christian," Lina wept. "I have no doubt, no doubt at all."

Peeters paused for a moment, then he looked to Clara.

"Ramon buried him here, it has to be. In the police report Father Howard mentioned how he had come across Ramon backfilling this hole and asked him if he had seen Father Lound. Whoever filled in this space was clearly responsible for putting the priest's body here too."

"And then Ramon was killed," Clara frowned. "That still makes no sense. Especially with the discovery of the British

225

pistol."

Clara, for a brief moment, wondered if Colonel Matthews had lied when he said he had not taken justice into his own hands and executed the person he suspected of being a traitor. But she dismissed the idea rapidly. A British colonel lurking about the woods would have been noticeable and Captain Mercier would have surely been in on the scheme. Brandt and Tommy had quickly updated her on what the Belgium soldier had told them, and he did not think the spy had been caught. Therefore, he did not know about Ramon's body being in the woods.

"Well, we can't ask Ramon what happened that day anymore, but I believe it mentioned in the police report that he had someone assisting him in filling this hole?" Clara said to Peeters.

"Louis Maes," Peeters nodded. "Wherever Ramon went, Louis followed. He was like a loyal dog, that boy."

Clara glanced to the street outside the Coppens' garden, and to the people there.

"What are the odds that talk of this has not already circulated through the entire town and reached Louis Maes' ears?"

Peeters snorted.

"This is a small town, and everyone knows how to talk."

"Then we need to hurry, before the only person who might be able to tell us what happened here disappears too," Clara glanced around her. Dr Jacobs was capable enough of seeing that the body was secured and respectfully removed from the garden. Colonel Brandt and Tommy would act as reliable sentries. She felt it was safe for her and Chief Inspector Peeters to leave. "Will you join me?"

Peeters was reluctant to leave his sister, but she pulled out of his grasp.

"Go. I want you to speak to Louis. I want to know why Christian died and who is truly to blame." She said.

Peeters turned back to Clara.

"I am ready. It is about time this mystery was solved."

Together they hurried out of the garden and towards the far side of town, hoping they were not too late to catch the one person who could tell them the truth.

Chapter Twenty-eight

Louis Maes lived in a cottage towards the edge of town. He was a farm labourer and the house came with the work. Peeters remarked that it was a way for the farmer to save on paying wages.

The cottage was tiny, smaller than Clara had expected, but it was very well maintained and every inch of the garden had been turned over to growing vegetables for the occupants. As Peeters and Clara drew near they could hear raised voices coming from inside, though it was impossible to make out words.

"Maes is married these days," Peeters added, in the process of opening the gate to the garden.

At the same moment the cottage door flew open and Maes stumbled outside; it almost looked like he was shoved out. He was carrying a haversack, the sort soldiers carried their belongings in, in his arms. Behind him a woman was yelling that she never wanted to see him again and calling him all manner of names.

Maes took a step onto the path that joined the narrow space between the cottage and the gate, then he came to a complete halt looking at Peeters. There was a moment when everyone froze, before Maes threw his bag at Peeters and took off across the garden.

Peeters was nearly knocked down by the heavy haversack which had taken him by surprise. Clara was quicker off the mark. She turned on her heel and ran alongside the garden fence, knowing that Maes' headlong sprint would require him to jump the fence at some point. She was banking on that slowing him down a fraction. She was still behind him when he reached the fence and attempted to leap it in one move. He clipped his knee and fell over onto his hands. Clara skimmed around the corner and dived at him. Maes wrestled with her, pulling at her dress and nearly ripping her clothes, but Clara kicked out at whatever part of him she could, and must have struck something important because he gasped and stopped fighting.

"Stay still!" Clara commanded him.

Maes was on the ground, groaning to himself. Peeters hurried to join them, while in the background Mrs Maes peered out of her front door.

"You are quite dangerous!" Peeters remarked to Clara as he grabbed Maes' hands and pulled him to his feet.

"You would be amazed at what I have to deal with," Clara shrugged her shoulders.

"As for you, Maes," Peeters addressed their groaning suspect, "I have quite a few questions. I am guessing you know what about, too."

Maes gave a miserable sniff and looked about ready to burst into tears. He briefly tried to grapple himself away from the Chief Inspector, then gave in.

"I didn't do anything wrong," he said bleakly.

"You and I both know that is a lie. Else you would not be attempting to run away," Peeters replied to him sternly. "Come on, let's get to the station."

Maes was defeated. The walk to the police station was uneventful and he seemed resigned to his fate, whatever he imagined that might be. Once at the station, he was escorted up to Peeters' office and offered a chair. He took it without hesitation, all his fight had evaporated. Peeters locked the door, all the same, and placed the key on his desk. Clara took a seat to one side, intending to ask her own questions when she got the chance.

"Well Louis," Peeters pulled some paper from a drawer

and began to take notes. "This is rather a pickle, isn't it?"

Maes hung his head and didn't answer.

"You know we have found the remains of Father Lound beneath the old Albion Hope?" Peeters continued.

Maes gave a small nod, so small it could have been mistaken for a twitch.

"I have a statement on file from Father Howard that you and Ramon Devereaux were responsible for filling in the excavated hole beneath the house. You were seen filling it on the day Father Lound disappeared. Would you care to explain how the priest ended up in your hole?"

"I never killed him," Maes lifted his head and begged them with his eyes. "I never hurt the man, never. He was a priest, I wouldn't dare. You go to Hell for things like that."

"But you were prepared to bury his body?" Clara pointed out. "I assume you were recruited by Ramon for the task."

"Ramon was my best friend," Maes agreed, turning to Clara. "He looked out for me."

"You mean he involved you in all his illegal activities," Peeters interjected. "I know all about you and Ramon. Every burglary we arrested Ramon for, you were somewhere nearby. You made your mother despair."

"I was only helping him out. He was my friend," Maes was pleading with them, trying to get them to see his point. "You help out friends."

"Is that what happened on that day in 1917? You were helping a friend?" Clara asked, her tone gentle. She was hoping that a soft, persuasive voice might appeal to Maes and make him talk. He seemed to be easily led and eager to please. Both things that Ramon had used to his advantage.

"Ramon said there had been an accident," Maes explained slowly. "Something awful, he said. And if I didn't help him, Ramon said he would be hanged for it. He was extremely upset. I have never seen him like that before. It scared me a little."

"What was this accident Ramon claimed had happened?" Peeters asked.

"Ramon said he had argued with Father Lound. The priest was always pressuring Ramon to change the way he lived his life. He didn't understand that Ramon had family to provide for and he did things for them. That day, Ramon had been so angry about everything and he had walked home after arguing with other lads at Albion Hope. I was there, I saw that part," Maes paused for breath, he was talking fast. "He just wanted to go home and forget about everything, but Father Lound followed him. He followed him to his house and they argued in the garden, before Ramon stormed indoors and refused to speak to him anymore.

"Ramon went upstairs, and he was there for a while. Then he had to go out again, and when he walked back into the garden, he saw Father Lound lying half under a bush. His head was all bloody and when Ramon tried to rouse him, he realised he was dead."

"Wait a minute," Peeters was stunned by this information. "You are saying that Father Lound mysteriously died in Ramon's back garden, while Ramon was inside the house?"

"That is what Ramon told me," Maes answered. "Why would he lie?"

Peeters glanced at Clara, his look incredulous. She just shrugged. Maes was either too stupid, or too loyal, to see how ridiculous the story sounded.

"What happened next?" Clara asked Maes.

"Ramon said we had to hide the body," Maes stated.

"Did he not suggest calling the police or a doctor?" Peeters asked in astonishment.

Maes shook his head and it was obvious he had thought nothing suspicious about his friend's plans.

"I went with him to his house. Father Lound was still under the bush. Ramon said we should transport him in a handcart, covered with rubble for the back-filling of the hole we had dug beneath Albion Hope. So, that is what we did. It took us a while to get the cart, and to suitably hide the priest in it," Maes paused. "I remember that Ramon's sister came to the door and looked out at us. She must have seen the body, but she just turned away and walked back in. Ramon said she was cold, so very cold. He hated her, he told me that as we place Father Lound in the handcart. He hated her, but she was family and that meant he had to look out for her.

"We pushed the handcart to the garden of Albion Hope. No one looked at us. I felt sick with nerves, but Ramon said no one would know. He was confident, as always. Once at the house, he said he was going to fetch Father Lound's suitcase, so it looked like the priest had left town. It was never hard to enter the priests' rooms at the house. They never locked the doors and people were always coming and going.

"Once that was done, we put Father Lound into the pit and covered him with rubble and then threw in the suitcase. I had never touched a corpse before. He was already quite cold and his skin looked so pale. I felt sick and Ramon slapped me, telling me I had to be strong, for his sake. We had barely put the priest in the hole when Father Howard and Father Stevens walked past and asked Ramon if he had seen Father Lound. He lied, of course."

Maes hefted his shoulders.

"That was it. We filled the hole and left."

"When did you last see Ramon?" Clara asked Maes.

The man looked miserable.

"About an hour later. I was fetching milk for my mother and I saw Ramon crossing the road. I went to stop him, and he was really upset and pushed me away. I tried to ask what was wrong, but he just told me to be quiet. I was going to tell him that I had seen his sister walking in the same direction a short time before. Ramon was always trying to keep track of her. She was in a lot of trouble with men," Maes looked sheepish at saying this of his friend's sister. "I didn't get a chance to tell him. That night he left."

"Only, he didn't leave," Peeters said solemnly. "We now know that the bones found in the woods are those of Ramon Devereaux."

232

Maes' mouth dropped open, he gaped at them like some strange gargoyle with a spout in its mouth. He shut his eyes and seemed about fit to collapse with the news. When he opened his eyes again, they glistened with tears.

"No…" he whispered.

"You must have always suspected, Louis?" Clara said softly. "You were the only one in town who knew the body could not be that of Father Lound. If it was not Lound, then who else could it have been?"

"Not Ramon," Maes' voice trembled. "He was my best friend. He looked out for me. I should have looked out for him."

"He was shot in the back of the head by a British revolver," Peeters laid the facts out before Maes, trying to draw something more from him. "Who was holding that gun, I don't know. But I do know that Ramon was holding Father Lound's crucifix and rosary. He must have taken them off the priest's body."

"No, Ramon took nothing from Father Lound. Lound was not wearing anything like that when we buried him," Maes insisted.

"Then he must have removed them before you arrived," Peeters continued. "Perhaps he was going to sell them."

Maes shook his head.

"You can't be blind to all this," Peeters persisted, his frustration growing. "Your friend Ramon was nothing more than a black-hearted traitor to his people. He was selling military information to the Germans. The reason he killed Father Lound was because the priest realised what he was doing. Ramon had to kill him to avoid being shot for treason."

"No!" Maes' head shot up, suddenly the meek man was gone, replaced by a furious man who was outraged at this talk about his friend. "Ramon was not a traitor!"

"He must have been," Peeters said sternly. "Who else? Ramon had access to Albion Hope. We know that Father Lound was protecting the traitor, and he argued with Ramon that day and was killed. Ramon hid his body to cover his tracks and then attempted to disappear. Someone caught up with him and dealt him the justice the authorities could not."

"NO!" Maes leapt from his chair and thumped both hands down hard on the desk, startling Clara and Peeters. "Ramon was never the traitor! I know this! I know this is true, because I know who really was betraying us back then! And I will tell you! I will break an oath I swore to my friend, because his name does not deserve to be tarnished by such lies. I'll tell you who was the real traitor in town, and then you can go and arrest them, and leave poor Ramon alone!"

Chapter Twenty-nine

Louis Maes sat back in his chair, some of his temper easing. He trembled a fraction at the violence of his emotions. Then he grew still and brought himself back under control.

"Ramon Devereaux was my closest friend in the world and everyone said that that blinded me to what he really was. They were wrong, they were all wrong. They were the ones who were blind," Maes held himself upright. The quiet, nervous man was gone. In his place sat one who was about to staunchly defend his friend. "Everything Ramon did was to try to help his family. Yes, he made mistakes. The burglaries were foolish, he said as much afterwards. But he only targeted people who could afford the loss.

"At the time he felt as if there was nothing else for him to do. There was no real work in the town, at least none that he was educated for. He considered joining the army, but he was too young and it was not easy to do back then, with the Germans everywhere. He had to look after his family. His younger sisters could not work, and his mother was breaking her back doing field labour she was not used to. His sister Elena refused to help. That left everything down to him.

"It helped so much when Albion Hope arrived and the priests were prepared to employ people to do odd jobs. Ramon would do anything and he finally persuaded Elena to do something too. She would collect the priests' rations every day from the local shops and deliver them to the house. Eventually, she also collected food for the workers too and delivered that. Ramon said he thought he was doing a good thing getting her work there, but in the end it was a bad thing. Elena got chatting to the soldiers. Many of them had not seen a girl in a while, being in the trenches or at barracks. They liked her company."

Peeters was taking notes and he nodded along.

"That is how it all began then?"

"Yes," Maes sighed. "At first Elena was just friendly with the soldiers and accepted any little gifts they gave her. The men could feel quite lonely and she would make them happy. I don't know when she started to sell herself to them. I just know when Ramon discovered this and blew his top. That was the late summer of 1916. He was so angry I thought he would kill her. He called her names, threatened to tell their mother. Elena told him their mother already knew and appreciated the money. That broke Ramon a little. You may not believe me, but Ramon had a strong sense of duty and honour. He had faltered, sometimes, and his temper could get the better of him, but he never forgot those things.

"He could do nothing about Elena. His mother would hear nothing on the subject and when he tried to stop Elena taking deliveries to Albion Hope his mother interfered again, saying they needed the money the priests paid Elena to bring food. In desperation, he confided everything to Father Lound.

"Ramon had never really seen eye-to-eye with the priests, but he valued the money they gave him for his work. He was not religious, not in the sense of going to church. He did believe, in his own way, but he couldn't explain it to me, I don't think he knew how to. Father Lound said he would try to help and started to call on the Devereaux family and talk to Madame Devereaux and Elena. It never went well, Ramon told me as much, but Father Lound never gave up. Ramon respected him for that.

"Like all things, after a while everything settled into a

routine. Ramon would accost his sister when he could, pull her away from the soldiers, but she would always go back. One time this big soldier beat him up. He thought Ramon was stealing his girl and Elena lied and said Ramon was a jealous ex-boyfriend. She watched on as Ramon was beaten. He said she grinned."

Maes came to a halt in his story. He had said so much in such a short space of time and it was cathartic to let out all these secrets, yet also overwhelming. He had kept so much stored up inside and now it was spilling out so fast he could barely keep track of it himself.

"This is all very sad," Clara leaned forward and spoke to him. "But it does not explain why Ramon was not a traitor. Seems to me he had every reason to be angry with the military and to want to spite them by selling their secrets."

"You have not been listening," Maes looked bleak. "Ramon was smart. So much smarter than me. He understood that one mean soldier is not representative of the whole army. And he did not blame the military for his sister's actions.

"Well… maybe a little. But he was more angry at her, and he would never have betrayed his country. Ramon loved Belgium. He wanted to fight for his homeland. His mother, on hearing his ideas of becoming a soldier, made him swear he would not go off to fight. She needed him more, she said, and that left Ramon very torn. He would have loved to have picked up a gun and shot at Germans. When rumours began to circulate about town of these strangers near the shrine of St. Helena, and everyone was saying they were Germans, Ramon said if he got the chance, he would shoot them. He even managed to get hold of a gun. A British revolver…"

Maes looked at Peeters sadly.

"I suspect the same gun you found in the woods near his body."

Peeters had paused over his paperwork. He was poised with his pen just above the paper. The gun had belonged to Ramon, which surely meant his killer had seized it off him.

"Could you identify this gun if we showed it to you?" Peeters asked.

Maes shook his head.

"I never saw it."

"You still have not told us who the traitor was, if it was not Ramon," Clara pointed out.

"I was trying to explain to you what Ramon was like," Maes looked hurt. "I wanted you to appreciate that he could never do such a thing. People judged him a lot. He did have a temper and he could be rash, but that did not make him a traitor.

"You know, when the rumours started to spread that there was a traitor in town, Ramon heard them as well as anyone, and he also heard that he was considered the traitor. That upset him more than anything, it upset him more than the thought that people considered him a rogue."

Maes shuffled in his seat, the storytelling was making him agitated.

"Ramon said he would find out who the real traitor was and kill him. I know that is murder, but I am being honest with you. Ramon thought it would be a civic duty to find and kill this traitor."

"Hence the revolver," Peeters made another note on his paper. "And, I suppose you are going to tell me Ramon did discover who the traitor was? Is that why he killed Father Lound, he thought he was the traitor?"

"He didn't kill Father Lound," Maes looked astonished. "Why would he? Father Lound was not a traitor."

"The secret papers stolen from an officer's pocket at Albion Hope were found in Father Lound's office," Peeters pointed out. "Ramon could have easily heard about that and made his decision to get rid of the traitor."

"Father Lound was not the traitor," Maes insisted. "I don't know about any papers."

Clara was listening intently.

"Ramon did not kill Father Lound," Maes was persistent, he was looking cross now. "I don't know why anyone would suggest Father Lound was a traitor, he was a good man. He spent a lot of time with Ramon's family, and I know it was not for pleasure. Ramon knew who the real traitor was, he told me and made me swear to keep the whole thing a secret."

"Because revealing the traitor would cause harm to Ramon's family?" Clara suddenly understood. "The traitor was close to the Devereauxs. No. The traitor was one of the Devereauxs."

Clara paused as the realisation struck her. It had been staring her in the face, utterly obvious.

"Elena Devereaux," Clara declared. "She was the traitor! She was in a position to listen to military talk, she hung around with the soldiers, went to bed with many of them. She overheard their conversations, or they simply told her stuff not thinking it mattered telling a prostitute about the situation at the Front. Men under stress, who are suddenly in a position where they can relax, will talk if they have someone who will listen and who appears innocuous."

Clara gasped.

"How obvious this has all been!"

Maes was nodding.

"Yes, you have it. Elena had found a way to make even more money. Ramon had known for a while, but he had no idea how to deal with the matter. He could not shoot his sister, as he had planned when he first realised there was a traitor. He also could not hand her over to the British. It would have killed his mother," Maes looked bleak. "All he could do was try to track down the Germans she was working for and shoot them."

"That day, when the papers went missing…" Clara was working things out in her head. "Father Lound was protecting someone, he was protecting Elena. Maybe he saw her take the papers, somehow he learned of what she was doing and so he took the blame on himself. Perhaps he was planning to talk with her family, have her leave town.

Did he imagine he could persuade her to stop?"

"He should have just handed her over to the British. Ramon should have done it too. The girl was clearly not going to stop and was a cold-blooded viper," Peeters interrupted, his tone surprisingly cruel. "Men might have died because of her. This town could have been overrun because of her."

"Blood is thicker than water," Clara said to him gently. "We do things for family we would not do for anyone else."

"If Elena was arrested and shot, Madame Devereaux would have given up," Maes said quietly. "Ramon's mother was clinging onto life by her fingertips, he was afraid what might happen to her, he was afraid what might become of his younger sisters. Ramon was scared he could not look after them himself and they would be taken away. He was trying to hold his family together. It was awful to watch the strain upon him."

"Elena killed Father Lound," Clara said sharply. "That was why Ramon was so secretive and hid the body. She came to the door, looked out on a body and did not react. You said that, Louis."

Maes looked startled. It was obvious he had never thought that Elena might be the murderer of Father Lound. He was not a person who made such connections. Things had to be very clear and plain for Maes to see them.

"That would make sense," he said slowly. "Ramon said she was so cold, and I thought he just meant she did not act like most women would around a body."

Clara smiled.

"I don't react like most women around a body," she said. "That is not what he was referring to, I see that now. Which also may mean…"

Clara turned to Peeters, waiting to see if he had reached the same conclusion. He put down his pen very deliberately and took a deep breath.

"That evening in 1917, Ramon went to the woods angry. Maybe he was looking for the German agents, he had the revolver with him," Peeters laid out his thoughts carefully, not wanting to look a fool by making another erroneous guess at how things happened. "Maybe he knew his sister had headed that way too. Could he have been intending to stop her? Whatever the case, he reached the woods and they argued. She got the revolver from him and shot him. Did he just kneel down and let her kill him? No, of course not. So, somehow he was incapacitated. And then she buried him?"

"I think we have to assume that the German agents were involved," Clara said. "That grave could not have been dug by one person alone, and not by a pregnant woman. I would think that Ramon came upon his sister meeting with the Germans, probably telling them about the incident at Albion Hope. I doubt Ramon reacted to the scene with caution. He probably tried to shoot them, but was overcome, the revolver stolen and he was shot."

Clara paused, the realisation of who had really been behind the betrayal and murder of two men that day in 1917 was hitting home.

"That was why the family had to leave in such a hurry. Elena had two deaths on her hands. Was she so cold she felt nothing at the execution of her brother?"

"Does that mean Madame Devereaux knows the truth?" Peeters mused.

"She probably knows some version of the truth. Elena could have told her that Ramon was the traitor and that they should all leave the town before the backlash of what he had done reached them. But that would not explain why Madame Devereaux pretended her son was still alive when she spoke to Dr Jacobs," Clara considered all this. "Elena certainly spun a good enough story that her mother rushed all her family into hiding, and they have been hiding ever since."

"Time we brought them out of hiding," Peeters said firmly. "I shall arrest Elena Devereaux as a suspect in the murder of Father Lound and her brother. Then maybe we can have the truth of this matter at last."

Maes gave a polite cough.

"Can I go now," he said meekly.

"You helped cover-up a crime," Peeters groaned at him in exasperation.

Maes frowned.

"Did I?" He said, innocently.

Chapter Thirty

Chief Inspector Peeters set off for Lugrule with a number of policemen. There was no police force in Lugrule itself, and Peeters was confident he was not going to be stepping on anyone's toes. Nonetheless, he aimed to be discreet in his dealings. Clara was to wait for his return at the police station.

Father Lound's full remains had been pulled from the rubble beneath the former Albion Hope. Dr Jacobs had had every bone carefully placed in a sturdy box and then brought to the police station, where he could lay it out in one of the rooms and examine it properly. He was satisfied that his earlier assessment had been correct and that Father Lound had died when someone struck him over the head with a heavy object. The blow had sent a shard of bone into his brain and killed him quickly.

Colonel Brandt, Tommy and Annie joined Clara at the police station to learn what she had discovered. She told them what Maes had said and what Ramon had suspected. Until they could talk to Elena, however, they would not know the whole of the story.

"What a miserable thing," Colonel Brandt seemed quite depressed by the whole affair. "A woman the traitor!"

"Women are no more honourable than men, on occasion," Clara replied to him. "She was driven by the desire for money. Such a mercenary person deserves no pity, she did not deserve the protection Ramon and Father

Lound afforded her. They may have said they were trying to spare her mother grief but, in the end, they did no one any favours. Madame Devereaux still suffered grief and ended up living a wretched life because of all this."

"Makes the blood run cold," Annie shuddered to emphasise her words. "What a horrid woman. Will she be shot?"

"I don't know. Chief Inspector Peeters thought that might be the case, but he was not clear on the law concerning treachery. The rule might be different now the country is at peace. People tend to feel more merciful about things in that circumstance."

Clara fell silent as Captain Mercier entered the building. He had been informed of the situation by Peeters and intended to be present when Elena was interviewed. Not catching the traitor had stung him all these years. He had not liked to think that Father Lound had got away, even when the bones were discovered in the woods and he thought they were the priest's, he felt he had lost. Someone else had reached the traitor before him. And then he had learned that Father Lound was not the traitor and he had felt even worse.

At last it looked like he was going to have the opportunity to resolve this whole sordid affair, and a living person could be properly tried for their crimes. He was feeling a lot better about everything. He acknowledged Clara and the others, but did not speak to them. Instead they all resolved to wait for Peeters silently. There seemed nothing left to talk about.

It was well into the night when Peeters returned. He had taken a police carriage and as it rolled back up to the door, Clara and the others looked up eagerly to see who would emerge. Could Madame Devereaux have refused the police to enter her home, as she had done with Clara?

It seemed the woman had not. As the carriage doors opened, Madame Devereaux and her daughter Elena stepped out. Madame Devereaux looked calm and composed, resigned to her fate. In contrast, her daughter wailed and swayed, almost collapsing. She was held up by two policemen who brought her into the station and straight through to Peeters' office.

"I'm going to have Dr Jacobs look her over first," Peeters told Clara as he stepped in behind.

Madame Devereaux was being escorted to a back room.

"She let you in, then?" Clara asked.

"Without complaint. I think she has been expecting this for a long time. Elena was harder to catch hold of, she tried to run, but didn't get far."

"What of the children?"

"I left a constable at the house," Peeters pulled a face. "If you can call it a house. One of the girls was too sick to be moved. Depending on what occurs tonight, I'll have to make other arrangements for them."

"Peeters, I want to be involved in the interview of Elena," Captain Mercier had stepped forward, his tone was firm and barred no opposition.

Peeters nodded at him.

"I thought as much. Right, shall we get this over with?"

Elena Devereaux was a good actress, but her apparent weakness and distress were no more than a pretence. Dr Jacobs informed Peeters that her pulse and heart rate were perfectly normal and there were no physical symptoms of the upset she was feigning. There was no reason to be concerned for her wellbeing. Clara was relieved about that as she did not want to have to delay their interview of Elena. She needed to know the truth. Waiting any longer would be torment.

Peeters, Captain Mercier and Clara entered the chief inspector's office and arranged themselves around Elena. Peeters faced her across his desk, while Clara and Mercier sat to one side. Peeters took out fresh paper and started making notes as he had done for Louis Maes.

Elena had her head dipped forward, almost to her chest, and was clutching her hands in her lap. She was sobbing softly, but Clara thought it sounded forced.

"Elena Devereaux, we know that you were selling

secrets to the Germans during the war," Peeters began bluntly. "We know you killed Father Lound, perhaps it was an accident, but the outcome was the same. Your brother, Ramon, covered the crime up for you. We also know that you were involved in his death. We have Ramon's body and we have the body of Father Lound. We also have a witness who can testify that you were guilty of these crimes."

That was stretching the truth. Louis Maes' testimony would never get into court, but it might be enough to startle Elena into confessing.

"Before he died, your brother told someone all about your crimes. That person has now come forward. This gentleman on my right is with the British military and was tasked with tracking down the spy in our town. After we talk, you shall go with him and be taken before a military tribunal. I don't know what the outcome of that will be, but I suggest a full confession would go in your favour."

Elena took a crackling breath. Clara was hopeful that she was not clever enough to know that silence was her best option. They had little real evidence against her. If she said nothing, they would never convict her of any crime. If Elena realised that, then there was no chance.

Elena scratched at her arm. She was thin and looked sickly. Whatever disease was eating her alive, it was certainly taking its toll.

"Now is the time to talk Elena, and get this all off your chest," Peeters continued. "It will make you feel better."

Elena lifted her head slowly. Her eyes burned like fire and there was something chilling about her stare. She first looked at Peeters, then at Clara and Mercier. There was nothing in her gaze to suggest she was afraid of any of them.

"I have nothing to say."

"Mademoiselle Devereaux," Mercier sat forward in his chair, "you think silence will do you a favour? It will not. There is mounting evidence against you. When I investigated this crime back in 1917, I helped to set a trap, a trap you walked into. Father Lound, rather foolishly, protected you. However, he was a patriotic man. He left behind a diary, I have it here."

Captain Mercier pulled a book out of his pocket. Elena had her attention fixed on him, her lips were parting slightly in her anxiety, revealing dull, brown teeth. There was, of course, no diary. Mercier was playing a game. Neither Clara nor Peeters were going to interfere.

"In this book, Father Lound wrote down what he had done for you. He wrote everything down in his diary. Until today, we did not have this book, because when your brother hid Father Lound's body, he also hid a suitcase containing the priest's belongings. We found that suitcase today and with it this diary," Mercier fixed Elena with his eyes. "He details everything. He had been tracking you, and he recorded every suspicion and every piece of information he collected in this book. This is the most damning piece of evidence against you. The words of a dead man."

Elena shot from her chair and tried to grab the diary, but Mercier quickly put it back in his pocket.

"Sit down, mademoiselle," Peeters said sternly.

Elena hovered for a moment, her hand still outstretched, then she sank back into the chair.

"Let's make a deal," Mercier told her calmly. "You confess and we shall make sure that your name does not end up in the papers. For the sake of your son, Ramon, and for your mother and sisters."

"But what about me?" Elena demanded.

Mercier had misread her. Elena did not care what became of her family, she never had.

"What do you want?" Mercier asked.

"Not to be shot," Elena snapped. "I want to walk out of here, go back to a normal life without fearing you people will follow me."

"That is impossible," Mercier explained to her. "You have committed at least two serious crimes. Never mind, the confession would have helped you, but if you do not want to help yourself…"

"How would it help me?" Elena asked. "I will still be

shot!"

She had a point.

"You would get to put your side of the story across," Clara spoke up. She thought she had an idea of how to appeal to Elena's vanity and self-obsession. "As it stands, the only part of this people will hear is the official side of things. No one will know the circumstances that placed you in such a position. The desperation, the difficulties. No one will get the chance to hear why you did this, why you had no choice."

Elena's eyes flicked to Clara. She seemed to be listening.

"Your son will grow up only knowing that his mother was a traitor to her country. He shall never learn that there was far more to you, that you had to do these things. If you want to have people understand, if you want people to appreciate the situation you were in, then you have to speak out now."

"They would have done the same," Elena murmured. "In the circumstances. No one understands that."

"I would like to understand," Clara said, and the response was honest. "I want to know what happened here and why."

Elena gave a little sniff, some of her arrogance was returning.

"This is all the fault of the Germans, anyway. I was only taking back the money they stole from my family."

"They did you a great disservice," Clara agreed with her. "And look at the position they left you in."

"Precisely," Elena was buckling. "I have lived in that pit of a town all these years because of them, and because of my stupid brother Ramon. And I have never told anyone."

"That must have been hard," Clara was sympathetic. "To say nothing, to want to explain what you went through, to let other people know how hard it was for you. That you were the victim. But knowing that there was no one to listen."

"This… this is true," Elena faltered. "I am so exhausted by it all, by my life. I have lived beneath this shadow so long."

"Well, you have an opportunity now to speak and have your side of things recorded officially. You shouldn't miss such a chance. This is the only way your words will be saved for history. Miss this moment, and no one will ever hear Elena Devereaux's voice."

Elena rocked in her chair, she gave a little tremble and her fingers crept to her bare arm and scratched painfully at the skin. She looked like she was used to taking substances to dull her misery, and she needed something right then. Captain Mercier spotted this.

"Dr Jacobs has things he can give you," he said, Elena cast a sharp glance in his direction, which was all the confirmation he needed of her problem. "If you talk to us."

Elena gave a heartfelt groan, rather like a child who has been told they must eat their greens before they can have dessert. Her groan turned to a soft wail and then she resigned herself. For a while she went back to rocking in her chair, her head down, her fingers clutched together. Then she took a breath and looked up.

"If I am to make a confession, I want it done right. I want everything written down, everything. Exactly as I say it. No mistakes," her voice was suddenly firm again, she did not sound like someone desperate for a high.

Clara was impressed by her strength of character. It was probably the reason she had lasted this long. Her life was one that would have destroyed most people rapidly; they would have descended into drugs, drink and despair. There was nothing but an endless slog through existence for Elena Devereaux, and she must have known that. But she hadn't given up, not completely at least.

"I shall record everything," Peeters promised. "And then you can read it through and make any alterations before it is signed as your official confession. That is your right."

Elena lifted her head up proudly and suddenly looked like the haughty young woman she might have been had circumstances been different.

"Then I am ready to begin," she said. "I shall tell you everything. And then you will know, it was not really my fault. None of it!"

Chapter Thirty-one

Elena's story was much as Clara had already surmised. The young girl raised in luxury and used to having everything done for her did not cope well with the sudden change in her family's circumstances. She was too proud to work. How could she lower herself to that? She had always been better than those who worked for a living.

Her mother had declared there was no money. She tried to sell things from the house, but there was no one to buy them. Not in the town, at least, where everyone was too worried about the war to want to buy antique vases or furniture. They could not advertise further afield for buyers, they did not have the means. It was the war, of course, it made things so hard. After a while her mother gave up and resolved herself to taking on some work. Elena had been appalled. Especially when her mother declared she would go to work in the fields; she had no talent for sewing or cooking and her cleaning skills were non-existent. But field labour was largely about stamina rather than skill, and at harvest time you could take home the gleanings for your family.

Madame Devereaux had implied that Elena ought to join her. Elena had stormed out of the house in horror. What a vile thing to even suggest! There had to be some other means of restoring the family's fortunes. Elena knew that if she did not bring money into the house, eventually her mother would insist on her working the fields.

It was then she found the soldiers. At first it was just a distraction to flirt with them, then one young man asked her to walk out with him. She did and it was fun. They did little more than stroll about the town talking and cuddling, but when he left to go back to the Front he gave her a gift to remember him by – a silver cigarette case. Unlike the big things in the Devereaux house that had been hard to sell, the cigarette case was readily bought by one of the shopkeepers in town.

When she brought the money home, Elena's mother was delighted. She avoided asking any questions but suggested that if Elena could keep bringing in money like that, there would be no more talk of field work.

For a while Elena carried on in this way. She would befriend a soldier, act like his girlfriend and make sure he gave her something valuable when he departed the town. Sometimes she would have to be quite blunt with her demands, but no one ever demurred, and they never got more than a kiss in return. Elena had decided on that early on. Until, that is, she met an older man named John. John walked out with her for a while, she played her usual games, but unlike the younger men she had strung along, John was not so soft or gullible. Whenever there was talk of gifts he would laugh or just grin. Then, one day, he laid his cards on the table. He wanted to go to bed with her and he was prepared to pay her for it. He laid out the terms like it was a business agreement and showed her the money he would pay her. Elena was hesitant until she saw the cash.

After that day she realised there was a quicker and easier way of earning money than pretending to be a man's girlfriend for a few days and prising a valuable keepsake from him. She could earn more in a few hours if she was prepared to ignore the principles she had been raised with.

Elena was not remorseful. The money was good and certainly in the early days she was the only girl offering such services in town. Business boomed. Eventually other women drifted there and would try to undercut her prices, but Elena was always popular because she dressed like a lady, spoke well, had a good education and exquisite manners. She was a cut above the rest and the men liked spending time with such a sophisticated prostitute.

The only real nuisance was Ramon. He disliked her whoring, but as her mother was tacitly approving of the situation, there was nothing much he could do.

The treachery business was Ramon's fault too. He had annoyed Elena when he attacked one of her man friends. Ramon had taken a pounding, but it was not enough to satisfy Elena's thirst for revenge. She wanted to spite him further. It was then she heard the whispers about German agents in the area and Ramon's determination to find them and shoot them. She decided to find them first. There was no real plan in her mind as to what she would do when she came upon them, though she did debate sleeping with them and taking their money. It would be amusing to be sleeping with the enemy.

It was never about the war, or about Belgium or about her town. It was always about Ramon. That was why it was never really treason, not in the proper sense of the word. Honestly.

Strangely, it was quite easy to find the German agents and Elena soon discovered they would pay her for information from the soldiers she slept with. Now she could earn twice as much by her night-time activities and every time she brought the money home, she would be spiting Ramon.

Elena freely admitted that she was using Albion Hope as her main base of operations; not just for information gathering, but also for touting for business. Father Lound discovered this and tried to get her to stop. He could not ban her from making deliveries to the house, as that was the only means she had of making legitimate money, but he tried to persuade her to give up her extra activities. He annoyed Elena as much as her brother. She would see them talking together and knew they were talking about her. It was unbearable!

And then the day came when she noticed some odd

papers in the pocket of a man's tunic and she stole them. Unluckily, or so she had imagined at the time, Father Lound spotted her. He made her give the papers to him. They argued, but she obeyed and stormed home. It was only much later that she learned the papers were part of a trap and she had been very fortunate not to stumble into it.

However, she didn't know any of that when she heard Father Lound and Ramon arguing in the garden of her home. It was the same argument they always had, over Ramon's behaviour towards the other lads and his temper. Ramon had finally stomped indoors and disappeared upstairs. He never noticed that his sister was present. She was supposed to be delivering bread at that time in the afternoon, but she had been feeling unwell due to her pregnancy and had stayed home.

Elena was in a foul mood because her swelling belly was putting off new customers. She was not earning money, aside from her deliveries. She had been convinced that the Germans would pay her handsomely for the papers she had tried to steal from Albion Hope, and she had been angry all afternoon because Father Lound had taken them away. Suddenly she wanted to tell him exactly what she thought of him. She walked outside and found him still in the garden. She yelled at him, told him he was making her life a misery, preventing her from supporting her family. When he tried to tell her once again that what she was doing was wrong, she lost her temper. Elena did not even remember picking up the stone, but she could vividly recall slamming it down on Father Lound's head.

He had crumpled to the grass. Elena stood for a while just looking at him, wondering if he was dead or not. She nudged him with her foot once or twice. He didn't respond. Maybe he was dead or maybe he wasn't, whatever the case, Elena didn't want anything more to do with the matter. Someone else could sort it out. Someone else had always sorted out Elena's messes in the past. Just before she left him, she stripped Father Lound of his crucifix and rosary. She was pretty certain she could sell them on the thriving black market, and he owed her for those papers.

She had been right, of course, someone else did sort out her mess. Ramon found the priest's body. Maybe he guessed what had happened. Certainly he disposed of the corpse and that satisfied Elena.

Later that night she went to seek out the Germans and tell them about the papers she had seen. She hoped they might pay her for that. The Germans usually loitered near St. Helena's shrine and Elena went there. She had not expected Ramon to follow her.

What happened next was close to what Clara had surmised. Elena was talking with the Germans when Ramon came upon them. He lost his temper and waved the gun about but, when it came to it, he could not shoot them. The Germans grabbed him, took the gun away and then they had to make a decision. The Germans could not let Ramon go, he had seen too much. Elena was worried that her brother would turn her in to the British. At last they were all agreed that Ramon had to be disposed of.

Elena had felt elated and scared by the decision. Ramon was sobbing as the Germans forced him to his knees. It was a test of Elena's loyalty to get her to fire the gun. She still had the rosary and crucifix on her, and when Ramon kept crying she felt a little bad. She put the crucifix around his neck and shoved the rosary in his hand as a sort of comforter. It made her feel a bit better. It certainly gave her the strength to shoot Ramon. It was only as his body hit the ground that the realisation of what she had done struck her. Suddenly she was not so cocky and confident. She started to scream and one of the Germans slapped her. He went to grab the gun, threatening to shoot her too. Elena managed to break open the chamber and dump the bullets, before dropping the gun and running off.

She thought the Germans would chase her, and she was certain they would come after her eventually. Back home, she persuaded her mother that Ramon had been working for the Germans, that she had witnessed him in the woods. He had threatened to kill her. Elena had to leave the town, but she could not go alone. Madame Devereaux, whether she believed the story or not, sided with her daughter and they left town that night, going to a place they thought no one would ever find them. They cut ties with their past, except for when Madame Devereaux needed the family medical records. Maybe she had guessed what her daughter her done. Even in Lugrule they had heard about the body in the woods. In any case, she had asked for Ramon's records as a precaution. To avoid people imagining he was not with the rest of the family.

And that was that.

Elena took a full hour to tell her story and when she was done she looked exhausted. There was no hint, however, of regret; not for Father Lound, not for Ramon and not for the betrayal of her country. She had done everything because it was necessary for herself, for bringing in the money she loved. Even the naming of her son had been the work of her mother. Elena could not care less about the boy's name.

When the interview was finished, Peeters agreed to hand Elena over to Captain Mercier. She had three crimes to answer for, and each carried a death sentence, but the betrayal of her people had come first and it was decided it would be the crime she would pay for. It would do more for Father Lound and Ramon, by clearing their names, than trying her for their murders.

Clara was glad to leave the matter in Mercier's hands. She had her answer at last, as did he, and she could go back to England knowing Lound's family would now have the truth. Emily had been right about her brother. He was not a traitor. Perhaps he had been too kind when he had attempted to protect Elena, he had certainly paid for it.

Back at the hotel, Clara outlined the whole story for the others. No one knew quite what to say. They had a solution to the mystery, that was it. It was rare to feel happy about the outcome of a case, as generally there was a sadness to the conclusion of such a story. The sadness in this instance was that two men had been murdered and their names sullied for trying to do the right thing. Ramon had hidden Lound's body, and that was both morally and legally wrong, but he was not a murderer or a traitor. That they had discovered who really was behind the crimes did not bring gladness, just understanding. Now they knew.

~~~*~~~

It was good to return to Brighton, to their house. Tommy seemed truly at peace with himself as they stepped through the front door. For the first time in years, a dark veil had lifted from him. Clara had never realised he was carrying a burden, until she now saw that it was gone. Annie strode straight into the kitchen and began making tea, insisting that Colonel Brandt stay for dinner. Clara excused herself. She had one last duty to perform.

Clara had sent a telegram to Emily to let her know they were heading home. They met at Clara's office in the early evening. Emily looked anxious.

"Well?"

Clara presented Emily with a letter from Captain Mercier. It outlined the entire case and explained that the real traitor had been discovered. It would take some time, but the Lound family would receive an official apology for the aspersions cast on Father Lound's name. He had been cleared of all wrongdoing.

Emily read the letter through twice and then clutched it to her chest.

"You did it," she said, tears softly falling down her cheeks. "I feared you would not be able to, but you did it."

"Your brother can now be remembered for all the good he did," Clara smiled gently, it was a bittersweet moment. "Captain Mercier has agreed to arrange for Christian's remains to be shipped to England. You can give him a proper burial."

"Thank you," Emily gulped, hardly able to speak through the tears. "I cannot thank you enough."

"Your brother was a good man. He deserves to be

commemorated along with all the others who fell in the war. His kindness touched so many."

Emily could speak no more, her tears fell freely. Clara put an arm around her shoulders and squeezed her gently.

"You never doubted him, all these years, you were loyal," Clara said, her own voice a little choked. "He could not have asked more from you."

"I… I have to get… home… and tell… my father," Emily managed to stutter out the words.

She gave Clara a firm hug, whispering further thanks in her ear and then hurried away.

Clara walked home, some of the sorrow she had felt on the ferry coming home lifting as she thought of the relief and gladness she had brought to Emily. She could not resurrect Christian Lound, but she had given him back to his family. They could now mourn him like everyone else mourned their lost loved ones. That was something.

As she walked into her house, she could hear Annie telling Colonel Brandt about a Belgium cake she had taken a shine to at the hotel. Janssen had given her the recipe and she was going to try it out soon. Clara stood in the hallway, listening to the sound, feeling so glad that her family and friends were all around her. Tommy emerged from the front parlour.

"All right, old girl?" He asked her, a slightly concerned look in his eye.

Clara smiled at him, her eyes bright with tears. She quickly went forward and hugged him tight. Tommy was momentarily startled, then he wrapped his arms around her. Clara started to cry.

"Don't ever scare me like you did that night on the bridge."

Tommy stiffened.

"It was you? How…?" He stopped talking and relaxed. "Never again."

"Promise?"

"Promise."

Tommy pulled back from Clara and looked her in the

face.

"Where did you get the wildflower from?"

"What flower?" Clara frowned.

Tommy paused and a smile crept onto his face.

"Never mind," he said. "I think I know where it came from."

He hugged Clara again, tightly this time.

"I'm going nowhere," he swore. "I vow to that."

Printed in Great Britain
by Amazon